SIDEWINDERS:
THE BUTCHER OF
BEAR CREEK

SIDEWINDERS:
THE BUTCHER OF BEAR CREEK

William W. Johnstone
with J. A. Johnstone

PINNACLE BOOKS
Kensington Publishing Corp.
www.kensingtonbooks.com

PINNACLE BOOKS are published by

Kensington Publishing Corp.
119 West 40th Street
New York, NY 10018

PUBLISHER'S NOTE
Following the death of William W. Johnstone, the Johnstone family is working with a carefully selected writer to organize and complete Mr. Johnstone's outlines and many unfinished manuscripts to create additional novels in all of his series like The Last Gunfighter, Mountain Man, and Eagles, among others. This novel was inspired by Mr. Johnstone's superb storytelling.

All Kensington titles, imprints, and distributed lines are available at special quantity discounts for bulk purchases for sales promotions, premiums, fund-raising, educational, or institutional use. Special book excerpts or customized printings can also be created to fit specific needs. For details, write or phone the office of the Kensington special sales manager: Kensington Publishing Corp., 119 West 40th Street, New York, NY 10018, attn: Special Sales Department; phone 1-800-221-2647.

ISBN-13: 978-0-7860-3120-7
ISBN-10: 0-7860-3120-4

First printing: June 2013

10 9 8 7 6 5 4 3 2 1

Printed in the United States of America

First electronic edition: June 2013

ISBN-13: 978-0-7860-3121-4
ISBN-10: 0-7860-3121-2

CHAPTER 1

Scratch Morton reined his horse to a halt, drew in a deep breath, let it back out in a gusty sigh of contentment, and said, "Smell that, Bo. Ain't it good to be breathin' the fresh air of Texas again?"

"We've been back in Texas for several weeks," Bo Creel pointed out dryly. "I've taken a few breaths in that time."

"Yeah, but we're closer to home now," Scratch countered. "As a matter of fact . . ." He rose in his stirrups so he could peer into the distance. "See that line of trees? If I ain't mistaken, that's where Bear Creek runs. Bear Creek!"

Bo smiled and told his friend, "I think you're right. It won't be long now."

"As the saloon girl said to the travelin' preacher," Scratch responded with a chuckle.

Scratch was right about one thing, Bo thought: it was good to get back to their old stomping grounds. They had grown up not far from here, in the plains and rolling hills of south central Texas. This was one of the areas that had been settled first, way back when Texas wasn't the Lone Star State or even an independent republic, as it had been for nine years, but before that, when it was still a part of Mexico. The Creel and Morton clans had been some of the first American families to immigrate here.

They hadn't been acquainted with each other at the time. The families had met during the Runaway Scrape, that terrible exodus during the Texas Revolution when the rebellious American settlers had been forced to flee before the wrath of Santa Anna's army.

Bo and Scratch, little more than boys at the time, had become fast friends, and when the Texicans had finally turned and made their stand on the plains of San Jacinto, the two youngsters had been right there on the field of battle.

That had been their baptism of fire. They had saved each other's lives that day, the first of many times in the more than forty years since then.

The thing of it was, that battle easily could have turned out to be the end of their adventuring. Once Texas was free, Bo and Scratch had grown into young manhood, and Bo had already settled down, with a wife and young child, when tragedy struck and took his family away from him.

Unable to stay there and face constant reminders of what he had lost, Bo had gone on the drift . . . and naturally enough, Scratch, his best friend and always the more footloose of the pair, had gone along with him. Probably neither of them had thought at the time that their odyssey would last for decades . . . but that was what fate held in store for them.

They had been back to Texas on a number of occasions since then. It had been about ten years, though, since they had visited their boyhood homes. The Creels and the Mortons still lived in these parts, most of them on farms and ranches scattered along the banks of Bear Creek. The stream gave its name to one of the settlements in the area. About five miles downstream from the town of Bear Creek was a smaller settlement known as Cottonwood that wasn't much more than a couple of saloons and a trading post.

At least that was all there was to it the last time Bo and Scratch had been here. Bo was curious to see how much, if any, it and the town of Bear Creek had grown.

"I think we've sat here long enough," Bo said. "Let's go see how the place has been getting along without us."

A grin stretched across Scratch's leathery face.

"I'm right with you, pard," he said.

The two Texans heeled their mounts into motion.

Despite the fact that the two men were edging past middle age, they both rode tall and straight in the saddle. Bo was dressed mostly in black, in a somber suit and hat that some said made him look like a preacher. He carried only one revolver, a Colt with well-worn walnut grips.

Scratch, on the other hand, was more of a dandy, sporting a cream-colored Stetson and a fancy fringed buckskin jacket. A pair of long-barreled, nickel-plated Remington revolvers with ivory grips rode at his hips in hand-tooled holsters. His hair had turned silver at a relatively early age, while Bo's dark brown hair was only touched here and there with gray.

They were both handsome men, and Scratch had romanced a number of widows from the Rio Grande to the Canadian border, sometimes having to leave town in a hurry when one of the "widows" turned out to have been lying about her marital status, resulting in an angry husband looking for Scratch.

Bo had a habit of being more discreet in his involvements with women, although there had been some along the way. He had no interest in getting married and settling down again, and at this late date, it wasn't likely Scratch would change his stripes and take that plunge, either.

Mostly they just drifted, taking work when they had to, usually as cowhands. But they had done other things, too, such as hiring on to help a federal marshal transport some prisoners from Arkansas to Texas.

That job had turned out to be pretty troublesome, but when it was over, Bo and Scratch found themselves at loose ends in their home state, so when the notion struck them to pay a visit to Bear Creek, it had been easy enough to amble in that direction.

Bo spotted something ahead of them in the trail, coming toward them and moving in and out of patches of shade cast by the trees on either side. After a moment he recognized it as a wagon being pulled by a team of mules.

Scratch had seen the wagon, too, and as he peered at the man on the driver's seat, he said, "Good Lord, is that old Avery Hollins?"

"Can't be," Bo said. "He'd have to a hundred and fifty years old by now. He was ancient when we were still youngsters."

"Well, he seemed ancient to us, anyway," Scratch replied with a grin. "But that thing on his head sure looks like that old stovepipe hat he always wore."

"It does," Bo admitted. "I reckon we'll find out, because whoever it is, he's coming this direction."

The two men kept riding, and within minutes the wagon rolled within hailing distance of them. Scratch raised a hand and called, "Hold on there, old-timer."

The man on the wagon hauled back on the reins and brought the mules to a halt. His body was so bony under his clothes that he looked like he was made out of sticks and leather. He wore baggy wool trousers and a homespun shirt with a long, black leather vest over it. The stovepipe hat perched on his egg-shaped head had an eagle feather stuck in the band. His face was a mass of wrinkles. Bushy white eyebrows and tufts of white hair sticking out of his ears seemed to be the only hair on his head.

"As I live and breathe," Scratch went on. "Avery Hollins. It *is* you."

"Of course it's me," the old-timer said in a high-pitched voice. "This is my wagon, ain't it? These is my mules. Who in blazes did you expect it to be?"

Scratch grinned.

"Well, to be honest," he said, "if anybody had asked me, I likely would've said that you'd been dead twenty years or more."

"Well, you'd have been wrong, wouldn't you?" Hollins demanded. His watery eyes squinted at them. "Do I know you? Who the hell are you boys?"

"You don't recognize us? I'm Scratch Morton, and this is Bo Creel. You knew us ages ago."

Hollins's eyes widened in surprise.

"Bo Creel!" he exploded. He reached for the whip in the socket at the edge of the seat next to him. "You stay away from me! Get out of my way!"

The whip popped like a shot next to the ear of one of the leaders. The mule surged forward in its traces, and the others followed suit. Bo and Scratch had to yank their horses hurriedly to the side of the trail to get out of the way.

"What the hell's wrong with you?" Scratch yelled at Hollins as the old-timer sent the wagon bouncing and rattling past them. "You nearly ran us down!"

"Leave me be!" Hollins shouted back at him. He shook the whip at the two men on horseback. "Keep your distance or I'll whip the hides off both of you!"

Scratch's face twisted in anger. He reached for his right-hand Remington.

"Hold on," Bo told him sharply, gesturing for Scratch to leave the revolver where it was. "You can't go threatening the old pelican with a gun."

"I don't see why not," Scratch said hotly. "He threatened to whip us."

Hollins kept urging his team on, faster and faster. Dust boiled up from the wagon's wheels now. The old man twisted on the seat to throw a look of fear over his shoulder.

"Something's wrong," Bo said. "He's really spooked."

"Well, I'm really confused, and a little mad, to boot. What a welcome home that was."

Bo frowned in thought as he stared after the wagon.

"He didn't really go *loco* until you mentioned my name," he pointed out to Scratch. "It's like when he realized who I was, it terrified him."

"I don't see why it would. You're pretty much harmless. We both are. Well, except to outlaws and rustlers and the like. We've tangled with a few of them."

"A few," Bo repeated, his voice dry with irony again.

In their wanderings, circumstances had forced him and Scratch to shoot it out with more lawbreakers than he could remember. Of course, the two of them had been accused of being outlaws more than once, he reminded himself.

"I guess we shouldn't let it bother us too much," Scratch went on. "Avery Hollins always was as crazy as a hoot owl. I remember he used to say that an old Indian had taught him how to turn himself invisible. Claimed he caught himself a ghost horse once, too."

"Those were just stories he made up to entertain the kids around here," Bo said.

Scratch let out a snort.

"I don't care. When a fella spends all his time makin' up stories, sooner or later he winds up touched in the head."

Bo couldn't argue with that.

The dust from the wagon had settled now. Bo lifted his reins, nodded toward the line of trees that marked the course of the creek, and said, "Let's ride on to town. Maybe when we get there somebody can tell us what put such a burr under old Avery's saddle."

CHAPTER 2

When they reached the creek they turned west, following the stream as it gradually curved south. The creek flowed lazily between eight-foot-tall banks lined with cottonwoods and live oaks.

A short time later, Bo and Scratch spotted the steeples of the Baptist church and the Methodist church, which sat at opposite ends of the settlement. That hadn't changed in the decade since they had been here last.

The town of Bear Creek had grown some, though, Bo saw as the trail he and Scratch had been following turned into the main street. A number of businesses stood on either side of the road, including the Bear Creek Hotel and the First State Bank. The office of the Bear Creek *Sentinel* was on the right. The town hadn't had a newspaper the last time the two drifters were here. Brantley's Livery Stable was still operating, but it had some competition now in the form of Hersheimer's Livery.

Old Doc Perkins's shingle still hung in front of his office, and it appeared that Ed Tyson was still practicing law.

The biggest change was on the east side of the creek, which was spanned by a sturdy wooden bridge. The last time Bo and Scratch had been in Bear Creek, there were two saloons over there, and that was all. Now there were more than a dozen buildings on that side of the stream, and even though it was just the middle of the afternoon, Bo heard the rinky-tink strains of piano music in the air. The so-called bad side of town had grown a lot.

Scratch licked his lips, nodded toward the proliferation of drinking establishments, and said, "Would you look over there? Progress has come to Bear Creek."

"Some people might argue about your definition of progress," Bo said. "Vice and respectability usually go hand in hand, though. They call it civilization."

That brought a laugh from the silver-haired Texan.

"Let's go across the creek and cut the trail dust," Scratch suggested. "You reckon Lauralee Parker still owns the Southern Belle Saloon?"

"One way to find out," Bo said. He headed his horse toward the bridge.

Several people were on the boardwalks of Bear Creek's business section. As he and Scratch rode past, Bo noticed the way they were looking at him.

Some shot apprehensive glances in his direction, while others stared in open disbelief. When they had ridden a few more yards, he said quietly to Scratch, "Looks like these people are just as spooked to see me as old Avery was."

"Yeah, you're right," Scratch said. "What in blazes is goin' on here, Bo?"

"I don't know," Bo replied with a shake of his head, "but I don't like it much."

"I don't cotton to it, either. You want to turn around and get out of here?"

Bo thought about it for a second, then shook his head again.

"No, we've come this far. I want to see my pa, and Riley and Cooper and Hank and their families. I'm sure you want to see your kinfolks, too."

"Yeah, that's true. Plus it'd sort of feel like we were running away from trouble, and you know how that rubs me the wrong way."

Bo smiled.

"Yeah, any time there's trouble, you generally light a shuck right toward it, don't you?"

Scratch didn't answer that question. Instead he said, "Look, there's Jesse Peterson." Without waiting for Bo to reply, he reined his horse toward the boardwalk on the left side of the street and hailed a man who stood there. "Hey, Jesse."

Peterson was about their age and owned a saddle shop. Bo and Scratch had known him since all three of them were youngsters. Peterson was a stocky man with graying red hair and bushy side whiskers. His beefy face wore a frown as Scratch rode toward him, followed by Bo.

"Scratch Morton," Peterson declared dubiously. "That really is you, isn't it?"

Scratch grinned and said, "Yep. And Bo's with me, too."

"I see him," Peterson said. The man's voice was as chilly as the blue northers that sometimes swept down across Texas from the Panhandle.

Bo brought his horse alongside Scratch's mount. He said, "What's going on here, Jesse? You act like you're not glad to see me, and when we ran into old Avery Hollins out on the trail, he seemed like he was scared of us."

"You didn't hurt him, did you?" Peterson asked with a note of alarm in his voice.

"Hurt him?" Scratch repeated. "Why in tarnation would we hurt a harmless old coot like Avery?"

"Figured you'd be just as bad as he is," Peterson snapped. "The two of you always were peas in a pod. Why don't you go away and leave us alone?"

Scratch flushed with anger. He started to swing down from his saddle, saying, "By God—"

Bo reached over and touched his friend's arm.

"Don't," he said. "Just let it go."

"But it's startin' to look like everybody in the whole town's gone loco," Scratch protested.

Peterson said, "You're a fine one to talk about somebody going loco." He slid a hand under his coat. "I've got a pistol here. If you try anything, I'll—"

"If we wanted to gun you down, some little pistol wouldn't stop us," Scratch said.

Peterson kept his hand under his coat and backed toward the doorway behind him.

"Leave me alone," he said. "The only reason I haven't started yelling for the marshal is because the two of you used to be my friends, but if you bother me, I swear I'll—"

Scratch interrupted him again.

"Come on, Bo," he said as he hauled his horse's head around. "I can't listen to any more of this craziness. Maybe if we get drunk enough, things'll start to make sense."

Peterson's florid face paled.

"You're going across the creek?" he asked in a hushed, frightened voice.

"What business is that of yours?" Scratch demanded.

Peterson didn't answer. Instead he turned abruptly and broke into a run along the boardwalk. Bo and Scratch were both startled. Scratch exclaimed, "What the hell!"

"Something's mighty wrong here, partner," Bo said. "Come on. Maybe we'll get some straight answers on the other side of the creek."

"Folks were always more plainspoken over there, that's true."

During the conversation with Jesse Peterson, the

boardwalks on both sides of the street had cleared out, Bo noted. It was like everybody had scurried for cover when they saw him and Scratch. That made no sense.

Scratch had come to the same conclusion. He said, "Folks cleared out like ol' Santa Anna his own self just rode into town with the whole blamed Mexican army behind him. None of this makes a lick of sense, Bo."

"Not so far," Bo admitted, "but maybe there's a logical explanation."

As they reached the western end of the bridge and started across it, four men on horseback were riding onto the bridge from the eastern end. Judging from the way a couple of them swayed in their saddles, they looked like they had been drinking. When they saw Bo and Scratch riding toward them, all four men stopped short.

The bridge was about sixty feet long. Despite their age, both Bo and Scratch still had excellent eyesight, so they could see the faces of the men at the other end of the bridge. Bo didn't recognize any of them, but they were all young, in their early twenties, he judged. That meant they would have been just kids the last time he and Scratch were in these parts, if they had even been around Bear Creek back then.

All four men wore range clothes and had lariats looped on their saddles. Bo figured them for cowhands who worked on the ranches along Bear

Creek. This was good, fertile rangeland around here, and the first herds of longhorns that had gone up the cattle trails to the railroad in Kansas after the war had come from this area.

Bo and Scratch kept riding. The cowboys stayed where they were, sitting in their saddles and regarding the two older men with hostile stares. Their horses blocked the eastern end of the bridge.

"I don't much like the looks of this," Scratch said under his breath. "Those fellas look like they're on the prod."

"Yeah, and I think they've been drinking, too," Bo said. "That's not a very good combination."

"Want to turn around and go back?"

"We talked about that," Bo said, his eyes narrowing. "I don't cotton to it, either."

Scratch chuckled.

"We're outnumbered two to one," he pointed out. "And they're a heap younger than us."

"That just means they'll underestimate us, doesn't it?"

They were in the middle of the bridge now. Suddenly one of the cowboys nudged his horse forward. The other three followed suit. Bo and Scratch had to rein in as the four riders clattered toward them. The cowboys didn't stop until they had closed the gap to about ten feet.

The one who had started forward first asked, "Is your name Creel?"

"That's right," Bo said. "Do I know you, son?"

"No, but you match the description," the young man shot back. He was slender, with a foxlike face and fair hair under his Stetson. Now that Bo was closer, he could see that the young man's clothes were a little cleaner and more expensive than a cowboy's usual garb. The fella might not be a typical forty-a-month-and-found puncher after all, although the other three certainly were. He went on, "And I'm sure as hell not your son, so don't call me that."

"No offense meant," Bo said. "If you and your friends will move aside a mite, we'll go on past. This bridge is wide enough for all of us."

"The hell it is," the young man snapped. "And if you think I'm gonna let you go across the creek after what you've done, you're crazy."

"After what I've—mister, you're the one who's crazy. My partner and I just rode into Bear Creek a few minutes ago. I haven't done anything around here for a long time."

The young man sneered.

"Yeah, it figures you'd lie about it," he said. "No-account bastard like you."

"By God, that tears it!" said Scratch. "Get out of our way, you young pup, or—"

"You're not going anywhere," the young man said. "We're holding you here for the law. Grab 'em, boys!"

With that the riders surged forward, charging the startled Bo and Scratch.

CHAPTER 3

The attack might have taken them somewhat by surprise, but they had ridden into trouble so many times they were in the habit of being ready for it. They yanked their horses apart, Bo going left, Scratch going right.

The youngster who had done all the talking so far hung back a little so that his three companions were in the lead. Typical of a troublemaker to start a fight and then let somebody else run the risk, thought Bo.

The only good thing about this confrontation was that they didn't seem to want to turn it into a gun battle. The nearest of the cowboys lunged at Bo, reaching out in an attempt to drag him from the saddle. Bo leaned to the side to avoid the grab, caught hold of the man's arm, and heaved. Instead of Bo being unhorsed, the cowboy suffered that fate, toppling from his mount as he let out a startled yell. He crashed down on the wide planks that formed the bridge. The impact cut short his shout and turned it into a pained "Ooof!"

Meanwhile, one of the other men forced his horse against Scratch's mount. Scratch's horse shied away so violently that the silver-haired Texan's leg was rammed against the railing on that side of the bridge. Scratch snarled a curse as he caught hold of the cowboy's shirt in his left hand and leaned across to slam his right fist into the man's jaw. The blow landed cleanly and caused the man to slew sideways as Scratch let go of him. The cowboy made a grab for his saddle horn but missed. He fell off his horse, too.

The third man left his saddle voluntarily in a diving tackle aimed at Bo. Unable to get out of the way in time, Bo barely had time to kick his feet free of the stirrups before the cowboy slammed into him. They both fell over the railing and plummeted toward the surface of the creek some ten or twelve feet below.

With the cowboy's arms wrapped around him, Bo twisted in midair so the other man hit the water first. A huge splash exploded around them as they went under. Bo had been able to grab a breath just before they landed in the creek, so he didn't have to worry about air for a few seconds.

His opponent, on the other hand, must have swallowed quite a bit of water, because he started thrashing and flailing and forgot all about hanging on to Bo. The creek wasn't that deep, only five or six feet. One good kick took Bo back to the surface, even with the weight of his boots and his wet clothes holding him down. As he broke into the air, he heard a shot.

So much for this not turning into a gunfight, he thought.

But as he looked up at the bridge, he saw that Scratch had one of the Remingtons leveled at the youngster who had provoked the ruckus. The young man thrust his hands in the air as he yelped, "Don't kill me!" Bo knew Scratch had only fired a warning shot over the man's head.

Scratch looked mad enough to ventilate the fox-faced troublemaker, but he held off on the trigger and glanced over the side of the bridge.

"Bo!" he called. "Are you all right?"

The man who had tackled Bo had fought his way back to the surface, but he was coughing and gagging and seemed to have lost any urge to fight. When Bo saw that he told Scratch, "Yeah, I'm fine," and started wading toward the bank. He spied his hat floating on the water nearby and snatched it on his way to shore.

With water streaming off of him, Bo climbed back onto solid ground. Two of the cowboys were lying on the bridge, momentarily stunned, and Scratch had the other man covered. Bo hurried to his horse and swung up into the saddle. He shook the water out of his hat and clapped it back on his head.

"Until we find out what the devil's going on, let's get out of here," Bo said.

"I think you're right," Scratch replied. "We don't want to have to shoot our way out of our own hometown!"

They wheeled their horses and galloped back the way they had come. Behind them, the young man jerked his gun from its holster and began firing after them.

"You won't get away!" he yelled. "You'll pay for what you did to those two girls, Creel!"

Bo and Scratch leaned forward in their saddles to make themselves smaller targets. They were already at the outer edges of effective handgun range, so they weren't too worried about the young troublemaker scoring a hit as he blazed away at them.

Still, lucky shots happened sometimes, so it didn't hurt anything to make it more difficult for a bullet to find them.

Bo didn't know who the marshal was in Bear Creek these days, but he was worried the lawman might try to stop them. He and Scratch didn't like to swap lead with a peace officer unless the man was obviously crooked. They had run into a few dogleg sheriffs and marshals in their time, but when a man wore a star you had to assume he was truly on the side of law and order until you knew different.

Nobody else tried to stop them as they reached the end of the bridge and turned south. The street was still deserted. As they left Bear Creek behind, Bo looked over his shoulder at the town. He didn't see any signs of pursuit.

"Now what?" Scratch called to him over the sound of their horses' hooves.

"Head for the Star C," Bo said. That was his father's ranch. He and Scratch ought to be safe there, Bo thought, and maybe his pa could tell them why the folks in Bear Creek seemed to have declared open season on Creels.

John Creel's ranch was located on the western side of the creek, where a smaller, nameless stream flowed in from the hills to the west and joined it. That smaller tributary watered the valley that formed the elder Creel's range. John had settled there in 1835, before the revolution, with his wife, Esther, and their three sons, Bo, Riley, and Cooper. The youngest son, Hank, had been born there after Texas won its freedom.

Esther Creel was buried there now, in the little family plot on the hill behind the ranch house. Alongside her were the two daughters who had died in infancy. It seemed that Esther had been destined never to know the joy of raising daughters, and that had been her particular burden to bear. Bo had gone on the drift with Scratch by then, but when the news caught up with him he had mourned the sisters he'd never met.

He had mourned his mother, as well, when a

letter from his father containing the news of her death finally caught up with him. As fiddlefooted as he was, getting word to him of anything was usually difficult and time-consuming.

He hoped that his father hadn't passed away, too, and he just wasn't aware of it yet.

His brothers were all married now and had families of their own, but as far as Bo knew, they all still lived on the Star C, helping old John Creel run the ranch. John had settled on the land intending to farm it, but over time he had discovered that it was more suitable to raising cattle. Longhorns ran wild on the range in those days. John had rounded them up, fashioned a brand, and burned it into the hides of the tough, rangy beasts.

Eventually he had built up a fine herd. The War of Northern Aggression had left him cash-poor, though, like everybody else in Texas, and those longhorns were the only asset he'd had in those postwar days, some fifteen years earlier.

At first he had driven them to the Gulf Coast, where the booming hide and tallow business in Fulton provided a market for them. Then, when the expansion of the railroad into Kansas opened up a route to the eastern half of the country, which was starved for beef, John had turned his eyes north-ward, like most of the other ranchers in Texas. They began driving their herds that direction, through

Indian Territory to the railheads over the line, and the true Texas cattle empire was born.

There were a lot bigger and more lucrative spreads than the Star C, but it had always supported the Creel family comfortably. And it was home, which was one reason Bo was looking forward to seeing the place again.

Replaying that family history in his head had helped distract him from the fact that he was soaking wet and utterly confused. He couldn't avoid facing the problem forever, so he said, "That young fella who was shooting at us yelled something about me hurting a couple of girls."

"I thought that's what he said," Scratch replied, "but I wasn't sure. That tells us right there this whole blamed mess is a big misunderstandin', Bo. For one thing, you and me haven't been anywhere around these parts lately, and for another, you'd never hurt a gal. That sort of sorry behavior just ain't in you."

"No, and I thank the Good Lord for that," Bo said. "But I reckon it's pretty clear folks around here *think* that I did. Whatever happened, it must have been something pretty bad, too. Avery Hollins and Jesse Peterson both acted like they were afraid I was going to haul out my gun and shoot them at any second, without warning."

"Plumb loco," Scratch said, shaking his head.

"What we need to do when we get to the ranch is

talk to my pa and find out exactly what happened. Then maybe he can ride to town and convince everybody that I didn't do what they think I did."

"We could always just ride on without stoppin' to see the folks," Scratch suggested.

Without hesitation, Bo said, "No, I don't want to do that. I want this cleared up. I don't fancy the idea of people believing that I would do such a thing. And you know that if we don't get it settled, some of them always will."

"Yeah, you're probably right about that," Scratch admitted. "Once some folks get an idea in their heads, no matter how crazy it may be, they won't ever let go of it unless you can show 'em absolutely, positively, that they're wrong."

"And even that doesn't always work," Bo said. "If it did, most politicians would never get elected a second time."

Scratch had to laugh at that, but it was a rueful laugh because he knew Bo was right.

The sun was bright and warm enough that Bo's clothes had begun to dry by the time they reached the smaller creek. They turned and headed west, following the stream toward the Star C headquarters, which lay a couple of miles in that direction.

"You don't have to come with me if you don't want to," Bo said. "You've got family to visit, too."

The old Morton home place lay on the other side of Bear Creek, several miles away. Both of Scratch's parents had passed away, but his sister and her family lived there now, and he had a brother close by, as well.

"There'll be plenty of time to visit once we get this mess squared away," Scratch said. "We're not in the habit of splittin' up when one of us is in trouble unless there's no way around it."

"Well, I appreciate that. I hope it won't take very long to put things right."

They began seeing cattle grazing almost right away. John Creel still ran some longhorns, but he had brought in Herefords and Angus as well to strengthen his herd. Some cattlemen resisted change, but John had always been open to experimenting with things to make his operation better.

"Those are some fat, healthy-lookin' beeves," Scratch commented. "Appears that the spring roundup ought to be a good one."

"That's because the drought hasn't been as bad here as it was up north," Bo said. Most of the upper half of Texas was scorched and dry because of lack of rainfall, leading to conditions that had caused a giant wildfire in which both of the trail partners had almost perished a few weeks earlier. Bo nodded at the fields they were passing and went on, "Everything's a lot greener down here."

"Yeah, and it's a pretty sight, too—"

Scratch's words stopped short at the sight of

several men on horseback emerging from a stand of trees about a hundred yards away.

"That must be some of your pa's riders," Scratch continued. "I expect they'll be glad to see you—"

His voice came to an abrupt halt again as the riders kicked their mounts into motion and started galloping toward the two drifters. Shots began to pop, and powder smoke spurted into the air from gun muzzles.

CHAPTER 4

Scratch let out a startled curse as he and Bo hauled back on their reins.

"They don't seem too fond of us here, either," Bo said. "Come on!"

He wheeled his mount and raced toward a wooded knob about a quarter of a mile away. He remembered that elevation well. When he and Scratch were young, they had waited up there with long-barreled, muzzle-loading flintlock rifles and shot wild turkeys that Scratch would call up with an uncannily accurate gobbling sound. Those birds had put food on the table for the Morton and Creel families more than once.

Bo and Scratch had snuck up there with jugs of corn liquor, too, and every now and then they'd even been able to persuade young ladies to accompany them to the top of Turkey Mountain, as they called it, for some sparking.

The important thing at the moment was that the

knob was the highest ground around here. If they could reach the top, they could throw a few carefully aimed Winchester rounds over the heads of their pursuers and make the men back off. Bo didn't want to hurt anybody who rode for his father if he could help it.

"Why'd they start throwin' lead at us?" Scratch called over the pounding rataplan of hoofbeats. "They weren't close enough to recognize you!"

"Don't know!" Bo replied. Scratch was right: this couldn't be the same sort of misunderstanding that they had run into in the settlement.

But no matter what had prompted the attack, Bo didn't want to let the men get any closer. So far they were just wasting bullets by blazing away with handguns, but if they stopped and pulled out rifles it might be a different story.

The drifters were mounted on strong, speedy horses, and they reached the knob well ahead of their pursuers. The horses took to the slope valiantly, but when it grew too steep, Bo and Scratch had to dismount and lead the animals.

While they were doing that, the gunmen thundered closer. Bo heard several slugs racket through the tree limbs, but none of the bullets came close enough to represent a real threat.

As soon as they reached the knob's fairly level top and hurried onto it, the shooting stopped. The men down below couldn't see them well enough from that angle anymore. Bo and Scratch dropped the reins and pulled their Winchesters from the saddle boots. They trotted back to the edge and crouched behind a couple of tree trunks for cover.

Bo aimed downslope and fired, keeping his barrel tilted enough that he knew the shot would miss the pursuers as they approached the knob. He levered another round into the rifle's chamber and fired again. Scratch followed suit. Bo wanted to get the attention of the men who had chased them, and he knew the shots ought to do it.

Sure enough, he heard shouted curses as the men reined in. One of them ordered, "Fall back, damn it! If we charge 'em, they'll cut us down!"

Bo cranked off another couple of rounds to re-inforce that idea. The men wheeled their horses and galloped back the way they had come, veering off into some trees.

"Looks like they're splittin' up," Scratch com-mented as the echoes of the shots rolled away. "Couple of 'em ridin' off to the east."

"They'll circle around and come up on the other side of the knob," Bo predicted. "That way they can keep us pinned down up here."

"Until it gets dark, anyway. Once it does, we can slip out." Scratch looked around. "You remember this place, don't you, Bo? This is good ol' Turkey Mountain."

Bo grinned and said, "I was just thinking about that. We had some mighty good times up here, back in the old days."

"Damn right. I recollect when you brought Mary—"

Scratch stopped short. Bo didn't want his old friend to feel bad about it, so he said, "That's all right, Scratch. It was a long time ago."

"So long that the hurt's wore off?"

"Well, no," Bo admitted with a shake of his head. "I don't reckon that'll ever happen, at least not completely. But it's not as bad as it once was. I can think back on how I brought Mary up here to ask her to marry me, and it puts a smile on my face and warms my heart. There's some pain there, too, but the warmth helps."

"Hard to understand all the twists and turns that life takes, ain't it? The sky pilots like to say that everything happens for a reason, even if we ain't wise enough to see it. I'd like to think that's true, but sometimes it's mighty hard to dab a loop on that idea."

"That's why it's called faith," Bo said. He leaned forward suddenly and peered into the distance to the west. "Somebody else is coming."

Two more riders had come into sight. Maybe they had heard the shots and wanted to find out what was going on, Bo thought.

His eyes narrowed as he realized that something was familiar about one of the newcomers. The man was still too far away for Bo to make out any details. He said, "Keep an eye on those varmints in the trees, Scratch. I want to get my spyglass."

"You recognize one of those other fellas?"

"Maybe."

Bo hurried back to where they had left their horses with the reins dangling. He took a telescope from his saddlebags and returned to the tree. Leaning his rifle against the trunk, he extended the spyglass and lifted the lens to his right eye. It took him a minute to locate the two riders through the glass, but when he did their faces sprang into sharp relief.

Bo felt a sharp tingle of recognition go through him. One of the men had craggy, powerful features and crisp white hair under a black Stetson. His face was the color of old saddle leather, a permanent tan that testified to how many years he had spent working outdoors. He still rode tall and straight in the saddle despite his obviously advanced age.

It had been ten years since Bo had seen his father, but John Creel hadn't changed a whit.

Before Bo could tell Scratch what he had seen through the glass, one of the men in the trees yelled, "Hey! You *hombres* up there on the knob! Come on down with your hands in the air, and I promise we won't hang you!"

"Hang us for what?" Scratch shouted back. "We ain't done anything!"

"That's just what I'd expect one of Fontaine's men to say, you lyin' cattle thief!"

Scratch looked over at Bo and said in amazement, "They think we're rustlers."

"That would explain why they started shooting at

us," Bo said. "I think they must be Star C punchers. One of those men riding up from the direction of the ranch is my pa."

Scratch let out a low whistle.

"So the old man's still alive," he said. "I'm mighty glad to hear it, Bo. Mr. Creel ought to be able to straighten all this out."

One of the men who had taken cover in the trees suddenly galloped out into the open and raced back to intercept John Creel and his companion. For all he knew, he was risking his life by doing so, but clearly he wasn't going to let his boss ride right into danger without being warned.

"I'm going down there," Bo declared.

"They're liable to start slingin' lead at you," Scratch said.

Bo shook his head.

"I don't think so. You heard that fella say that if we surrendered, they wouldn't hang us. I'm hoping the same holds true for shooting us."

"It's a big risk."

"I'm willing to run it." Bo tossed his rifle over to Scratch. "You stay here until you see it's all right, then you can come down and bring the horses."

"Are you sure about this, Bo?"

Bo stepped out from behind the tree, held his hands out at his sides where they were in plain sight, and started walking down the slope.

"I'm sure," he said over his shoulder to Scratch.

"I'll cover you," the silver-haired Texan said. "If any of those varmints gets trigger-happy, I'll part his hair with a slug and make him duck."

Bo walked a few more steps, maintaining a steady pace, then raised his voice and called, "Hold your fire! I'm coming down!"

"Keep your hands in the air!" ordered the spokesman for the group in the trees. "I'll blow a hole through you if you reach for a gun!"

"Take it easy. My name's Bo Creel."

Although he couldn't make out the words, he heard the sound of several men exclaiming in surprise. Then the spokesman said, "Keep comin', and keep those hands in sight."

He didn't sound much more friendly now than he had before Bo revealed his identity. Bo wasn't sure the man sounded *any* friendlier, when you got right down to it.

A hundred yards away, John Creel had stopped long enough to listen to whatever the man who'd ridden out to warn him had to say. Then he promptly ignored it and kept riding. That came as no surprise to Bo. His father had never been one to let somebody else tell him what to do.

Bo reached the flat and started forward with his hands still half-raised. The men who had shot at him and Scratch emerged from the trees and rode toward him. John Creel and the other two men came on in that direction, too. Bo stopped and waited where he was, figuring he might as well let everybody come to him.

They did. The two groups rode up and reined in. Several men had their guns out and held the weapons leveled at Bo.

John Creel's blue eyes, set deep in pits of gristle, stared at Bo for a few long seconds before he barked, "Put those guns down, you blasted fools! That's my son."

A big redheaded man in the other bunch said, "You mean he was tellin' the truth about that?" Bo recognized the voice as that of the man who'd been doing the talking.

"I think I know my own flesh and blood." John moved his horse forward a couple of steps and rested his hands on the saddle horn. He gave Bo a curt nod and said, "Bo."

"Pa." Life on the rugged Texas frontier had made them not very demonstrative with family. "Good to see you again."

"Hendry, why were you shootin' at my son?" John demanded of the redhead.

"When we spotted him and his friend, we figured they were some of Fontaine's men," Hendry replied. "We weren't tryin' to kill 'em, just chase them down so we could find out what they were doin' on Star C range, boss."

At the time it had sure seemed to Bo that Hendry and the other men had been trying to kill him and

Scratch. But he didn't see any point in continuing that argument.

John repeated, "Friend? Scratch is with you?"

"Sure," Bo said.

The corners of John's mouth twitched slightly in what passed for a smile. He said, "Be good to see that rapscallion again. I reckon he's still as feisty as he ever was?"

"Pretty much."

Hendry said, "I'm sorry we threw lead at your boy, Mr. Creel. We didn't know it was him."

Hendry was twenty-five or thirty years younger than him, thought Bo, and yet the fella was calling him a boy. He supposed he understood, though, considering that Hendry worked for Bo's father.

"Anyway," the burly redhead went on, "you know what they've been sayin' in town. It ain't like Bo Creel is exactly welcome around here!"

John's leathery face hardened even more than usual. He glared at Bo and demanded, "What do you have to say for yourself about that, son?"

"What I have to say is that I don't know what in blazes is going on around here," Bo responded. "Avery Hollins and Jesse Peterson acted like they thought I was some sort of monster, and some fox-faced young firebrand sicced his friends on us and said he was going to hold us for the law. Then he yelled something about a couple of girls who got hurt . . . ?"

John didn't answer Bo's implied question. Instead he said, "That fox-faced gent you mentioned . . . did he have blond hair? Dressed sort of like a cowboy, but fancier?"

"That sounds like him, all right," Bo said.

"Danny Fontaine!" Hendry spat out the name as if it tasted bad in his mouth.

"And some of that salty Rafter F crew, more than likely," John said.

"He's the one you've been having trouble with?" Bo asked.

"He's one of 'em," John answered in a flinty voice. "Mostly it's his pa. Damn carpetbaggin' Yankee."

"The war's been over for fifteen years, Pa," Bo said.

"A Yankee's always a Yankee, no matter how many years go by," John said.

"Maybe so." Bo was getting mighty impatient. "But you still haven't told me why everybody in these parts seems to think it's all right to use me and Scratch for target practice."

"It's mostly you," John said. "Scratch just happened to be trailin' along with the wrong hombre. And you can't blame people for bein' scared and upset. I reckon everybody in the county has heard about what happened by now."

"And what is it I'm supposed to have done?"

Bo's father squinted at him and said, "A fella matchin' your description killed a couple of saloon girls, one in Cottonwood and one right there in Bear Creek. Choked 'em and then hacked 'em to pieces with a knife."

Bo was so shocked by what he'd just heard that he almost missed what his father said next.

"That's why they've started callin' the killer The Butcher of Bear Creek."

CHAPTER 5

For a long moment, Bo could only stare at John Creel and feel horrified. Finally, when he was able to speak again, he said, "Do you really believe I'd ever do a thing like that?"

John snorted.

"No flesh and blood of mine'd be capable of such a thing," he declared.

"Well, I'm glad to hear you feel that way," Bo said. "You understand there's been a mistake somewhere."

The redheaded cowboy, Hendry, said, "Maybe. But you got to admit, the fella Barney Dunn described sure looks an awful lot like your boy here."

Bo couldn't restrain his irritation anymore. He said, "I'm old enough to be your daddy, so I'd appreciate it if you'd stop calling me a boy . . . son."

Hendry flushed with anger and started to goad his horse forward. John Creel moved his mount to get in Hendry's way.

"Settle down," he snapped. "There's no point in startin' another ruckus. We'll get to the bottom of this, don't you worry about that."

"If the shooting's over," Bo said, "I want to let Scratch know it's all right to come on down."

"Go ahead," John said with a nod. "There won't be any more gunplay."

Judging by the glare on Hendry's face, he wasn't necessarily in agreement with that statement. Bo could tell the redhead wanted to reach for the Colt on his hip.

Turning to face the knob, Bo took off his hat and waved it over his head so Scratch would know it was all right to come down the slope. He put the hat back on and swung around to face his father again.

John nodded toward the redhead and said, "This is Pete Hendry. He signed on to ride for the Star C a while after you were here the last time, Bo. Your brother Riley's my foreman, but Pete's *segundo* these days."

Before Bo could respond to that introduction, Hendry said, "Don't bother tellin' me you're pleased to meet me, mister. The feelin' ain't mutual."

"Then I won't waste my breath," Bo said. To his father, he went on, "Tell me more about the trouble you've been having with those Fontaines, Pa."

John shook his head.

"We can talk about all that later, back at the ranch house. Pete, you and the boys go on about your business."

Hendry didn't look pleased about being dismissed, but he said, "Sure, boss." With another sullen glare directed at Bo, the segundo turned his horse. He told the other punchers, "Come on. We need to check those hill pastures to make sure no more stock has *strayed* onto Rafter F range."

Bo knew from Hendry's tone of voice that the man wasn't worried about the cattle straying. What he really wanted was to see if any of them had been driven across the line by Fontaine hands. From the sound of it, John Creel had a rustling problem on his hands.

The cowboys rode away, leaving Bo standing there alone with his father while they waited for Scratch. The silver-haired Texan had led the horses down from the knob and now walked toward them, leading the two mounts.

"Scratch still carries them fancy guns, I see," John said. "Most of the time when a fella packs an ivory-handled iron, it's mostly for show."

"Not Scratch. He's mighty good with those Remingtons."

"I remember," John Creel said with a nod. "You were always pretty fast, too. It's a wonder the two of you didn't wind up as gunfighters. Hired killers."

"We were both raised better than that," Bo pointed out.

John grunted in acknowledgment of that comment.

"Howdy, Mr. Creel," Scratch said as he walked up.

"Scratch," John said with a nod of greeting.

"It's mighty good to see you again. Were those some of your hands takin' those potshots at us?"

"That was all a misunderstanding," Bo said. "They thought we were rustlers working for a fella named Fontaine. Seems it was his son who started that ruckus on the bridge in town."

"You mean there's a feud between the Creels and these here Fontaines? That'd explain some of it, I guess." Scratch frowned. "But not the way Avery Hollins and Jesse Peterson and all the other folks in town acted."

"That's because that's not all of the story," Bo said. His face and voice were grim. "It seems that most of the people in these parts are convinced that I'm a murderer. They think I killed a couple of saloon girls."

"What! That's crazy. You never done such a thing!"

"You know that, and I know that," Bo said dryly. "Convincing everybody else will be the trick."

Scratch looked up at John Creel, who was still mounted.

"You don't believe that, do you, Mr. Creel?" he asked.

"Of course not," John said gruffly. "But enough people do that it's gonna cause a heap of trouble around here if you stay, Bo."

"Are you telling me to run, Pa?" Bo sounded like he couldn't believe it.

"You ought to know better than that," John snapped. "Creels don't run from trouble. Sometimes, though, it's smarter to ride around it." He lifted his reins. "For right now, both of you come on back to the ranch with me. You ought to know the whole story before you make up your minds what to do next."

"That sounds good to me," Bo said. He took the reins of his horse from Scratch and swung up into the saddle. Scratch mounted, as well, and the two of them fell in alongside John as the patriarch of the Creel family started west along the stream toward the headquarters of the Star C.

Bo tried to bring up the subject that was uppermost in his mind, the accusations leveled against him, but John wasn't having any of it.

"Wait'll we get back to the ranch," he said, and Bo knew his father well enough to be aware that there was no point in arguing.

"Well, how about the rest of the family?" he asked. "Will you at least tell me how everybody's doing?"

"Reckon I can do that. They're all fine. Riley and Julia are grandparents."

"Is that so?"

"Yeah, their boy Chad and his wife, Sunny, got themselves a little boy."

"That makes you a great-grandpa."

"Yeah, I know, and I will be again, sometime in the fall. Davy's wife, Hannah, is in the family way, too."

"I'm glad to hear it," Bo said. "Davy is Cooper and Desdemona's boy, right?" He had close to a dozen nieces and nephews, and it was hard for him to keep up with all of them, what with him being away from home so much. He supposed he had missed out on a lot by drifting for all those years . . . but he had experienced a lot of things he would have missed out on otherwise, too.

"Yeah, Davy is one of Cooper's sons," John went on. "He's got the twins, too, and that girl, Barbara Sue."

For the next quarter of an hour, John brought Bo up to date on all the family happenings. Bo enjoyed hearing about it, even though nothing really exciting had happened to the Creel family, just the mundane things that wove together to form the tapestry of life.

Clearly, though, other things had been going on around here that weren't so mundane. When Bo was caught up on all the lives of all his kinfolks, he said, "What about this trouble with the Fontaines? Are you going to tell me about that?"

"I don't see why I should," John replied bluntly. "There's not a blamed thing you can do about it."

"Scratch and I aren't exactly strangers to trouble, you know."

"That's right," Scratch added. "We been known to walk right up and introduce ourselves to it."

"I don't doubt it," John said. "But you've got

your own problems right now, Bo. You don't need to be takin' on anything else."

"If it has to do with my family, then the decision's already been made for me," Bo insisted. "I'm involved."

John sighed and said, "All right, you might as well know what's been goin' on. About five years ago a fella named Ned Fontaine bought the Winthorp spread."

"What happened to Jim Winthorp?" Bo asked, referring to the cattleman who had owned the range to the west of the Star C. "I didn't think that old-timer would ever sell out. He'd been in these parts just about as long as we have."

"He wouldn't have sold out," John said, "but his widow did after the consumption took Jim."

Bo shook his head solemnly.

"I'm sorry to hear that. Jim was a good man. Pioneer stock, all the way to the bone."

"That's true. Fontaine's a different story. He's from back East somewhere. Fancies himself a shrewd businessman."

Scratch put in, "Every Yankee I ever saw who called himself a shrewd businessman was really just a cheap crook."

"That's Ned Fontaine," John said. "He stays just inside the law, as far as anybody's ever been able to determine, but I'm damn sure some of my cows have wound up with his brand on 'em. Not only that, but his sons are always stirrin' up trouble with our men. It's got to where our crew can't hardly go into Bear Creek without windin' up in a ruckus of some sort."

"We saw one of the Fontaine boys, according to your segundo," Bo said.

John nodded and said, "Danny. He's the younger one. The older one is Nick. There's a girl in between 'em in age, Samantha. Danny's a hothead, always lookin' for a fight. Nick's quieter, but he's the more dangerous of the two. He's killed three men in gun-fights. Fair fights, accordin' to the law, but every time the other fella was pushed into it. Nick Fontaine is pretty slick on the draw."

"Sounds like you've got the makin's of a range war here," Scratch said.

"Not if I can help it." John Creel's voice was emphatic. "Nobody wins in those damned things. A lot of innocent folks die, that's what happens. But if Fontaine pushes me hard enough, he won't leave me any choice."

Bo said, "I hope it never comes to that."

"You and me both, son." John nodded ahead of them. "There's the ranch."

Bo had already seen it, and he felt the warmth of memory spreading through him as he gazed at the old home place. The original ranch house was built of logs and sat atop a rise that sloped up gently from the creek. Several additions constructed of roughly planed and whitewashed lumber sprawled around it, connected to the main house by covered dogtrots.

Beyond the house was a large barn surrounded by corrals. A blacksmith shop and smokehouse were also on this side of the creek, which could be crossed by means of a sturdy footbridge, although the stream's banks were low enough and it was shallow enough that it could be waded or ridden across without any trouble except during spring floods.

A long, low bunkhouse sat on the other side of the creek, along with a cook shack for the hands. A short distance upstream was another large frame house where Bo's brother Riley and his family lived. Bo knew that a couple more houses belonging to his brothers Cooper and Hank lay out of sight around a bend in the creek. His nieces and nephews who were married probably had cabins scattered over the range.

Several men stood at the corral fence, watching a rider try to stay on the back of a pitching, sunfishing bronc. The cowboy lost his seat and sailed into the air, drawing groans from the spectators as he crashed to the ground. Two more punchers dashed forward and lassoed the bronc, pulling it away so it couldn't trample the cowboy who'd been thrown.

The approach of Bo, Scratch, and John caused several dogs to bound toward them, barking. One of the men who stood at the corral fence turned to look and then started toward them. He was tall and slender, with a loose-jointed stride that Bo would have recognized anywhere. He knew the man was his brother Riley.

As Riley came up to them, he asked his father, "Did you find out what all that shooting was about, Pa?" Without waiting for an answer, he swung his gaze to the two men who had ridden up with John Creel, and his face hardened to stone as he said, "Bo?"

"That's right, little brother," Bo said with a smile. He was the oldest, so all his brothers were "little brother" to him. "It's mighty good to see you."

Riley Creel didn't return the greeting. Instead, he turned back to his father and said harshly, "I thought you said that if he ever dared to show his face around here again, you'd tell him to rattle his hocks off Star C range, Pa. You said as far as you were concerned, he wasn't even a Creel anymore!"

CHAPTER 6

It seemed that there was no end to the surprises he was going to encounter today, Bo thought as a bitter taste welled up in his throat. He looked at his father and asked, "Is that what you said, Pa?"

He knew better than to expect John Creel to be embarrassed about anything, so he wasn't disappointed when John returned his look squarely and answered in typically blunt fashion, "Damned right I did. And when I said it, I meant every word of it, too."

"Then what's he doing here?" Riley asked.

"It's his home just like it is yours, no matter what he's done. I realized that when I saw him."

Anger flashed in Riley's eyes as he said, "The hell it is. He ran off ages ago, while me and the rest of the boys stayed here and worked our hind ends off and helped you make the Star C one of the best spreads in Texas!"

"I'm right here, you know," Bo said coolly. "If

you've got a problem with me, Riley, you can tell me about it to my face."

Riley's jaw jutted out defiantly.

"All right," he said. "That's just what I'll do. As far as I'm concerned, Bo, you're nothing but a low-down—"

"That's enough!" John's voice cut across his son's words. "Bo, you and Scratch go on in the house. I'll join you directly. Riley, you take care of their horses."

"The hell I will," Riley said. "Get somebody else to do it."

He turned on his heel and stalked off toward the bridge over the creek. John's face flushed a dark red with fury. Bo knew his father wasn't accustomed to being spoken to that way, least of all by one of his own sons.

One of the hands came up and said, "I'll tend to the horses, Mr. Creel."

"I'm obliged to you, Steve," John said as he jerked his head in a nod. He dismounted, along with Bo and Scratch, and turned to follow Riley.

"Maybe I ought to go after him, too," Bo mused as he handed his reins to the young cowboy called Steve.

Scratch shook his head and said, "Right now I reckon there's a good chance you'd just make things worse. Let the two of them sort it out, if they will."

Bo knew that was good advice, but it still wasn't

easy for him to take it. He sighed and forced himself to walk toward the big ranch house.

The front of the house had a low porch on it. As Bo and Scratch stepped up onto that porch, the front door opened and a woman said, "Bo Creel and Scratch Morton. Land's sake, I'd just about given up on ever seeing you two boys again."

The tiny owner of that voice stepped out onto the porch to meet them. Idabelle Fisher barely topped four feet. She had been John Creel's cook and housekeeper for fifteen years. Her gray hair was pulled into a tight bun on top of her head. Spectacles perched on the end of her nose. She lifted her arms to hug Bo and Scratch in turn as they bent down to embrace her.

"Howdy, Miz Fisher," Scratch said, grinning. "You don't happen to have any peach cobbler cookin', do you?"

"No, but if I'd known you were coming, Scratch, I would have had one in the oven. I'll whip one up tomorrow. You *are* staying awhile, aren't you?"

"I reckon that depends on Pa . . . and Riley," Bo said. "He wasn't too happy to see me."

"Don't worry about that stiff-necked brother of yours," Idabelle said. "He'll do whatever John says."

"Then maybe I should worry about Pa. According to Riley, Pa said I wasn't welcome here anymore."

"Your father says a lot of things. It means about as much as an old bull bellowing in the pasture."

A troubled look came over the old woman's face. "Blood's stronger than, well, just about anything."

"You're probably wondering—"

She stopped him by shaking her head.

"I'm not asking any questions."

"Well, I'm telling you," Bo said. "I didn't do those things folks are saying I did."

"And I can vouch for that," Scratch added. "Bo and I just rode in today from up north. Neither of us has been anywhere around here since the last time we saw you, ten years ago."

Idabelle looked relieved.

"Thank the Lord for that," she said. "I never believed those terrible things people claimed you did. When Barney Dunn told everybody about the man who killed poor Rose, somebody said that description sounded just like Bo Creel, but I knew that was pure foolishness. I knew you'd never hurt anybody unless it was a bad man who had it coming. Nobody was willing to listen to reason, though. You know how people are. Once somebody said your name, so many of them latched on to it and decided you had to be the killer. You hadn't been around here for so long, it was easy to blame you."

"But we hadn't been here, like you just said," Scratch pointed out. "Why would folks think that Bo had snuck back to Bear Creek and turned into a mad dog?"

"Well . . . that was easier for folks to believe than to think that one of their neighbors . . . maybe even somebody in their own house . . . was to blame, I suppose," Idabelle said.

She was probably right about that, Bo thought. Nobody wanted to believe that someone capable of such brutal violence lurked among them.

"I've heard this Barney Dunn mentioned a couple of times," Bo said. "Who is he? I don't remember him."

Idabelle waved a hand and said, "Oh, I suspect your father will want to explain everything to you. There's coffee on the stove. Come on in, and I'll pour a cup for both of you."

Scratch said, "That's an invitation I won't turn down."

They followed the diminutive woman into the house, which was almost exactly as Bo remembered it. The flintlock rifle his father had used during the revolution hung over the mantle above the massive stone fireplace. A couple of sets of longhorns were mounted on the wall flanking the rifle. Thick woven rugs were scattered around on the puncheon floor. The furniture was heavy and comfortable. There was a certain air of gloom in the place because it was rather dark, and that was because the windows were small. Big enough to fire a rifle out of, but too small for a Comanche warrior to climb through. More than once in the old days, the family had been forced to fort up in here and fight off a marauding war party.

Bo and Scratch hung their hats on pegs near the

door while Idabelle went into the kitchen. She came back with steaming cups of Arbuckle coffee. Scratch took a sip of his and said, "Strong enough to get up and walk off on its own hind legs, just the way I like it."

"That's the only way any of you cowboys drink it," the old woman said. "Although I guess you and Bo aren't really cowboys, are you?"

"We've done our share of working cattle," Bo said. "Just not here."

"Well, from what your pa told me about what happened, I don't suppose I blame you for leaving, Bo. Might've been nice if you'd been here to lend John a hand over the years—"

"He's done all right for himself, and he's had plenty of help from Riley and the other boys."

"Yes, but I know he's missed you," Idabelle said.

From the gentleness of her tone whenever she spoke about his father, Bo had a pretty good idea that Idabelle was in love with John Creel, even though he would have bet not only his hat but his boots and saddle, too, that nothing improper had ever taken place between the two of them, and almost certainly never would at their age.

Bo's mother had been dead for several years when Idabelle came to work at the Star C. John had gone through a succession of cooks and housekeepers before finding one who could put up with his sometimes irascible ways. Idabelle had filled that bill. She wore a wedding ring but never said anything about a husband, so Bo had always assumed she was a widow.

All he knew for sure was that she took good care of his father, and that was all that mattered.

John came in, stomping his boots on the porch before he did so to get some of the dust off them. That had been a habit of his for as far back as Bo could remember, stomping off dust in the summer and mud in the winter. John hung up his hat and walked over to join them near the fireplace.

"I tried to talk some sense into your brother," he said to Bo. "Don't think I did much good, though."

"Riley was always pretty stubborn," Bo said. "He comes by it honest. We all do."

John snorted. He gestured toward a couple of chairs and said, "Sit down. Idabelle . . ."

"Already going to get your coffee," she said over her shoulder as she swept out of the room.

The men sat down. Bo said, "If you think it'll help, I'll talk to Riley."

"You leave your brother to me," John said. "I'll make him understand."

"Making somebody understand something and making him believe it are sometimes two different things," Bo pointed out.

John scowled.

"I reckon I'm partly to blame for this. When folks in Bear Creek started talkin' about how it must've been you who killed those girls, I didn't put a stop to it right away like I should have. I knew better than to think that my own son would do such a thing. But I hadn't seen you for so long . . . and folks change some over the years—"

"Not that much," Bo said.

"No, not that much," John agreed. "You're right. But you know how I am."

"You get a burr under your saddle and say things you don't mean."

"That's right, but you needn't sound so disrespectful about it. I'm still your pa, remember?"

"Why don't you start at the beginning?" Bo suggested. "I'd really like to hear about these things I'm suspected of doing."

"Once you've heard it, you may not feel that way."

"I'll take my chances," Bo said.

Before John could begin, Idabelle came back from the kitchen with a cup of coffee for him. He took a couple of sips, then said, "About a month ago, a girl who worked at one of the saloons down in Cottonwood turned up dead. Her name was Sara, Sally, something like that. She had her own shack where she lived, and when she didn't turn up for work the fella who owns the saloon went looking for her. He found her in the shack . . ."

John stopped and glanced at Idabelle, who had taken one of the other chairs. She said, "If you're thinking to spare my delicate sensibilities, John, it isn't necessary. I've heard the story, too. I know what happened to the poor girl."

"All right," John said. He went on, "The gal had

been choked to death, Doc Perkins said when they brought the body up here for him to look at, and after she was dead whoever killed her took a knife to the body. A big knife with a heavy blade, from the looks of it, accordin' to Doc."

"A butcher knife," Bo said.

"More than likely. The sheriff sent a deputy down to ask around about what happened, and a couple of people said they saw the girl talkin' to a tall fella in a dark suit the night before, but nobody seemed to get a real good look at him. The girl worked at the saloon, but she, uh, sometimes . . . uh . . ."

John hesitated and glanced at Idabelle again. She said, "For goodness' sake, John, I know what whores are. I'm not going to roll my eyes and faint just because somebody says something about what men and women do together."

"All right, all right," John muttered. "Sometimes this gal would take men back to her shack, too, as well as consortin' with 'em at the saloon. Everybody figured the fella she was with went a little loco—"

"More than a little," Idabelle put in.

"Yeah, more than a little. It shook up the folks in Cottonwood when she was killed, but the people in Bear Creek weren't that worried about it. Then a couple of weeks ago, Rose Delavan was killed the same way. She worked for Lauralee Parker at the Southern Belle."

Scratch asked, "Lauralee wasn't hurt, was she?"

"No, she's fine. Just upset and scared, like everybody else."

"So who's Barney Dunn?" Bo asked.

"He's a bartender who works for Lauralee, too. On the night that Rose was killed, he stepped out in the alley behind the saloon for a minute, after most of the customers had gone home, and he spotted something going on in the shadows. He said it sounded like a couple of people strugglin', so he went to get a better look. Then he heard this sound like . . . well, like somebody cuttin' meat. He struck a match to see what was goin' on, and he saw a man bendin' over what was left of Rose, choppin' her to pieces. The fella stopped cuttin' and looked right up at him."

"And it was me," Bo said heavily.

"Well, he said it was a fella who wasn't young, who had brown hair with a little gray in it and wore a dark suit. You've got to admit, that sounds like you, Bo."

Scratch said, "It sounds like thousands of other hombres, too."

"Yeah, but Dunn, he's sort of good at sketchin' things, so he made a drawin' of the man he saw killin' Rose, and I got to admit, Bo, it looked just like you. Dunn was showin' it around at the saloon, and Avery Hollins saw it and said, 'Good Lord, that's Bo Creel,' and other folks who know you took a look at it and agreed. It didn't take long for the story to get around town, and everybody figured you had come back to Bear Creek and started killin' soiled doves."

Bo drew in a deep breath and blew it back out in an exasperated sigh.

"Did anybody bother to stop and ask themselves why in blazes I'd do a thing like that?" he wanted to know.

"I'm sure some did. I guess most folks just assumed you'd gone mad."

Scratch said, "That's a heck of a conclusion to jump to."

"Yeah, but mobs don't stop and think, and that's what the population of Bear Creek is these days, a mob. It don't help matters that the Fontaines keep stirrin' 'em up. Danny's always in one of the saloons harpin' on the killin's and sayin' that something ought to be done about them."

"Getting back to Barney Dunn," Bo said, "what happened after he struck that match and saw what had happened? How come this so-called Butcher of Bear Creek didn't come after him?"

"According to Dunn, he did. He swung that big ol' knife at him. Dunn claims he jumped higher and farther than he ever did in his life and barely avoided gettin' his head chopped off. He made it to the back door of the saloon and tumbled through it just in time to kick it closed behind him and drop the bar across it. Then he started hollerin' his head off for help. The place had cleared out by then, but a few people were still movin' around town and they came a-runnin'. When they heard Dunn's story, they got shotguns and lanterns and went out to search that alley, and they found Rose's body back there, but no sign of the killer."

"That's mighty convenient," Scratch said. "Anybody stop to think that maybe Dunn killed her his own self and made up that business about the other fella?"

John Creel's bushy white eyebrows rose in surprise.

"That's mighty smart of you, Scratch," he said. "You thought of that right away. It took Marshal Haltom three or four days to have that same idea. But Dunn's a little fella, and Rose was a pretty strappin' gal. I'm not sure he could've strangled her. Not only that, Dunn was workin' at the Southern Belle with plenty of witnesses when the gal was killed down at Cottonwood, so he couldn't have done that. Doc Perkins said that from the looks of it, he was sure the same varmint was responsible for both killin's."

"That's probably true," Bo said. "But either way, I didn't have anything to do with them."

"No, but you can see how come folks were

spooked when you rode into town, bold as brass. The question is, what are you gonna do now?"

"I came to visit you and the rest of the family," Bo said. "The real question is, what do you want me to do?"

"I can answer that," Riley said from the doorway. "Get out. That's what we want you to do."

CHAPTER 7

John Creel bolted up out of his chair and said, "Damn it, Riley, we talked about this. You told me you'd back off—"

"That was before he talked to me."

The new voice came from a man who'd stepped up onto the porch behind Riley. As this man followed Riley into the house, Bo recognized his brother Cooper, who had their mother's blond hair and wore a handlebar mustache with the tips waxed. Cooper had inherited his brawny build from John Creel, just like Bo had, instead of Riley's lankiness, which came from their mother.

"I'm sorry to have to say it, Bo," Cooper went on, "but with that trouble hanging over your head, there's no place for you here. We have enough problems of our own these days without shielding a murderer."

"You, too?" Bo said. "You really believe your

own brother is capable of doing such terrible things?"

"You may be our brother by blood, but you haven't spent more than a month here, total, in the past forty years. How the hell are we supposed to know what you're capable of?" Cooper glanced over at Idabelle, who was glaring at him, and added, "Pardon my language, ma'am."

Scratch said, "You know what Bo was like when you were all kids."

"People change," Cooper said, unknowingly repeating what his father had said a few minutes earlier. "And that picture Barney Dunn drew was the spitting image of you, Bo. Tell me how he was able to do that if he didn't see you like he said he did."

Bo couldn't answer that. The same mystifying question had occurred to him. As far as he knew, he had never met Barney Dunn. There was no way the bartender could have drawn a picture of him without seeing him.

But he hadn't been there in that alley behind the Southern Belle, and he sure hadn't killed any saloon girls. None of it made sense.

"I don't have any explanation," Bo said. "You'll just have to take my word for it."

"And he's your brother," Scratch added, "so you damned well ought to."

"Stay out of this, Scratch," Riley said. "It's none of your business."

"It sure is. Bo's my friend, and I'm his, what do

you call it, alibi. He's been with me the whole time, a long way from Bear Creek, so I know he didn't kill those gals."

"Then why don't the two of you go back to the settlement and explain all that to Marshal Haltom?" Cooper suggested. "Maybe he'd believe you."

Scratch shook his head and said, "Nobody in Bear Creek seemed to be interested in believin' anythin' except the worst."

"You can't blame them," Riley said. "All the evidence says Bo's guilty."

"We're just goin' 'round and 'round in circles here," John growled. "Bo's stayin' right here for now. I'll go into town tomorrow and have a talk with the marshal. Like I said before, we'll get to the bottom of this."

Riley and Cooper didn't look happy about that decision, but evidently they knew better than to continue arguing with their father. Being told he was wrong always made John Creel dig in his heels and get even more stubborn. A mule could be downright open-minded in comparison to his pa, thought Bo.

His brothers turned and left the house without saying anything else.

"This hasn't been much of a homecomin' for you, has it?" John asked.

"Maybe not," Bo said, "but I'm glad to be here anyway. I'm glad I found out what people have been saying about me. I don't like the idea that folks believe I'm a murderer. I'd rather clear my name once and for all so I can ride free wherever I want to without that hanging over my head."

Scratch added, "Yeah, the way things are goin', there'll be wanted posters out on Bo before much longer, and then bounty hunters might come after him. If we hadn't ridden down here, we wouldn't have had a clue why he was bein' chased."

"That's a good point," John agreed. "We got to get things straightened out before anybody prints up some of those 'Wanted Dead or Alive' posters."

Idabelle got to her feet.

"I'm going to get started on supper," she said. "Are you staying, Scratch?"

"Yes'm," he replied. "Figured I'd ride across Bear Creek and see my brother and sister tomorrow."

"Do you still have as big an appetite as you used to?"

Scratch grinned and said, "Gettin' older ain't done anything to change that yet."

"Then I'll be sure to fix plenty of food," Idabelle told him with a smile.

When she had gone out to the kitchen, John went over to a big rolltop desk in the corner and opened it. He took out a corked jug and said, "We'll just sweeten this coffee a mite."

Bo and Scratch held out their cups and let John add a dollop of whiskey to each of them, including his own. After he had replaced the jug in the desk, he took a sip of the spiked coffee, licked his lips in appreciation, and said, "There's nothin' wrong with Idabelle's coffee, but there ain't many things in life that a little corn liquor won't improve."

"You know she probably knows you've got that jug hidden in the desk," Bo said.

"Oh sure, but she don't say anything about it and neither do I. As long as I don't flaunt it in front of her, she lets it slide. If she ever let on that she knew about it, then her bein' a good Christian woman, she'd have to do something about it." John sat down in his chair, stretched his long legs out in front of him, looked at Bo and Scratch over his coffee cup, and went on, "All right, you two. Tell me all about your adventures since the last time you came home to Bear Creek."

If not for the worry lingering in the back of his mind, Bo would have thoroughly enjoyed the rest of that day. He and Scratch spent a couple of hours spinning yarns for John Creel. There were plenty of them to choose from, because trouble had never been shy about roping in the two drifters from Texas.

At one point, John commented, "If I didn't know better, I'd say you've been makin' up stories like old Avery Hollins. You've been in so many fights you ought to be dead a hundred times over."

"We've been lucky," Bo acknowledged.

"Luck's got nothin' to do with it," Scratch insisted. "It just stands to reason that a couple of Texans are tougher than any of the varmints they might run into somewheres else."

"Damn straight," John agreed with an emphatic nod.

Idabelle brought in food from the kitchen and called them over to the big dining table on one side of the room.

"Do the boys and their families eat with you?" Bo asked.

John shook his head.

"They've got their own houses and take their meals there."

"Except on holidays and other special occasions," Idabelle said. "Then the house is full of children and laughter."

"I'd like to see that," Bo said. "Maybe we'll make a point of drifting this direction some Christmas."

"Don't wait too long," John said. "I ain't gettin' any younger, you know."

Scratch said, "Shoot, Mr. Creel, you'll outlive us all. Everybody knows that."

John grunted as if to say that he wasn't so sure of that.

It was hard to imagine a world without his pa in it, mused Bo. But that day was coming. John Creel was already older than most men ever lived to be, and while he seemed hale and hearty, that could change with little warning.

Bo told himself not to think about that. Instead he just enjoyed the meal and the evening that followed. When it came time to turn in, in one of the guest rooms upstairs, he slept well, although his dreams were haunted at times by gruesome images of dead women and blood dripping from a butcher knife.

He woke early the next morning, as was his habit, but not as early as Idabelle Fisher, who had breakfast ready for the men when they came downstairs. Ham and eggs, biscuits and gravy, mountains of flapjacks, plenty of steaming hot coffee . . .

Bo had never minded the rough meals that he and Scratch prepared on the trail, but this home cooking was a world of difference. It was almost enough to make a man think about settling down and staying put.

Almost.

After Scratch had heaped effusive but well-deserved praise on the meal, he said, "I reckon I'll saddle up and head on across the creek this mornin'."

"Keep your eyes open," Bo warned. "Folks around here know that you were with me yesterday. They might hold a grudge against you because of the things they think I did."

"I'll take my chances," Scratch said. "Anyway, if

I run into anybody, I'll just tell 'em that they're all wrong about you."

"I'm not sure that would do any good."

"It's a start," Scratch insisted. "We got to make people see the truth."

"It would help if we knew what that truth was," Bo said.

Scratch frowned and asked, "Are you thinkin' about tryin' to find out who really killed them gals?"

"I'm no Pinkerton detective," Bo said, "but it seems to me that the best way to make folks believe I'm innocent would be to figure out who's really guilty."

"Yeah, that makes sense, I reckon. We'll talk about it when I get back."

Bo nodded and lifted a hand in farewell as Scratch headed out to the barn to saddle his horse. A short time later the silver-haired Texan rode away with a clatter of hoofbeats.

John Creel got ready to leave a short time later for Bear Creek, heading out on his errand to talk to Marshal Jonas Haltom. Bo didn't know the marshal, who had taken the job since the last time Bo and Scratch had been there, but his father assured him that Halton was an honest lawman.

"He'll listen to reason," John said. "At least I hope he will."

"He hasn't done anything about the stock you're losing to the Fontaines, has he?" Bo asked.

John shrugged and said, "There ain't much he can do. He's the town marshal, got no jurisdiction outside the town limits. It's up to the sheriff to stop the rustlin', and to tell the truth, he don't seem to care all that much about it. Makes me wonder if Ned Fontaine didn't slip him a little somethin'."

"That's a pretty serious accusation."

"Maybe so, but I wouldn't put it past Fontaine." John sighed. "And we don't have any proof that Fontaine's to blame for what's been goin' on. If we did, hell, I'd send for the Rangers. They'd come in and clean things up, by gum."

"Maybe that's what you ought to do," Bo suggested.

John's eyes narrowed as he said, "I'm used to stompin' my own snakes without hollerin' for any help." He swung up into the saddle. "We'll talk about it later. For now, you stick close to home, Bo. Don't go wanderin' around the countryside where somebody could jump you."

"I plan to stay right here," Bo promised.

With both Scratch and his father gone, he was sort of at loose ends, so a while later he gave in to his restlessness and walked out to the barn. The hands had already left on their daily chores, so he didn't think anybody was around. But when he stepped into the barn he saw a man sitting on a stool, mending a saddle.

"Hello, Hank," Bo said, warmth going through him at the sight of his youngest brother.

Hank was stocky and awkward. He had never been much good as a cowboy, but he was good with numbers and kept up with the ranch's books. He was a decent craftsman, too, and could be counted on to keep the saddles and other tack in good repair. With his brown hair, close-cropped beard, and sad eyes, he had always reminded Bo a little of an overgrown puppy.

Hank smiled now and set the saddle aside. He stood up and hugged Bo.

"Riley and Cooper told me you were here," he said.

"Did they mention how they weren't happy about that situation?"

"Those two are always worked up about something. This time it just happens to be you, Bo."

"You're bound to have heard what people are saying, Hank."

"I've heard it. That doesn't mean I have to believe it. Right from the start, I've said that the whole idea is crazy."

"You weren't much more than a boy the last time you saw me," Bo pointed out. "We don't really know each other that well."

"Well enough," Hank said. "We're blood kin, Bo. I believe in you."

Bo put a hand on his brother's shoulder and said, "I appreciate that, Hank, I really—"

The sudden thud of hoofbeats made him stop. The pounding grew louder as Bo turned. A group of riders swept into the yard between the main house and the barn and reined in with dust swirling around the hooves of their horses. Bo and Hank stepped out of the barn.

A big, barrel-chested man with a prominent nose was in the lead. He sat his saddle and glared down at the two men on the ground.

"Bo Creel?" he demanded.

Bo moved forward, ignoring the warning murmur that came from Hank. He said, "I'm Bo Creel."

He had already spotted the tin star pinned to the big stranger's vest, so he wasn't surprised when the man said, "I'm Marshal Jonas Haltom from Bear Creek. You're under arrest for murder." Haltom put his hand on the butt of his holstered gun. "And I don't reckon there's anybody here who'd be too damn upset about it if you wanted to put up a fight."

CHAPTER 8

Hank took a hurried step and put himself in front of Bo.

"See here, Marshal," he began, "you can't—"

"Get out of the way, Hank!" Haltom snapped. "Nobody wants to hurt you. It's this mad dog killer brother of yours we're after!"

Bo had strapped on his Colt that morning even though he was home. Wearing the gun was purely a matter of habit. Since he could tell the members of the posse were eager for trouble, he made sure his hands were in plain sight as he stepped around Hank. He didn't want to give any of those trigger-happy hombres an excuse to start blazing away.

"Take it easy, Marshal," he said. "And, Hank, do what the man says and move back."

"But, Bo, it's not right—"

One of the possemen said, "Defending a killer, that's what's not right."

Until now, Bo hadn't spotted the man in the

cluster of riders, but when he looked closer he recognized the speaker as Danny Fontaine, the fox-faced youngster who'd instigated the battle on the bridge the day before.

Danny went on, "Of course, that's just about what I'd expect from one of you no-account Creels." He smirked at Bo. "And you, I told you you'd pay for what you've done."

"That's enough," Marshal Haltom snapped. "Now, are you coming along peacefully, Creel, or do we have to lasso you and drag you back to town?"

"My father's gone to Bear Creek to talk to you, Marshal," Bo said. "You must have run into him on your way out here."

Haltom shook his head stubbornly.

"We didn't see him. Anyway, there's nothing to talk about. You're wanted for murder, and you've got to answer for it."

"Who swore out the charge?"

"I did," Danny said.

"I'm not sure that's legal."

The marshal said, "We'll let the judge sort all that out once you're behind bars where you can't hurt anybody else. Now, I'm tired of messin' around with this. One way or another, you're coming with us."

"Say the word, Bo," Hank breathed. "I'll back your play."

And get yourself killed, Bo thought. Even though the charge against him was bogus, the last thing in the world he wanted was to be responsible for his little brother's death.

"Stay out of it, Hank," Bo said. "Marshal, I'm going to take out my gun and give it to you—"

"Cover him!" Haltom snapped, and several of the men yanked out their revolvers and leveled them at Bo. "But nobody fire unless I give the order!" To Bo, he went on, "Use your left hand, Creel, and take that hogleg out nice and easy."

Bo did as he was told, even though his every instinct rebelled against surrendering like this. He still believed in the law, still believed there had to be a way to work this out. Having the townspeople and even the marshal all riled up was one thing, but surely once a judge heard Scratch's testimony, he'd have to realize that Bo was innocent and dismiss the murder charges.

He reached across his body, took his gun out of the holster with his left hand, reversed it, and held it out to Haltom butt-first. The marshal took the weapon, unloaded it, and stuck it behind his belt.

"Where's your horse?" he demanded.

"In the barn," Bo replied, inclining his head that direction.

"Hank, go saddle it up," Haltom ordered.

"I'm not your damn flunkey," Hank said, letting his anger boil over.

Bo said, "You know which horse and saddle are mine, Hank, and I can trust you to do a good job. Take care of it for me, will you?"

Hank turned to him.

"Bo, you can't really mean to do this," he argued. "I know you didn't hurt those girls. It's loco!"

"It'll all get hashed out," Bo said, keeping his voice calm and level despite the fact that his insides crawled at the thought of being locked up in Bear Creek's jail. He looked into his brother's eyes and nodded to let Hank know that it was all right.

"I'll get Cooper and Riley, and when Pa gets back, we'll ride to town and get you out of there," Hank said miserably.

The marshal said, "Anybody who tries to mess with one of my prisoners will get a damn faceful of buckshot, and don't you doubt it!"

"Just get the horse," Bo told Hank.

Looking stricken, Hank did as Bo asked. He came out of the barn a few minutes later leading the saddled mount.

"What about my hat and coat?" Bo asked Marshal Haltom.

"You won't need 'em where you're going," the lawman snapped. "Get on that horse, and then I'll cuff you."

"You won't need the handcuffs. I'm not going to give you any trouble."

"If you do, you'll be sorry."

Bo had no doubt about that. He had been studying the faces of the posse members. Many of them were unfamiliar to him, citizens of Bear Creek who had moved into the area since the last time he'd been here. They all believed he was a vicious, cold-blooded murderer, and if he made any move to escape, they wouldn't hesitate to fill him full of lead.

On the other hand, half a dozen of the men were hombres he knew, honest men who lived and worked in Bear Creek and wouldn't stand for any illegal shenanigans. They wouldn't allow Danny Fontaine or any of the others to gun Bo down without provocation . . . and he didn't intend to give them that provocation.

So he felt reasonably certain that if he went with the posse, he would make it to Bear Creek alive. More important, Hank wouldn't get hurt, and neither would anyone else on the Star C. With the posse covering him, Bo grasped the reins and the saddle horn and swung up onto his horse.

"Get word to Scratch about this," he said quietly as he looked down at Hank. "Tell him what happened. Tell him he's going to have to take care of the chore we talked about earlier."

"What's that?" Marshal Haltom asked sharply. "Are you conspiring, Creel?"

"No, just asking my brother to let my friend know what's going on."

Danny Fontaine said, "If you ask me, we ought to arrest that partner of his, too. He had to know about Creel cutting up those women."

"You let me worry about who we're gonna arrest

and who we aren't," Haltom said. He had drawn his revolver, and he gestured to Bo with it. "Come on."

Bo heeled his horse into motion. The members of the posse closed in around him as he rode away from the ranch. He looked back over his shoulder and caught a glimpse of Hank standing there forlornly. Over at the house, Idabelle Fisher had come out onto the front porch and looked upset, too, as the men rode away.

Surrounded and unarmed like this, Bo felt helpless, and he didn't like the feeling, not one bit.

His best chance now was the hope that Scratch would understand the message Hank would deliver to him and be able to find the actual murderer of those saloon girls.

It was a pretty slim chance, especially when Bo knew that his life was probably riding on it.

Not much had changed in these parts, Scratch thought as he rode across Bear Creek at one of the places where the stream was easy to ford. About half a mile downstream was the old swimming hole where he had persuaded Betsy Hanrahan to go skinny-dipping with him when they were both sixteen.

Truth to tell, he hadn't had to try very hard to convince her. She'd been just about as eager as he was. The memory put a wistful smile on his face. The last he had heard of her, Betsy was married to a fella over at Hallettsville and had six kids and twenty grandchildren. Scratch doubted if she even remembered that hot summer day so long ago . . . but he did.

On the other side of the creek, he spotted the grove of trees where he and Bo had hidden one time when they were out hunting and almost ran smack-dab into a Comanche war party, back in the days when Texas was still a republic. They had made it to the trees barely in time to crouch down out of sight and hope that the Comanches hadn't seen them.

They didn't have any horses, so there wasn't any chance they could outrun the war party. If the Indians came after them, they'd have to make a fight of it. Armed only with single-shot rifles, they had known they likely wouldn't survive a battle. There were a dozen warriors in that bunch. They would be able to overrun the two young Texicans.

But Bo and Scratch were both confident that they would give a good account of themselves and kill some of the Comanches before they went down fighting. That was scant comfort when they considered how their hair would wind up decorating some warrior's lance, but on the frontier you took what consolation you could when it came to dying.

Of course, the Comanches had ridden on without ever noticing them, and when the war party was gone, the two youngsters had lain down on the ground and laughed at their close call, both of them pretending not to see the tears of relief they were crying. They still had a lot of living to do.

And they had done it, Scratch thought now. By God if they hadn't.

He came in sight of a frame farmhouse, built in the early Texas style with the two parts of the house separated by a covered dogtrot. The thick planks were unpainted, gray with age, and slightly warped in places but still sturdy. It was the old Morton home place. Scratch rode toward it with a warm feeling inside him and the tightness of nostalgia in his throat.

A man was plowing in the fields near the house. That was his brother-in-law, Eben McCoy, Scratch thought, recognizing him. Eben saw him coming and left the plow and the mule where they were. He trotted toward the house and called, "Dorothy! Dorothy!"

Scratch's sister came out of the house, drying her hands on the apron she wore. As Scratch reined in and dismounted, she hurried forward.

"Baby brother!" she cried. She threw her arms around him and hugged him.

"You're only a year older than me," Scratch reminded her as he returned the embrace.

"That's enough to make you the baby of the family," Dorothy said. She stepped back and put her hands on Scratch's shoulders. "Let me take a look at you. Handsome as ever, just like all the Mortons."

Scratch chuckled and said, "We were blessed with good looks, weren't we?"

He shook hands with Eben, who said, "It's good to see you again, B—"

Scratch held up his other hand to stop Eben before he could pronounce Scratch's real name. He had gotten the moniker he carried when he wasn't much more than a baby and his folks had found him scratching around in the yard with the chickens. That had been back in Alabama, quite a few years before the family had come to Texas. The name had stuck, and he sure preferred it to the one his parents had given him. Nobody knew his real name except a few family members, not even Bo, and that was the way Scratch planned to keep it.

As a matter of fact, he had made it plain to Bo that if he died first, he wanted *Scratch Morton* put on his tombstone. If he had a tombstone, that is. Given the life he led, it was more likely he would wind up being laid to rest in a lonely, unmarked grave that would soon fade away as if he'd never been here on this earth.

Scratch shook that thought out of his head, slapped his brother-in-law on the back, and said, "Dang, it's good to be home!"

CHAPTER 9

The next hour was mighty pleasurable for Scratch, as he sat in the shade of the dogtrot with his sister and brother-in-law and caught up on things in their lives, including how all his nieces and nephews were doing.

Dorothy and Eben's kids were grown, married, moved out, and making their own way in the world. Scratch asked about his brother Gideon, too, along with Gid's wife, Helen, and *their* kids. He took it all in, glad to know that the family was doing so well. He knew he had missed out on a lot by not being part of it for most of his life, but he wouldn't trade the existence he'd led for anything.

Inevitably, the subject of Bo came up. Dorothy asked hesitantly, "I suppose you've still been riding with . . . with Bo Creel."

"Yeah, and I don't mind tellin' you, everythin' that folks around here are sayin' about him is as plumb loco as anythin' can be. When those two gals were killed, Bo and I were all the way up in Indian Territory, helpin' a deputy federal marshal deliver some prisoners. Anybody who don't believe that can get in touch with Marshal Brubaker and ask him. And if that ain't good enough, Judge Parker in Fort Smith will back up our story, too."

"The famous Hanging Judge?" Eben asked.

"One and the same," Scratch declared. Even as he said it, he realized that was the key to putting a stop to all the wild rumors about Bo being a killer. Even if folks didn't believe him, they'd have to take the word of Judge Parker and Forty-Two Brubaker.

The problem there was that he'd have to send a wire to the judge, and the closest telegraph office was at Hallettsville. And there was no telling where Brubaker was by now. Judge Parker might have sent him back out chasing outlaws, so he could be anywhere in Indian Territory, unable to get a message for days or even weeks.

But the judge's statement ought to be enough, Scratch thought. He and Bo would ride to Hallettsville and send that wire as soon as they got the chance, he told himself. If Parker could get word to Brubaker, then so much the better.

Scratch felt more relaxed about things now. He was confident that within a few days, a week at the most, he and Bo would have everything cleared up and they could just enjoy their visit.

"You're going to see Gid while you're here, aren't you?" Dorothy asked.

"Sure. I'll ride over to his place this afternoon, or maybe tomorrow," Scratch said.

"Make it tomorrow," Eben suggested. "Spend tonight here with us." He laughed. "To tell you the truth, there's a stump I could use some help with."

Dorothy slapped him lightly on the arm.

"Eben McCoy!" she said. "When my baby brother comes to visit, you can't put him to work."

Scratch chuckled and said, "That's all right, Dorothy. I don't mind. If a fella's gonna get fed, he's got to expect to help out a mite."

Eben stood up from the stool where he was perched.

"Come on, Scratch," he said. "I think maybe we can get that stump pulled up before lunch if we try."

"Let me unsaddle my horse and put him in the shed, and I'll be right with you," Scratch said.

A few minutes later Scratch walked out to the field where Eben waited for him. Eben had unhitched the mule from the plow he'd been using earlier and led the animal over to the stump, which was about two feet in diameter and stuck up three feet from the ground. Eben brought out a length of chain, which he wrapped around the stump, then attached the other end to the mule's harness.

"You can see where I've been digging up around the roots," Eben said to Scratch as he gestured at the base of the stump. "It's stubborn as all get-out, though."

"We'll get it," Scratch said. "You lead the mule, and I'll push."

"Once I get him going, we'll both push."

Eben grabbed the mule's harness and tugged. True to its nature, the mule was balky at first, but finally it leaned forward and the chain tightened around the stump.

"Come on!" Eben urged the mule.

Scratch lowered his shoulder and placed it against the stump. He braced his feet on the ground and heaved. The stump didn't budge. Long seconds ticked by. Scratch couldn't be sure—he might have imagined it—but he thought the stump moved slightly. Just a fraction of an inch, but that was a start.

He grunted with effort as he continued to push. He said, "We've got . . . a little play . . . in it now."

The mule kept straining against the chain. Eben let go of the harness and hurried to join Scratch. He put his shoulder into the task, too, and side by side they struggled against the stump.

It definitely moved, but then it sagged back as the mule stopped pulling. Scratch and Eben rested against the stump.

"Dang," Eben said. "I thought for a second there we had it."

"We made some progress," Scratch said. "We'll get it next time."

"You handle the mule this time. I'll push."

Scratch nodded. He was too out of breath to talk

anymore. When he had gotten some of his wind back and his pulse wasn't hammering quite as hard in his head, he went around the stump and took up his position beside the mule's head.

The varmint lived up to its kind's reputation for stubbornness. Scratch had to work hard just to get the beast to pull. When it was finally pulling, Scratch ran to the other side of the stump and threw his weight against it alongside Eben. The stump was looser now, leaning over as the mule continued pulling and the two men kept pushing.

When the roots tore loose, it happened suddenly, just as Scratch expected. The stump rolled out onto the ground and left a gaping hole behind it. Big chunks of dirt clung to the broken roots. The abrupt lack of resistance threw both Scratch and Eben off balance. They fell to the ground as the mule dragged the stump a few feet before coming to a halt.

Eben pulled himself up to a sitting position and let out an exultant whoop.

"We got it!" he said triumphantly. "I knew we would."

"Yeah, but the dang thing put up a good fight," Scratch said as he sat up, too. He turned his head as the sound of hoofbeats reached his ears.

Eben heard the running horse, too. He said, "Somebody's in a hurry. Who's that coming this way?"

Scratch's gaze followed his brother-in-law's

pointing finger. He spotted the rider galloping toward the old Morton place. Something about him struck Scratch as familiar, but he didn't recognize the man right off.

The two of them climbed to their feet. Somebody moving that fast usually meant trouble, and Scratch was glad he hadn't taken off his gun belt and hung up the Remingtons. He watched tensely as the rider veered away from the house and came toward him and Eben. The man must have spotted them in the field.

Scratch relaxed a little as he realized why the rider looked familiar. He wasn't sure, but he thought the man was Hank Creel, Bo's youngest brother. When he came closer, Scratch was sure of it. He lifted a hand in greeting.

"That's Bo's brother Hank," he told Eben.

"Yeah, I recognize him now, too. But he looks mighty upset about something."

Scratch agreed with that. And considering all the crazy things that had taken place since he and Bo returned to Bear Creek, he wasn't even too surprised that something else must have happened.

He just hoped it wasn't too bad.

"Howdy, Hank," he called as the younger man hauled back on the reins and brought the horse to a skidding stop. Hank was red-faced and out of breath. He had never been a good rider, and Scratch thought that the way he'd been bouncing up and down in the saddle should have been a dead giveaway as to his identity.

Hank dismounted awkwardly and stumbled toward them. He said, "Scratch, Bo needs your help. The marshal arrested him a little while ago."

"What!"

Hank nodded and swallowed hard.

"Marshal Haltom brought a posse out from Bear Creek," he said. "Bo wouldn't put up a fight against the law, and he wouldn't let me, either."

"No, he wouldn't," Scratch said. "Bo's always been the law-abidin' sort, except when there wasn't any other way to make sure the right thing got done. He didn't do anythin'?"

Hank shook his head and said, "No, he just handed over his gun and went with them peacefully."

Scratch knew how difficult it must have been for his old friend to do that.

"I thought your pa was goin' to town to talk to the marshal," he said to Hank.

"Yeah, he did. He left the ranch not long after you did. But he and the posse must have missed each other somehow. Marshal Haltom had to have been on his way to the Star C by the time Pa left for Bear Creek."

There were three or four different trails a man could use to get to the settlement from the Creel ranch, Scratch thought, so the idea wasn't too far-fetched. But it was bad luck for Bo, even though

John Creel might not have been able to talk the lawman out of making an arrest if he'd been there.

"Who swore out the charges against Bo?" Scratch asked as his eyes narrowed in anger.

"Danny Fontaine."

Eben made a disgusted noise and said, "Those damn carpetbagging Fontaines are nothing but trouble."

Scratch turned to his brother-in-law.

"I've got to head for town and see if I can talk some sense into the marshal," he said.

"It won't be easy," Eben warned. He put a hand on the mule's shoulder. "Jonas Haltom is honest, as far as I know, but he's also stubborn as the day is long. If he's convinced he's done the right thing by arresting Bo, you won't be able to talk him out of it."

"We'll see about that." Scratch was still thinking about Judge Parker and Deputy Marshal Brubaker. They were the key to this . . . but only if he had time to get in touch with them and get a reply back.

With the way everybody in the settlement was so up in arms against Bo, Scratch worried about his old friend being locked up in jail. The situation was ripe for a lynch mob to form. That was another good reason to get to town as fast as he could.

"Tell Dorothy I'm sorry I couldn't stay and visit any longer than I did," he said to Eben as he started walking toward the house.

Eben and Hank hurried along with him, Hank leading the horse he had ridden so hard to get there.

"Don't worry about that," Eben told Scratch. "She'll understand. I'll explain everything to her. Is there anything we can do to help?"

Scratch shook his head, then said, "Maybe say a prayer or two. With the way everybody's got Bo tried and convicted and all but strung up from a hangin' tree, he's liable to need all the help he can get."

CHAPTER 10

The worst part of the ride into town was having to listen to the taunts from Danny Fontaine, Bo thought. The young man had plenty to say about how Bo was going to wind up kicking at the end of a hang rope. He was looking forward to the spectacle, he declared, and the punchers from the Rafter F who were riding with him laughed in agreement.

Bo ignored them as much as possible. He tried to talk to Marshal Haltom, to make him understand that it was impossible for Bo to have committed the crimes everyone believed he had, but the lawman told him to be quiet.

"You'll have a chance to tell your side of the story to Judge Buchanan," Haltom said.

Bo remembered Judge Clarence Buchanan. He said, "Judge Buchanan's just a justice of the peace."

"He's what we've got in Bear Creek," Haltom snapped. "He'll decide whether to take you over to the county seat and turn you over to the sheriff."

Right now that didn't sound like such a bad idea to Bo. He figured he would be safer in jail at the county seat than in the little crackerbox hoosegow in Bear Creek. He suspected that as soon as they got back to the settlement and he was locked up, Danny Fontaine would head for the saloons on the other side of the bridge and start trying to stir up support for a lynch mob.

Thinking about how the Fontaines were feuding with his family put an idea in Bo's head. Having one of the Creels suspected of being a particularly brutal murderer made it easier for folks around here to support the Fontaines. Was it possible that wasn't just a coincidence? Bo knew it was a stretch to think that the Fontaines might have had something to do with the killings, but he couldn't deny that the whole situation was mighty convenient for them.

That was something else he could talk over with Scratch when his friend came to town . . . providing that Marshal Haltom allowed Scratch to visit him.

Bo kept an eye out for his father as the posse rode into town. It was bad luck that John Creel hadn't been able to get a word with Marshal Haltom before the lawman set out to make an arrest. It might not have made any difference if he had, but at least John could have tried. Bo assumed that Haltom and the posse had taken a different trail from Bear Creek.

When they reached the settlement, Haltom rode straight to the marshal's office and jail with the posse and the prisoner behind him. The group's arrival in town caused quite a commotion. People hurried out of the buildings to follow along the boardwalks on both sides of the street. Some of them yelled questions at Haltom, but the marshal ignored them and kept his gaze fixed on their destination.

He reined to a stop in front of the building. A crowd had formed on the boardwalk by the time Haltom dismounted. He raised his voice to be heard over the hubbub and said, "All right, you folks get back! Make room, I say! I've got a prisoner to lock up!"

Without waiting to be told, Bo swung down from the saddle. He looked around the posse members, and his gaze settled on Silas Brantley, the owner of the livery stable.

"See that my horse is taken care of, would you, Silas?" he asked.

Brantley nodded and said, "Sure, Bo." The man looked vaguely embarrassed to have gotten caught up in the fever that gripped the town. "Don't worry about the critter."

"Thanks," Bo told him with a smile.

Well aware that at least a dozen men were pointing guns at him, he stepped up onto the boardwalk after Marshal Haltom, who spread his arms wide to keep the townspeople back.

"I'm not sure folks would be this worked up if it

was ol' Santa Anna himself you were locking up," Bo commented.

"Shut up and get inside."

Danny Fontaine holstered his revolver and said loudly, "All you men who rode out to bring in this mad dog killer, drinks are on me at the Southern Belle!"

That brought cheers of appreciation from the Rafter F hands and from some of the other posse-men, as well.

Bo heard that as he stepped into the jail and tried not to think about what it meant. One way to get a lynch mob eager to take the law into its own hands was to prime the pump with liquor first.

The front room was the marshal's office, complete with a scarred wooden desk, a rack of rifles and shotguns on the wall, a potbellied stove in the corner, a couple of armchairs with sagging seats, and a cabinet.

One unusual touch was a large painting that hung on the wall. The scene it depicted was that of a group of men on horseback, dressed in fancy red jackets, galloping across a bucolic countryside in pursuit of what appeared to be a fox. The picture was so out of place in this frontier lawman's office that Bo couldn't help but stare at it, even though he had more important things to worry about at the moment.

Marshal Haltom saw where Bo was looking and said, "Some artist fella who was passing through here got drunk one night, and when I arrested him he didn't have enough money to pay the fine the judge levied on him, so he offered to paint pictures for us instead. This is what I got."

"Looks nice," Bo said, struck by the bizarre nature of this conversation.

Haltom put his hand on the butt of his gun and nodded toward the door that led into the cell block.

"Get in there," he ordered. "We're not here to talk about art."

The cell block door was open, which told Bo that there were no other prisoners at the moment. The door was thick and sturdy, with a small, barred window in it to provide ventilation and a way to look into the cell block from the office.

The short aisle on the other side of the door had two cells made of iron bars on each side of it. Each cell had a bunk with a thin mattress attached to the wall, with a bucket shoved underneath the bunk. That was all. The accommodations sure weren't fancy, thought Bo. But they weren't any worse than plenty of other jails he had seen during his wanderings with Scratch.

Come to think of it, they had been locked up in worse places than this.

The cells were all empty, so Marshal Haltom followed Bo into the cell block and said, "Take your pick."

There was a vacant lot to the left of the jail, with

a narrow alley to the right. So the cells on the left ought to get more air coming through their windows, Bo decided. He walked into the first cell on the left.

Haltom clanged the door shut behind him. Bo didn't like the sound.

"I'll bring you some dinner after a while," Haltom said. "Until then you might as well sit down and take it easy."

"When's the hearing going to be?" Bo asked. "There has to be a hearing with the judge."

The marshal snapped, "Don't get uppity with me, Creel. You're not a lawyer, so don't go acting like one. You'll see the judge when the judge is ready to see you, and not before."

"Just want to make sure things are done properly," Bo said in a mild voice.

"They will be. You can count on that."

Haltom went out and swung the cell block door closed with a heavy thump. The key turned in the lock. Those sounds were pretty depressing, too, Bo thought as he sighed and sat down on the bunk. It wasn't any more comfortable than it looked.

He had never liked having to depend on other people, but there was no getting around it. Right now his fate rested in the capable hands of Scratch Morton.

* * *

Scratch didn't waste any time getting to town. He didn't slow his horse until the settlement came in sight.

As he rode into Bear Creek he passed a wagon that was also entering town. Scratch's mind was filled with thoughts of the danger facing Bo and what he was going to do about it, but even as distracted as he was by that, he couldn't help but notice the gaudily painted vehicle.

The back of the wagon was enclosed, and painted on its sides in bright red letters was THE LEGEND PROFESSOR THADDEUS SARLAT AND HIS TRAVELING PHARMACOLOGICAL EXPOSITION AND EMPORIUM. A medicine show, in other words, Scratch thought. That was confirmed by a painting of a bottle, and underneath it in smaller letters *Professor Sarlat's Miraculous Elixir and Curative—Restores Vitality—Ameliorates Disease—Replenishes Bodily Fluids—Try It Now!*

Scratch had made the mistake of falling for the pitch of more than one snake oil salesman. Every bottle of so-called miracle cure he had ever tried, though, was nothing more than a mixture of foul-tasting stuff spiked with alcohol. And not good whiskey, either. He wouldn't be buying anything from Professor Sarlat.

He couldn't help but look at the woman on the seat next to the tall, skinny man who had to be the professor, though. Fiery red hair was piled high on her head, above a strikingly beautiful face. A small beauty mark near her mouth made her looks that much more compelling. Although she wore a rather simple gray dress, her lushly elegant figure made it seem like a fancy ball gown. She was the sort of woman to take a man's breath away.

She certainly kept Scratch from paying much attention to her companion. Professor Sarlat had sallow features under a black top hat. Scratch thought the man's pointed goatee made him look vaguely European. Other than that he couldn't have said much about Sarlat's appearance.

The team of four black horses pulling the wagon were decked out like circus horses, with fancy rigging and feathered plumes. Scratch glanced at them as he went around them. From the looks of the outfit, the medicine show did a pretty good business.

Then Scratch forgot all about the other new-comers to Bear Creek, because he saw the marshal's office up ahead and knew that his best friend was locked up in there. He angled his horse toward the hitch rack in front of the jail.

Quite a few people along the boardwalks were watching him, Scratch realized as he reined in and dismounted. That had to be because they knew he was Bo's friend. That made him suspicious in their eyes. Scratch never would have dreamed that their old hometown would turn on them like this, but that was what had happened.

Once Bo's name was cleared, it would be a

different story, he told himself as he looped his horse's reins around the hitch rail. Then folks around here would feel mighty foolish about the way they had rushed to judgment.

He went into the office and found a barrel-chested, big-nosed hombre in a brown vest sitting behind the desk. The tin star pinned to the man's vest told Scratch he had found Marshal Jonas Haltom.

The lawman glanced up, grunted, and asked, "Something I can do for you?"

"My name's Scratch Morton."

Haltom set aside the pen he'd been using to scrawl something on a piece of paper and frowned.

"I reckon I know that name from somewhere," he said.

"You ought to," Scratch snapped. "Bo Creel's my friend."

"That's right," Haltom said. "You're the fella who's been riding with that murderer. The one he claims can clear his name." The marshal's frown deepened. "There are plenty of people around town who think I ought to arrest you, too, Morton. They say you must've been in on those killings with Creel, or at least known about them."

"My word's not good enough for you, is that it? You don't believe me when I tell you that Bo's innocent?"

"Why in blazes should I?" Haltom demanded. "I

don't know you for Adam. For all I know, you're even more loco than Creel is!"

Scratch controlled the anger that welled up inside him and drawled, "So if my word ain't good enough, how about that of a federal judge and a deputy United States marshal?"

Haltom's eyebrows climbed up his forehead. He put his hands on the desk and heaved himself to his feet.

"What are you talking about?" he asked. "What judge?"

"Isaac Parker, up in Fort Smith, Arkansas."

"The Hanging Judge." Nearly everybody in this part of the country had heard of Judge Parker, and Haltom was no exception. "What's he got to do with this?"

"He can tell you that Bo and I weren't anywhere around Cottonwood or Bear Creek when those gals were killed," Scratch said. "And so can that federal marshal I mentioned, because we were helpin' him out with a little chore at the time."

For a second Haltom looked like he wanted to accept what he was hearing. The evidence that Scratch claimed to have was pretty convincing.

But then a fresh wave of stubbornness washed over Haltom's rugged face, and he yanked open one of the drawers in his desk.

"How about this?" he asked as he took out a sheet of paper and slapped it down on the desk. "How do you explain this picture?"

Scratch stepped closer to the desk and looked at the drawing. Marshal Haltom rested his fingertips on the paper and rotated it so that Scratch could see it better.

The face that looked up at him from the paper, sketched there with what appeared to be a piece of charcoal, was undoubtedly that of Bo Creel.

CHAPTER 11

Scratch stared at the drawing in silence for a long moment, then said, "I don't care what it looks like, Bo didn't hurt those women. It just ain't possible, I tell you."

Marshal Haltom let out a contemptuous snort and swept the piece of paper back into the desk drawer.

"You get me sworn statements from Judge Parker and that federal marshal you were talking about, and then I might believe you."

"Might?"

Haltom shrugged and said, "I've got to admit, evidence like that would carry a lot of weight. But I'd still like to know how Barney Dunn could draw a picture of your friend like that if he'd never seen him before. I looked mighty close at Creel when I arrested him. He's the man in that drawing, all right."

Scratch just shook his head, but he was expressing his confusion as much as he was disagreeing with the marshal.

"I want to see Bo," he said.

"There's no law says I have to let you see him."

"No, but there's no law that says you have to keep me from it, either."

"All right," Haltom said, turning to snag a ring of keys off a peg on the wall behind the desk. "Take off that fancy gun rig first. I'm not letting you go back there armed."

Scratch unbuckled his gun belt and set it and the pair of holstered Remingtons on the marshal's desk.

"You don't have a hide-out gun you plan on slipping to Creel, do you?"

"If I did, I don't reckon I'd tell you about it, do you?" Scratch asked, not bothering to keep the scorn out of his voice.

Haltom flushed angrily.

"Just for that, I'll have to search you."

He patted Scratch down and didn't find any other weapons. The silver-haired Texan said, "I never ran into anything yet I couldn't handle with those two Remingtons of mine, and maybe my Winchester, which is outside on my horse."

"All right, you made your point." Haltom picked up the key ring again and went over to the cell block door. He unlocked it and swung it open. "Five minutes." He paused, then added, "And I'll be right out here, so don't try anything funny."

"Wouldn't dream of it," Scratch said. He went into the cell block. Haltom left the door open behind him.

Bo was sitting on the bunk in the first cell to the left, leaning forward with his hands clasped together between his knees. He stood up as Scratch came into the cell block.

"I thought I heard your voice out there," he said. "I'm glad to see you, Scratch. I think maybe you're the only friendly face in the whole county, except maybe for my little brother Hank."

"Miz Fisher's on your side, too," Scratch said, "and I think your pa wants to be. He's just mighty confused by the whole thing, and I got to admit, I am, too."

Bo smiled and asked, "You don't think I've figured out how to be in two places at once, do you?"

"It'd be a neat trick if you could," Scratch said with a smile, "but no, I don't reckon you could manage that, Bo, even as smart as you are."

"I don't feel so smart now. I can't think of any way that bartender ought to be able to draw my picture without ever seeing me."

"The marshal just let me take a gander at that picture." Scratch sighed. "It sure looks like you, Bo."

"I haven't seen it yet, but I don't doubt it. If it wasn't the spitting image of me, I don't think everybody around here would have been so quick to make up their minds that I'm guilty."

"They'll soon know better. I'm headin' over to

Hallettsville this afternoon to send a wire to Judge Parker. With any luck I'll be back with his reply before nightfall."

Bo nodded and said, "I thought about that, too, and was going to suggest it. The judge's testimony ought to clear me of any wrongdoing."

"I don't know if a telegram will be enough to satisfy the marshal," Scratch said uneasily. "He said he wanted a sworn statement from Parker, and from ol' Forty-Two Brubaker, too. That's liable to take time."

"Yeah, but even a telegram from Judge Parker ought to be enough to slow things down until that statement can get here."

"That's what I'm worried about," Scratch said. "I'm not sure this jail would stand up to a lynch mob."

"Marshal Haltom won't let that happen."

Even though Scratch could tell that Bo was trying to sound confident, he knew his old friend was worried about the same possibility.

Bo went on, "That Fontaine kid was a member of the posse. When we got back to town he offered to buy drinks for everybody at the Southern Belle."

"Damn it, that ain't good," Scratch said. "Most of the people in Bear Creek are decent folks—or at least they used to be, I ain't so sure anymore—but if they sit around drinkin' all day with Danny Fontaine eggin' 'em on . . ."

"That's exactly what I was thinking," Bo said. He lowered his voice so Marshal Haltom couldn't overhear as he went on, "It sure works out well for the

Fontaines that there's all this sentiment against one of the Creels, doesn't it?"

Scratch leaned closer to the bars and asked, "You think they're behind all this trouble somehow?"

"The thought occurred to me," Bo admitted. He shook his head. "But then something else started nagging at me. Once Barney Dunn drew that picture and somebody said it looked like me, the Fontaines may have tried to take advantage of the situation . . . but there's no way they could have set it all up beforehand. In order to do that, they would have had to know that you and I were coming back to Bear Creek. And when that first girl was murdered, you and I didn't even know that yet."

Scratch grimaced and said, "Dadgum it, Bo, we keep comin' up with these ideas, and then they don't pan out."

"That's what makes the whole thing a mystery, I reckon."

"Well, I know one thing that ain't a mystery," Scratch said. "It ain't gonna be safe to leave you here, not with a lynch mob in the makin' across the creek."

"You're not thinking about trying to bust me out of jail, are you?" Bo asked with a frown.

"If that's what it comes down to—"

"No," Bo said. "You'll just get yourself hurt . . . or killed. I don't want that."

"I don't want those varmints stringin' you up,

either, and that's what's liable to happen if you have to stay in here for very long."

Wearily, Bo scrubbed a hand across his face and then said, "Let's see what happens when you get back from Hallettsville with that wire from the judge. That's the next step. I think I'll be safe enough this afternoon."

Scratch thought it for a moment and then nodded.

"Yeah, it'll probably take until after dark for that bunch across the creek to soak up enough liquid courage," he said. "I'll be back before then, one way or another."

Bo extended his hand through the bars.

"Thanks, Scratch. I knew I could count on you."

Scratch gripped his friend's hand and said, "Just like I know I could count on you if it was me on the other side of those dang bars."

From the office, Marshal Haltom called through the open cell block door, "Are the two of you about done back there? You're trying my patience, Morton."

Scratch nodded to Bo and said, "I'll see you later."

"*Hasta la vista, amigo.*"

Scratch walked into the marshal's office. Haltom glared at him and said, "I was starting to think I might have to run you out of there at gunpoint."

Scratch ignored that comment.

"Do you have any deputies, Marshal?" he asked.

Haltom frowned and shook his head.

"No, the town doesn't see fit to pay for any. But I've never had any trouble doing my job without them," he said. "What business is it of yours?"

"It's just that I'd feel a little better about you protectin' this jail if you weren't by yourself."

The lawman snorted contemptuously.

"I don't need any help doing what needs to be done. No lynch mob is getting in here. Me and my shotgun will see to that."

Scratch just hoped that Haltom was right. He thought the man's overconfidence might turn out to be dangerous for all concerned, especially Bo.

"I'll be back," he said as he buckled on his gun belt. "And when I get here, I'll have a wire from Judge Parker with me."

"You do that," Haltom said, but Scratch could tell from the marshal's condescending tone that Haltom didn't expect him to be successful. Haltom's mind was set so firmly in its belief that Bo was guilty, he couldn't allow himself to believe even for a second that he might be wrong.

Scratch left the office, pausing on the boardwalk to heave a sigh. He and Bo had found themselves neck-deep in trouble many times before, but usually he'd been able to rely on Bo to figure out what they should do next.

This time it was all up to him, and Scratch didn't care for the feeling.

One step at a time, he told himself, and as Bo

had said, the next step was getting in touch with Judge Parker. Scratch stepped down from the boardwalk and reached toward the hitch rail for his horse's reins.

A sudden outbreak of loud voices from down the street made him pause again.

Scratch turned his head to look toward the disturbance. The wagon he had noticed as he came into town was parked in front of the general store. The top-hatted driver stood beside the team of fancy-rigged horses. The good-looking redhead was on the seat. Scratch figured they had just come out of the store.

Three men in range clothes stood on the boardwalk in front of the store, having followed the professor and the redhead out. Even from a distance, Scratch could tell they were troublemakers just by looking at them. Their tense, aggressive attitude was a giveaway.

The man in the top hat—Professor Sarlat, that was the name painted on the wagon, Scratch recalled—reached for the team's reins to untie them from the hitch rail.

At the same time, one of the men stepped down from the boardwalk, reached over the rail, and grabbed the reins before the professor could take hold of them.

"You ain't goin' anywhere, you damn medicine show quack!" the man yelled.

Scratch sighed. He didn't even come close to

having time for a distraction like this. He needed to get to Hallettsville as quickly as possible and send off that telegram to Judge Parker in Fort Smith. The sooner he did that, the sooner he would be back with Parker's answer . . . the answer that might be enough to free Bo.

But the redhead looked scared, and the tall, skinny professor was no match for a trio of burly cowboys. Despite the urgency of his mission, Scratch knew he couldn't just mount up and ride away from this confrontation.

He left his horse tied where it was and walked toward the medicine show wagon.

Other people were on the street and the boardwalks, but they ignored what was going on in front of the general store. Obviously they didn't want to come to the defense of the two strangers. Maybe they were scared of the cowboys, or maybe they just didn't care what happened to the professor and the redhead.

Either way, Scratch was disappointed in the way Bear Creek had changed over the years while he and Bo were gone.

As Scratch approached, one of the cowboys still on the boardwalk said, "Tell your daughter to come down off of that wagon and give us a little sugar, old man, and maybe we'll let you go."

"The young lady is not my daughter," Sarlat said stiffly. "She's my assistant."

"Well, then, in that case it shouldn't bother you for her to give us a kiss," the puncher insisted.

Sarlat squared his shoulders, gave the three men a haughty look that probably didn't help matters, and declared, "I wouldn't subject her to that indignity."

"You think it wouldn't be dignified for her to kiss three fine, upstandin' fellas like us? Hell, we ride for the best outfit in these parts, the Rafter F!"

So they were some of Fontaine's men. Somehow that didn't surprise Scratch at all.

One of the other cowboys said, "Anyway, callin' her an assistant don't mean anything. Everybody knows that all medicine show gals are nothin' but thievin' whores! If they don't steal your money one way with that snake oil they sell, they'll steal it another way!"

"By God, sir!" Sarlat exclaimed. He reached back to the floorboard of the driver's box and picked up a cane that had been lying there. Scratch hadn't seen it until now. He brandished the walking stick at the men and went on, "If you don't leave us alone, I'll—"

The man who had been holding the team's reins let go of them suddenly and lunged at Sarlat. He grabbed the cane and twisted it. Sarlat let out a pained cry as the cowboy wrenched the cane out of his hands. On the seat, the redhead pressed the back of her hand to her mouth in fear, either for herself or the professor or both.

"Threaten me, will you?" the cowboy said. "I'll give you a taste of your own medicine, old man, and it won't be that damn snake oil you sell!"

He lifted the cane, ready to swing it at Sarlat's head in what was bound to be the first blow of a painful thrashing.

CHAPTER 12

Scratch's right-hand Remington came out of its holster in a smooth, fast draw. He eared back the hammer with an audible ratcheting sound that made the cowboy with the cane freeze.

"I wouldn't do that," Scratch said. "Give that walkin' stick back to the professor, and be careful how you do it, too."

One of the men on the boardwalk said, "Back off, you crazy old coot! This is none of your business."

"Yeah," his companion added. "And there's three of us and only one of you!"

"There'll only be two of you once I've put a bullet through that hombre with the walkin' stick," the silver-haired Texan drawled. "I'll just go ahead and shoot him as soon as either of you boys makes a move toward your gun. And you may not have noticed, but I've got a second Remington. I'm pretty good at gettin' it out and usin' it, too, if I do say so myself. I'd bet this Stetson of mine that I can get lead in both of you before you put me down. Feel like riskin' it?" A cold, dangerous grin stretched across Scratch's face. "Remember, I've got a lot less years to lose than you hombres do. But it's up to you."

The atmosphere in the street was tense now, heavy with the feel of impending violence as the seconds ticked by. The man with the cane broke that stalemate by throwing the walking stick on the ground at Sarlat's feet.

"There!" he said. "Now put that gun up before it goes off by accident."

"Oh, if it goes off, it won't be no accident," Scratch said.

He didn't holster the Remington. He knew that all three men wanted to slap leather. He could tell it by the hatred and fury he saw in their eyes. None of them wanted to back down, especially from a man who was so much older than they were.

But they knew that if they started shooting, one or two of them, possibly even all three, would die here today, and none of them wanted to chance that.

One of the men on the porch spat disgustedly and said, "Come on, fellas. Gettin' a kiss from some medicine show whore ain't worth it."

He turned and stalked off along the boardwalk. The other two joined him, but not without casting venomous glances over their shoulders at Scratch.

He considered making them stop and apologize

to the redhead for what they had said, but decided against it even though such unchivalrous language definitely rubbed him the wrong way. He'd been willing to throw lead to protect somebody from a beating, but with Bo depending on him, he didn't want to get himself shot over some gal's hurt feelings.

Anyway, she didn't seem all that offended. When the Rafter F hands were gone, she said, "Professor, you are all right?"

"Of course, my dear," he answered in his deep voice that held a hint of a Southern accent. He bent and picked up the cane. As he straightened, he went on, "Thanks to our friend here, I came to no harm. Although if that miscreant had attacked me, he might have been surprised. You know that my elixir gives me the vigor of a much younger man."

Even under these circumstances, the fella had to get in a pitch for his snake oil, Scratch thought. He supposed it was a matter of habit for the professor to always be selling.

The three cowboys reached the bridge and started across it. Not trusting them, Scratch didn't holster his gun until then.

"Professor Thaddeus Sarlat, sir," the goateed huckster introduced himself. "Purveyor of the greatest boon to mankind since the invention of fire and the wheel. I'm pleased and honored to make your acquaintance."

"Scratch Morton," Scratch replied with a nod. "Purveyor of, well, not much of anything."

"On the contrary, Mr. Morton, you brought salvation to us. I would have given a good account of myself in battle, but in the end I'd have been no match for those ruffians. There's no telling what they might have done to me and my lovely assistant Veronique. Speaking of which . . . Mr. Morton, allow me to present Mademoiselle Veronique Ballantine."

Scratch tugged his hat brim and nodded to her.

"Ma'am," he said. "It's my honor."

"And my pleasure, M'sieu Morton."

Scratch had already noticed the French accent. He doubted if she had ever set foot in France, though. She looked more like the sort of gal who hailed from New Orleans.

"Do you live here in Bear Creek, my friend?" Professor Sarlat asked.

"Used to," Scratch replied. "I grew up in these parts. But right now my pard and I are just visitin'."

"Returning to old haunts, eh? A worthwhile endeavor. If you're going to be here tonight, I hope you'll attend our exhibition. I'm quite the expert in prestidigitation, you know."

Scratch frowned and shook his head.

"Magic," Sarlat explained.

"Oh. Card tricks and such-like."

A pained expression came over Sarlat's face for a second before he banished the reaction. He said, "I suppose you could put it like that. I prefer to think of it as a demonstration of dexterity and the power of illusion." He waved a long-fingered hand toward Veronique. "And if magic doesn't interest you, I'm sure you'd be enchanted by the lovely Mademoiselle Veronique's performance. She's a superb singer and dancer. When the show concludes, I'll be offering bottles of my elixir at such a low price that the members of the audience will practically be losing money if they *don't* purchase a bottle or two." He paused in his spiel. "In your case, however, I wouldn't feel right about charging you for this miraculous, health-giving liquid after what you've done for us. Mr. Morton, I'd like to give you a bottle right now, absolutely free of charge. If you have a chance to try it between now and this evening, perhaps you would be willing to stand up and offer a testimonial to its absolutely splendid benefits."

Scratch was beginning to wonder if he was ever going to be able to get a word in edgewise. The professor spewed words like a politician.

Sarlat had to take a breath eventually, though, and when he did, Scratch said quickly, "You don't have to do that, Professor. I was glad to help. And right now I've got somewhere I need to be, so I'd best be movin' along. I don't know where I'll be tonight."

"Please, sir, take a bottle of my elixir and tonic for later," Sarlat insisted. He reached inside his long, swallowtail coat. "I happen to have an unopened bottle right here."

For a second Scratch wondered if the professor might have paid those three cowboys to cause a commotion, just so somebody like him would come to their aid and wind up being given a bottle of elixir, in the hope that the Good Samaritan would then help them sell some more of the concoction.

He discarded that idea, though, as he remembered how the Rafter F hands had looked at him. There was nothing phony about the anger they had felt.

But even though Sarlat hadn't set up the confrontation, he was still going to try to take advantage of it.

Since Scratch was in a hurry and had already spent too much time on this, and because he could tell that Sarlat wasn't going to take no for an answer, he accepted the pint bottle that the professor held out to him. The bottle was made of dark brown glass and had a cork in its neck.

"I'll give it a try later," Scratch said as he slipped the bottle into the pocket of his buckskin jacket. He might take a small sip of the stuff when he got a chance, just to see how vile it was, but he figured he would wind up pouring out most of it. He sure wasn't going to get up at the medicine show and tell people they ought to buy it.

"Excellent," Sarlat said. "I hope we see you tonight, Mr. Morton."

"Yes," Veronique said as she gave Scratch a

sultry smile. "I would be very pleased to see you again, m'sieu."

Scratch knew she was just flirting with him and it didn't mean anything, but he still enjoyed having a gorgeous redhead smiling at him that way. He touched a finger to his hat brim and said, "The feelin' is mutual, mademoiselle."

With that he lifted a hand in farewell and headed back to his horse. He didn't look behind him, because he didn't want to take a chance on being delayed again.

He mounted up and rode out of Bear Creek, taking a road that led northeast toward Hallettsville. There was a telegraph office at Victoria, too, southeast of Bear Creek, but Hallettsville was slightly closer.

Scratch kept his eyes open. He wasn't expecting any trouble, but it sometimes jumped out at a man when he wasn't looking for it.

His horse had plenty of stamina and maintained a ground-eating lope for miles. Scratch pulled the animal back to a walk every now and then to let it rest. He paused once for half an hour, a delay that chafed at him even though he knew it was necessary to keep from riding the horse into the ground.

It was well past midday by the time Scratch reached the good-sized town of Hallettsville. He glanced down at the Lavaca River as he rode across the bridge that spanned it. As usual, there wasn't much water in the twisting stream. Bear Creek was bigger and flowed more. It was common in Texas to find creeks that were bigger than the so-called rivers.

The courthouse and the business section of town perched atop a small hill. The railroad ran south of it, and the telegraph office was inside the train station. Scratch dismounted, tied his horse, and went into the depot.

A counter on one side of the big waiting room had telegraph flimsies and pencils on it. Scratch got one of the yellow pieces of paper and printed on it:

JUDGE ISAAC PARKER FORT SMITH ARK
STOP URGENT YOU REPLY WITH
CONFIRMATION THAT BO CREEL
WORKING FOR YOU IN INDIAN
TERRITORY ONE MONTH AGO STOP
MATTER OF LIFE AND DEATH STOP
SCRATCH MORTON

He addressed another telegram to Deputy U.S. Marshal Ed "Forty-Two" Brubaker and put the same message on it. Then he took both of them over to the window and slid them across to the telegrapher.

The man's brows rose under the green eyeshade he wore as he scanned the words.

"Are you a federal lawman?" he asked Scratch.

"Would I be sendin' wires to those fellas if I

wasn't?" Scratch replied, which wasn't exactly a lie since he was just asking the telegrapher a question and letting the hombre draw his own conclusions. But if the man thought Scratch packed a badge for Uncle Sam, it might make him more efficient.

"I'll send these right away," the telegrapher said. "Sorry, I've got to charge you for them, though."

"That's fine," Scratch said. "Just get 'em on the wire as fast as you can."

The telegrapher counted up the price, and Scratch paid it. Then the key started clattering as the man tapped out the messages.

"Are you going to wait for the replies?" he asked when he was finished.

Scratch hadn't taken the time to eat anything before he left Bear Creek, and it had been a long time since breakfast, his stomach reminded him.

"Is there a hash house close by?"

"A block up toward the courthouse," the telegrapher said. "Mighty good food there."

"That's where I'll be, then," Scratch said. "If a reply comes in to either of those wires before I get back, can you send a boy to deliver it?"

"Sure," the telegrapher said with a nod. "I'll do that immediately, Marshal."

"Much obliged," Scratch said, letting the man go on thinking he was a lawman. As long as nobody asked to see his badge and bona fides, he didn't see where it would hurt anything.

The hash house was owned by a Swedish couple.

There were a lot of Scandinavian settlers in this part of Texas, Scratch recalled. North of here a ways there were entire communities made up entirely of Swedes and Norwegians. They were mighty good folks, too, he thought. Salt of the earth.

The man and woman who ran the little café served good old American food, though, including a thick, juicy steak that went a long way toward restoring Scratch's energy and his spirits. He washed the meal down with several cups of black coffee and was about ready to head back to the train station when a towheaded youngster came in carrying a couple of telegrams. Scratch spotted the yellow flimsies and knew the replies to his wires had come in.

"Over here, son," he called to the boy as he stood up. "I'll take those."

"You're Marshal Morton?" the boy asked.

"That's right." Now that *was* an outright lie, but Scratch figured he could be forgiven for it, since he was just trying to help Bo as quickly as he could.

"Here you go, then," the youngster said as he held out the telegrams. Scratch took them and flipped a half dollar to the kid, who snatched it out of the air and stared at it in awe as he realized how rich he was. He turned and ran out of the café, no doubt headed for the nearest place that sold licorice whips and penny candy.

Scratch unfolded the first telegram, thinking that he'd been lucky to hear back from both Parker and

Brubaker. Their word ought to carry enough weight to get Bo out of jail. At least Scratch hoped that would be the case.

His spirits plummeted as he read the words printed on the paper.

JUDGE PARKER UNAVAILABLE STOP
IN ST LOUIS ON BUSINESS STOP
WILL RETURN IN ONE WEEK STOP AMBROSE
PENNINGTON CHIEF CLERK

A growl of disappointment came from Scratch. That was bad luck, pure and simple. But maybe Brubaker's wire would be enough to help clear Bo's name.

MARSHAL BRUBAKER UNAVAILABLE STOP
PURSUING FUGITIVES IN INDIAN TERRITORY
STOP DATE OF RETURN UNKNOWN STOP
AMBROSE PENNINGTON CHIEF CLERK

So both messages had been delivered to Pennington at the big redbrick courthouse in Fort Smith. Scratch bit back a curse as he read the second reply, then impulsively crumpled both flimsies in his fist. He had known there was a possibility he wouldn't be able to get in touch with Brubaker, but he had been counting on Judge Parker's help.

Thinking about his next course of action, he smoothed out the telegrams on the table, then paid the proprietor for his meal and headed back to the depot. When he got there, he hurriedly printed another message.

AMBROSE PENNINGTON CHIEF CLERK
FEDERAL COURTHOUSE FORT SMITH ARK
STOP URGENT YOU CONTACT JUDGE
PARKER WITH PREVIOUS MESSAGE
AND FORWARD REPLY TO ME AS SOON
AS POSSIBLE STOP
SCRATCH MORTON

The telegrapher read it and asked, "Are you going to wait here in Hallettsville for a reply to this one, too?"

Scratch shook his head. If he left now, he would get back to Bear Creek about dark. He didn't want to arrive any later than that. He had to be on hand in case a lynch mob tried to storm the jail.

"No, you're gonna have to send a rider to Bear Creek with it," he told the telegrapher.

The man frowned.

"I don't know if I can—"

Scratch slid a double eagle across the counter.

"That'll cover sendin' the message and the trouble it'll be to get the reply to me, won't it?"

The telegrapher tried not to grin as he scooped up the twenty-dollar coin.

"Yes, sir, it sure will. Will the rider find you at the marshal's office in Bear Creek?"

"Yeah, that'll do," Scratch said. He planned to stick pretty close to there as long as Bo was locked up.

"I'll take care of it, then," the telegrapher promised. "I hope you get your reply soon, Marshal."

"Yeah, me, too," Scratch said. There was no telling how long it might take for Ambrose Pennington to send a wire to Judge Parker in St. Louis, get a reply back from him, and then send that reply on to Scratch.

And that was assuming that Pennington would even cooperate, Scratch thought bleakly. The clerk might decide that the matter wasn't pressing enough to bother Judge Parker with, even though Scratch had said it was a matter of life and death. Clerks who worked for the government usually thought they knew better about everything, whether they really did or not.

Scratch left the train station and heaved a sigh before he untied his horse and swung up into the saddle. All he could do now was head back to Bear Creek.

And hope that he got there before lynch mob hell broke loose.

CHAPTER 13

The sun had dipped below the horizon by the time Scratch approached the settlement, but a proscenium arch of reddish-gold light still hung in the western sky.

He had pushed his mount hard and the horse had responded gallantly, although he could tell that it was tired. The horse could rest in Silas Brantley's stable, since Scratch wouldn't be returning to the Star C or to his sister's place tonight.

He just wished he had better news to deliver to Bo.

With dusk settling down over Bear Creek, the street and the boardwalks weren't very busy, although some of the businesses were still open. More noise and light came from the other side of the creek where the saloons were located.

Scratch thought he might take a pasear over there later. He wanted to say hello to Lauralee Parker at the Southern Belle, who was an old friend. Also, he thought he might have a talk with Barney Dunn, the witness against Bo who was supposed to work as a bartender at Lauralee's saloon. First, though, he would try to find out from her just how trustworthy the man really was. Lauralee was smart, and Scratch put quite a bit of stock in her opinion.

He noticed Professor Sarlat's medicine show wagon parked at the far end of the street, near the public well. Scratch hoped the three cowboys from the Rafter F hadn't come back later and given Sarlat and Veronique any more trouble. He didn't have time to check on them at the moment, though. He headed straight for the jail.

The place looked peaceful and quiet. Scratch was grateful for that, but he knew it might not last. The darker the night got, the greater the potential for trouble.

He dismounted and went to the door of the marshal's office, only to find that it wouldn't open. Haltom must have it barred on the inside, thought Scratch. Actually, that was a good sign. He hammered on the door with his fist and called, "Marshal? It's me, Scratch Morton."

A moment of silence went by before Haltom answered, "Are you by yourself, Morton?"

"That's right."

"You'd better not be lying to me. You'll get a double load of buckshot if you try anything funny."

"Just open the door, Marshal," Scratch said, trying to keep the impatience and annoyance he felt from being heard in his voice. "I need to talk to you and Bo."

Scratch heard a scraping sound on the other side of the door as the bar was lifted from its brackets. Then Haltom called, "Come on in, slow and easy."

Scratch opened the door, being careful as he'd been told, and stepped into the marshal's office with his hands in plain sight. With Haltom obviously holding a scattergun, Scratch didn't want to do anything to spook the lawman.

Haltom had backed away from the door after lifting the bar and now stood beside the desk with a double-barreled Greener in his hands. He gestured with the shotgun's twin barrels as he told Scratch, "Put the bar back in place."

Scratch did so, saying, "I'm glad to see you're bein' this careful. Any trouble so far?"

"Not a bit," Haltom replied. "You got that telegram from your friend the Hanging Judge?"

The marshal's skeptical tone bothered Scratch, but he knew things were likely to get worse when he told Haltom about the responses he had gotten from Fort Smith.

Postponing the inevitable wouldn't change anything. He said, "Judge Parker's out of town, gone to St. Louis for a week, and Marshal Brubaker's somewhere over in Indian Territory chasin' after outlaws." Scratch took the two telegrams from Ambrose Pennington out of his pocket and set them on Haltom's desk. "I got those back from the chief clerk of the judge's court."

Haltom grunted, obviously unimpressed.

"So you don't have any more proof Creel's innocent than you did when you rode out of here this morning."

"Maybe not, but damn it—"

Haltom lifted the shotgun a little and said, "That's enough. I told you it'd take a sworn statement from the judge to get Creel out of jail. You don't have that. You don't even have a telegram that amounts to anything. So he stays locked up and you can get out of here."

"You got to at least let me talk to him again," Scratch argued.

A stubborn frown appeared on Haltom's face, making Scratch think that the lawman was going to deny him that privilege, but then Haltom shrugged.

"I suppose it won't hurt anything. Take those guns off again."

Scratch complied with the order. Haltom tucked the shotgun under his arm and unlocked the cell block door.

Bo must have heard Scratch's voice in the office. He stood at the door of the cell, his hands loosely holding the bars. He seemed relaxed, but an undertone of tension lurked in his voice as he asked, "Good news from Fort Smith?"

"No news from Fort Smith," Scratch said, unable

to suppress the disgust he felt. "Judge Parker ain't there, and neither is Forty-Two."

Bo's expression didn't change, except for a brief flicker of disappointment in his eyes.

"Where are they?" he asked.

"The judge is in St. Louis on business. Legal business, I reckon, since I don't know what other kind he'd have. And Brubaker's off gallivantin' around the Territory somewhere."

Bo smiled and said, "I'm not sure I'd call chasing fugitives gallivanting. How did you find out about this?"

"I got telegrams back from the clerk in Judge Parker's court. I asked him to wire the judge in St. Louis and try to get a reply from him, but I don't know how long that'll take, or if he'll even do it."

Bo nodded slowly and said, "I guess we'll have to just wait and see."

"Blast it, I ain't much good at waitin'," Scratch burst out. "I hate to see you behind bars like this, Bo."

"The view's not very good from this side, either," Bo said. "But you did everything you could for now."

"I ain't so sure about that," Scratch said, thinking about Barney Dunn. He wanted to ask that bartender some questions, and he was going to make damned certain that Dunn came up with the answers.

Hoping that it might help to get Bo's mind off his plight, even for a few minutes, Scratch went on,

"There's a medicine show in town, you know. Came in earlier today. I met the folks who run it."

"Medicine show, eh?" Bo chuckled. "You're not going to fall for that cure-all pitch again, are you, Scratch? I remember you guzzled down a bottle of so-called elixir once, and it made you sick as a dog for two or three days."

Scratch shuddered.

"I ain't likely to forget about that," he said. "I don't even like to think about how bad I felt. It was like the old joke about bein' afraid you were gonna die . . . then bein' afraid that you *weren't*."

"Is there a girl with this show?"

Thinking about Veronique Ballantine made a grin appear on Scratch's face.

"I'll say there is. As pretty a red-haired gal as I've seen in a long time. You know I'm partial to redheads."

"Yeah . . . and blondes and brunettes, too," Bo said dryly. "Are you going to their show?"

"Hadn't really thought about it. I don't reckon I've got time, though. I need to get busy findin' out who really killed those gals, so we can get you out of here."

"I wouldn't mind being out," Bo admitted. "I never have liked being locked up."

Scratch lowered his voice and said, "I still reckon we could do somethin' about that, especially if I rode back out to the Star C and talked your pa and brothers into givin' me a hand."

"Absolutely not," Bo said.

Scratch blew out an exasperated breath.

"You sure are a stickler for the law," he said.

Smiling, Bo said, "One of us needs to be. Anyway, Cooper and Riley would never help you. Hank probably would, and my father might, but I won't risk them getting hurt. Everything's all right so far. For the time being we'll just wait and hope that you hear back from Judge Parker."

"All right," Scratch agreed grudgingly. "Did the marshal feed you?"

"A waitress brought a couple of meals over from the café."

"I hope she was pretty, anyway."

"I wouldn't know. She never came back here. I heard her voice out in the office, but Marshal Haltom was the one who brought in the trays."

"And he ain't what you'd call pretty."

"No," Bo said, "not unless you were blind. And probably not even then, with that gravel voice of his."

Scratch promised to keep an eye on the jail all night, just in case there was any trouble. Bo told him to get some supper and some rest. Scratch shrugged noncommittally, lifted a hand in farewell, and left the cell block.

Marshal Haltom got up from behind the desk, closed and locked the cell block door, and asked, "Did I hear you say something about that medicine show that came into town?"

"Yeah," Scratch said. "I talked to the folks who run it."

"I knew it was here, but I haven't had a chance to lay down the law to them yet. Medicine show people are as bad as gypsies, as far as I'm concerned. I can't run 'em out of town as long as they haven't broken the law, but the sooner they're out of Bear Creek, the better. You tell 'em that for me, if you talk to them again."

"Why, Marshal, are you deputizin' me?"

Haltom stared at him for a second, obviously confused by the question, then glared and said, "Get on out of here before I lock you up, too."

"On what charge?"

"I'll think of something!"

Scratch put on his guns and left, momentarily pleased by the fact that he had gotten under the marshal's skin.

Then his attitude grew more sober again. He had spent the day trying to help Bo, but for all practical purposes he hadn't accomplished a blasted thing.

But the day wasn't over yet. Scratch was hungry, but he could get something to eat on the other side of the creek. Leading his horse, he walked down the street toward the bridge.

CHAPTER 14

The Southern Belle was the oldest and most successful saloon in Bear Creek, and the best as far as Scratch was concerned. Lauralee Parker's father had started it more than twenty-five years earlier, when Lauralee was just a little girl. She had literally grown up in the saloon because her mother had passed away when Lauralee was an infant.

Most folks thought it was shameful for a child to be raised that way, especially a girl child. But Lauralee had turned out to be a fine woman. Smart, honest, and tough-minded, there had never been any question that she would take over the saloon when the time came, as it had when Samuel Parker's heart gave out on him with no warning one summer day.

The Southern Belle was closed for a period of mourning, but then Lauralee had reopened it and operated it ever since. She didn't water down the whiskey, and any gambler who wanted to play in the Southern Belle had to deal an honest game. No tinhorns allowed. Some of the girls who worked there were soiled doves, no doubt about that, but it wasn't a requirement and they conducted that part of their business away from the saloon.

The ladies who attended services at the Baptist, Methodist, and Lutheran churches considered all the saloons in Bear Creek to be abominations unto the Lord, of course, including the Southern Belle, but if you forced them to be honest, most of them would admit to having a soft spot in their hearts for Lauralee Parker no matter what her business was.

That was because anybody in Bear Creek who needed help could always count on Lauralee. She sat up with the sick and the dying, she helped make sure that anyone who was hungry got fed, and some of the saloon's profits always ended up in the coffers of those churches. The donations were anonymous, of course, but most people knew where they came from.

Bo and Scratch had known Lauralee ever since she was a little girl. They had been friends with her father. They had watched her grow up into a beautiful young woman.

During one of their previous visits to their old hometown, Scratch had seen a little something going on between Bo and Lauralee. He had the idea that she had pretty much thrown herself at his trail partner. As gently as possible, Bo had put a stop to that before it ever got started, for several reasons.

Most important, he wasn't interested in settling down, and there was no getting around the fact that he was old enough to be Lauralee's father himself. Plus, he suspected that her attraction to him was more a case of hero worship than anything else, and he knew that wouldn't last.

Scratch was glad that it wasn't him Lauralee had set her cap for. He wasn't sure he would have been able to resist the persistent temptations of such a fine gal, no matter how much difference in their ages there was.

He was looking forward to seeing her, though. He suspected the ten years that had gone by since he had last laid eyes on her had just made Lauralee that much more beautiful.

The hitch racks in front of the Southern Belle were nearly full, but Scratch found a place to tie his horse. Laughter and music and loud talk, the siren song of good saloons everywhere, drifted over the batwings at the Southern Belle's corner entrance. Scratch stepped up onto the boardwalk and pushed those batwings aside.

Inside, the air was blue with smoke from pipes, cigars, and quirlies. The tobacco scent mingled with that of beer and sawdust. Lauralee saw to it that the Southern Belle was swept out and mopped good every morning, so some of the more offensive odors that often lurked in saloons weren't present here.

The long hardwood bar was to Scratch's left. On the wall to his right a staircase ascended to the second floor. More than a dozen tables for the drinkers sat in between. Poker tables, faro and keno layouts, and a roulette wheel were in the back, along with a small stage where a slick-haired piano player tickled the ivories. There was nothing really unusual about the Southern Belle except that everything was clean and in good repair.

A woman with blond curls spilling down her back, as opposed to the more elaborate braids and buns that most women preferred, stood at the far end of the bar talking to one of the bartenders. When her eyes swung toward Scratch, they widened with recognition.

"Scratch Morton!" she exclaimed as she hurried along the bar toward him. "I'd heard you were back in these parts. It's so good to see you again!"

She threw her arms around him in an enthusiastic hug that immediately made Scratch the envy of just about every man in the place. He knew they were all thinking about what it must feel like to have that enticing bundle of female flesh in his arms.

It felt mighty good, he had to admit. The scent of that thick hair the color of sunshine as she pressed her head against his chest was downright intoxicating, too. He thought it would be a good idea to step back a little, so he did and rested his hands on Lauralee Parker's shoulders as he gazed at her.

"Dang it, gal, I don't think you've aged a day in the past ten years!"

She smiled and slapped a hand lightly against his chest.

"You always were full of flattery, Scratch," she said.

"That's a generous way of puttin' it," he said with a grin. "People are all the time sayin' that I'm full of somethin'."

Lauralee grew serious as she went on, "I heard about Bo being in jail. That's terrible. I just can't believe it."

"Neither can I. And it never should've happened. I told that marshal and everybody else in earshot that Bo never hurt those gals. He couldn't have."

"I know it doesn't sound like him."

Scratch shook his head.

"No, I mean he *couldn't* have done it. He was with me, and we were a long way from Bear Creek when those girls were killed."

"And you say you told the marshal about that?" Lauralee asked with a frown.

"I dang sure did. He didn't believe me, because of that picture one of your bartenders drew."

Lauralee glanced toward the bartender she'd been talking to when Scratch came in, and he realized the man was probably Barney Dunn.

"I saw that picture," Lauralee said quietly. "I don't know if you've seen it, Scratch, but it does look an awful lot like Bo. Exactly like him, in fact."

"Yeah, the marshal let me take a gander at it," Scratch admitted. "And I know things look bad for Bo. But I know for certain sure he's innocent, and not just because we weren't anywhere around here. I know it because I know Bo."

Lauralee nodded.

"I feel the same way," she said. "That's why I told Danny Fontaine and his friends to take their business elsewhere. They were in here earlier, getting drunk and saying awful things. I thought they might start a brawl when I told them to leave, but they finally went on without starting any trouble."

Scratch had noticed when he came in that the crew from the Rafter F was nowhere to be seen. Now he knew why.

But there were plenty of other places on this side of the creek where the men could continue getting liquored up. The danger of a lynch mob forming remained high.

"Come and sit down with me," Lauralee said as she took hold of Scratch's arm. "We need to talk."

"I was thinkin' the same thing."

They went to a table in the rear corner. This was where Lauralee held court, Scratch recalled, laughing and telling stories and generally being the beautiful queen of the Southern Belle.

"Do you want something to drink?" she asked him.

"Maybe some coffee. I need to keep a clear head tonight. And something to eat, if you've got it."

"I can always rustle up something for you," she told him with a smile. "How about a roast beef sandwich?"

"Sounds mighty good," Scratch told her.

She left him sitting at the table and went through a door at the end of the bar, coming back a few minutes later with a cup of coffee and a plate with the sandwich on it. The thick slices of roast beef nestled between equally thick slices of bread. The long ride had left Scratch hungry, so he dug in eagerly.

Lauralee sat with him and let him get several bites down before she said, "Tell me the whole story, Scratch."

He drank some of the coffee and then said, "There ain't much to tell. Bo and I rode in, thinkin' we'd have a nice visit with our families and old friends, and found the whole dang county's gone loco."

"People are upset about the killings," Lauralee said. "Those girls may have been soiled doves, but they had friends, especially Rose. She'd worked here for a long time. But it's more than that. People are scared, too."

"Because they don't know when the killer's gonna strike again," Scratch said.

Lauralee nodded.

"That's right. People have been afraid to step out of their houses at night because they think somebody's lurking in the darkness with a knife, just waiting to murder them, too." She shrugged. "Maybe now that Bo's locked up, they'll rest a little easier."

"They'll be makin' a mistake if they do," Scratch

said, "because whoever killed those gals is still out there somewhere."

"You and I know that. Most of the people in Bear Creek will want to believe that the danger is over, though."

Scratch grimaced and shook his head. He ate some more of the sandwich before he asked, "What about that fella Dunn?"

"Barney?" Lauralee looked toward the bar again. The object of her scrutiny was a short, stocky man with a round face, a double chin, and a mostly bald head that shone pinkly in the light from the chandeliers. "He's been a good bartender, always shows up on time and does what he's supposed to do. I don't know much about him. He's from back East somewhere. I hired him about a year ago and haven't had any problems with him."

"You trust him?"

"He's never lied to me as far as I know. That's all I can tell you, Scratch."

"So you don't know of any reason he might lie about what he claims he saw out back in the alley that night?"

Lauralee shook her head.

"It doesn't make any sense to me that he would. And I sure don't see how he could have drawn such an accurate sketch of Bo if he hadn't . . . well, if he hadn't seen him." She added hastily, "I know you say that's impossible, Scratch, and I want to believe it is, too, but I still don't see any other explanation."

Scratch finished off the sandwich and washed it down with the rest of the coffee. As he set the empty cup on the table, he asked, "Do you mind if I talk to Dunn?"

"No, of course not." Lauralee hesitated. "You won't threaten him or anything, will you?"

"Forcin' him to change his story wouldn't do any good," Scratch said. "Folks would know he was doin' it because he was scared of me, and they'd still think Bo is guilty. That ain't what I want. I want proof to convince everybody that Bo's innocent."

"I agree." Lauralee stood up. "I'll send him over here."

"I'm obliged to you."

"It's the least I can do. You and Bo were always good friends to my father . . . and to me." A pink flush spread across her face. "You may not know this, Scratch, but there was a time when I had sort of a crush on Bo."

"Never dreamed of it," Scratch lied with a straight face. "And Bo never said nothin' to me about it." That part was true.

"He wouldn't have. He's too much of a gentleman for that. He always has been." Lauralee's tone became more brisk as she went on, "I'll get Barney."

She went over to the bar and spoke to Dunn. He glanced nervously at Scratch, but Lauralee seemed to be trying to reassure him. After a moment Dunn nodded and came out from behind the hardwood.

The two of them walked back to the table in the corner.

"Scratch, this is Barney Dunn," Lauralee said. "Barney, Scratch Morton, an old friend of mine."

"Pleased to meet you," Dunn said, and Scratch heard the eastern accent in the man's voice.

Scratch stood up and shook hands with the bartender, then said, "I'm obliged to you for talkin' to me, Dunn. I reckon this must be a mite awkward for you. You're bound to know who I am."

"Yeah, the friend of the guy the marshal's got locked up," Dunn said. "The guy I drew the picture of, the one who . . ."

From the uncomfortable look on Dunn's face, Scratch knew what he'd been about to say before his voice trailed off.

"We might as well put our cards on the table," Scratch said as the three of them sat down. "You're the reason my pard's in jail."

"Yeah, but you gotta understand. When all that happened with . . . with Rose . . . I didn't know who the guy I saw was. I'd never even heard of Bo Creel. I just described him as best I could, and then I got the idea that maybe I could draw a sketch of him. I used to be pretty good at that when I was a kid, you know."

"You mind goin' over the story again with me, about what you saw that night?"

"Well, I hate to think about it . . . It ain't a

pleasant memory, you know? But sure, I can tell you what I saw."

It was the same thing Scratch had heard before, but the tale had more immediacy and impact coming from the man who had lived through it.

"I've never been so scared in my life," Dunn concluded. "I swear, that big knife came within a whisker of getting me. I don't want to ever come that close again."

Scratch had to admit that the bartender's story sounded convincing. Anyone who listened to it and saw the sketch Dunn had made would have a hard time believing that Bo *wasn't* the Butcher of Bear Creek.

And yet Scratch knew that was impossible. He said, "What if I was to tell you that Bo was more than two hundred miles away from here when that happened?"

Barney Dunn shrugged.

"I don't know what to tell you, Mr. Morton. Remember, it wasn't me who said your friend was the killer. Other people did that. I just told what I saw and let somebody else figure it out."

"Yeah, that's where we stand, all right," Scratch said with a sigh. "I know Bo's innocent, but there's no way to prove it right now."

Lauralee said, "And meanwhile you've got Danny Fontaine stirring up the town against him even more. I worry that this isn't going to end well, Scratch."

"So do I, but we'll do everything we can to get to the bottom of it."

Dunn said, "If there's nothin' else I can do to help you, I oughta get back to work."

Lauralee looked at Scratch, who shook his head. She told the bartender, "Thanks, Barney."

"Anything for you, ma'am, you know that."

Scratch wasn't surprised by that sentiment. Lauralee inspired a lot of loyalty among her employees.

"What are you going to do now?" she asked Scratch when Dunn had gone back behind the bar.

"Keep an eye on the jail, I reckon, just to make sure nobody tries anything."

"You'll have to sleep sometime."

"Not for a while yet." He smiled. "One good thing about gettin' older is that you don't need as much sleep. Fact of the matter is, I spend a lot of nights tossin' and turnin' anyway."

"Not everybody in Bear Creek has turned on Bo. I can put the word out and find some men who'd be willing to help guard the jail. Marshal Haltom won't like that when he finds out about it, but I don't care. Let him be stubborn. He can't keep Bo safe alone."

Scratch nodded and said, "That sure might help. But you be mighty careful about what you say and do, Lauralee. There's one thing we got to remember about this."

"What's that?"

"As long as Bo's in jail," Scratch said, "nobody but us is lookin' for the real killer. He's safe for now."

"Unless we can prove that Bo isn't guilty."

"Yep. Which means the varmint's got a powerful strong reason for makin' sure Bo stays behind bars . . . even if it means gettin' rid of the folks who are tryin' to help him."

CHAPTER 15

Scratch talked to Lauralee for a while longer, turning to the things that had gone on in her life in the years since he had last seen her. They caught up like two old friends will, and under normal circumstances Scratch would have enjoyed the conversation a great deal.

There was nothing normal about the circumstances, though, and he was too distracted by worrying about Bo to really concentrate on what Lauralee was saying.

Finally she told him, "Go on back to the jail, Scratch. That's where your mind is, already."

He shook his head and said, "Never thought I'd have so much trouble payin' attention to what a beautiful blonde was tellin' me. That just goes to show you how shook up this dang business has got me."

"I appreciate the compliment, but I understand why you're distracted. Go on, now. I'll see if I can find somebody to spell you later." She gave an unladylike snort. "Shoot, if it comes to that, *I'll* help you guard the jail. I can handle a gun, you know."

"Bo wouldn't stand for that, and you know it."

Lauralee grinned.

"Bo's in jail. He wouldn't know about it, now would he?"

Scratch chuckled and shrugged. He got to his feet and said, "I'll see you later."

"Be careful. If you're right about the real killer wanting to put a stop to any investigation, then you're in danger, too."

"Let him come after me," Scratch said. "That'd be plumb welcome as far as I'm concerned. That's one way of skinnin' the varmint's hide."

"Or getting your own hide skinned."

Scratch inclined his head in acknowledgment of that point and left the Southern Belle. As he walked back toward the bridge, leading his horse, he wondered in which of the other saloons Fontaine and the rest of the Rafter F punchers were drinking and raising hell.

Music drifted to Scratch's ears as he crossed the bridge, but it wasn't coming from the saloons behind him, he realized. It sounded like an accordion. Whoever was playing the squeezebox was doing so with both talent and enthusiasm.

The medicine show, Scratch thought. That had to be the source of the music.

A turn to the right when he reached the foot of

the bridge would take him toward the jail. The public well was the other way, and that was where he had seen Professor Sarlat's wagon parked earlier.

He was tempted to walk down and check out the show. He figured the professor was playing the accordion, which meant Veronique was probably dancing. Scratch had a feeling that would be a sight well worth seeing.

But Bo was counting on him, and Scratch knew good and well he couldn't ignore what he needed to do just so he could go see a pretty redhead dancing around, possibly in some sort of skimpy getup. He didn't hesitate for a second when he reached the end of the bridge.

He turned toward the jail.

But he hadn't gone more than a few steps when the music at the other end of the street suddenly stopped and a woman's scream ripped through the night.

Scratch stopped short and swiveled around, unable to ignore the sounds of trouble. Lanterns hung from the corners of Professor Sarlat's wagon and created an oasis of light at the far end of the street. The glow revealed a crowd of people around the wagon, mostly men although a few women were in attendance, too.

The wagon's tailgate had been lowered. Veronique Ballantine stood on it, cringing away from hands that reached up and tried to grab her. She wore a short, spangled dress that was cut low enough to expose the upper swells of her breasts.

"Leave her alone!" Sarlat shouted. Scratch saw the professor's top hat bobbing around as he struggled in the grip of the two men who were holding him. Scratch was too far away to get a good look at the men wrestling with Sarlat, but it didn't take much guesswork to figure out who they were, or who the man grabbing at Veronique was.

Those three cowboys from the Rafter F had come back looking for more trouble.

It didn't appear that any of the townspeople in the crowd around the wagon were going to try to help Sarlat and Veronique. They were probably afraid of the Fontaine punchers, who had struck Scratch as ruffians from way back.

That left it up to him again. He knew he needed to get back to the jail, but he also knew what Bo would want him to do in a situation like this.

Scratch started jogging toward the wagon, hanging on to his horse's reins and leading the animal behind him.

Veronique wasn't able to avoid the pawing hand of the cowboy who clutched at her. He got hold of her ankle and gave it a jerk that stole her balance from her. She cried out again and waved her arms in frantic circles, but she was unable to recover. She toppled off the tailgate.

The cowboy was there to catch her. He laughed raucously as he wrapped his arms around her.

"Got you this time!" he crowed triumphantly.

"Put her down and let her go!" Scratch shouted as he reached the edge of the crowd and dropped his horse's reins. He knew the animal was well-trained enough not to run off.

People got out of his way as he strode forward. He didn't reach for his Remingtons, because he didn't want this to turn into a gunfight. There were too many innocent folks around who might get in the way of any flying lead.

"It's that old geezer!" one of the men holding the professor exclaimed.

"Teach him a lesson!" ordered the puncher holding Veronique. "I'll hang on to the girl."

The other two men slammed Sarlat back against the side of the wagon. As the professor fell to his knees, stunned, they charged Scratch.

The two burly cowhands were a lot younger than Scratch, but he had the experience of decades when it came to brawling. As a punch came at his head, he stepped nimbly aside and let the man's fist whip past his ear. That made the cowboy stumble forward, momentarily blocking the other man.

Scratch bored in, hooking a right into the cowboy's belly and then a left to the jaw as the first punch made the man gasp and lean forward. The second blow landed just as cleanly as the first and jerked the man's head to the side. Scratch kicked his feet out from under him, and as the cowboy fell Scratch shoved him into his companion. Their legs tangled and both men went down.

He knew they wouldn't stay down long, though. Neither man was out of the fight by any means. As one of them started to get up, Scratch kicked him in the chest and knocked him sprawling. Kicking a man while he was down went against the grain, but when a fella was outnumbered by younger opponents, some of the niceties had to go by the wayside.

The second cowboy made it to his feet while Scratch was dealing with the first one. He tackled Scratch and drove the silver-haired Texan against the wagon. Scratch's hat flew off as the impact jarred through him. He lifted an uppercut that caught the man he was battling under the chin.

The punch jacked the man's head back and gave Scratch a little room. Unfortunately, as he tried to move to a better position he stumbled over Professor Sarlat, who was still lying on the ground where he had fallen next to the wagon. A fist hammered against Scratch's head while he was off balance from that and sent him to the ground.

The first cowboy was back on his feet and rushed at Scratch alongside the second one. Both of them looked ready to stomp him into the ground. Scratch rolled aside desperately as a boot came at his face. He grunted in pain as the other man kicked him in the shoulder. Scratch tried to ignore that as he grabbed the man's leg and heaved, upending him.

The next second, a boot toe slammed into Scratch's ribs and sent him rolling again. The man who had just kicked him rushed after him. Scratch recovered just in time to avoid another swinging kick. He brought his own leg up and sank the heel of his boot in the man's groin.

That brought a high-pitched scream of agony from the hombre. He staggered, clutched at himself, and collapsed. That was one varmint down who wouldn't be getting back up again anytime soon, Scratch thought as he slapped a hand on the ground and pushed himself up.

He sensed as much as saw the fist rocketing toward his head and ducked under it. His right fist shot out in a counterpunch that landed on the man's chest. Scratch followed with a left that clipped the man on the ear, probably painfully but without doing much real damage. A flurry of punches from his opponent forced Scratch backward as he tried to block the blows.

One of the punches got through and tagged him on the jaw. Scratch fell back against the wagon again. He probably would have fallen all the way to the ground if the vehicle hadn't caught him. He twisted aside so that another punch narrowly missed him. The cowboy's fist crashed into the thick sideboard instead. He howled in pain. Scratch knew the man might have busted a knuckle or two because of the missed blow.

Seizing the advantage, Scratch waded in, swinging

a left and then a right, both of which connected and sent the cowboy stumbling backward.

The crowd had backed off to give the combatants plenty of room, although no one had left. A knock-down, drag-out, bare-knuckles fight like this was just as entertaining as any medicine show.

Scratch went after his opponent, landing a left jab and then a roundhouse right. That finally did the trick and sent the cowboy to the ground. He rolled over once and came to a stop on his belly. He lay there limp and unmoving, obviously out cold.

That left the man who had dragged Veronique off the tailgate where she'd been dancing. As Scratch turned in that direction, the man shoved Veronique away and dragged his gun from its holster. Scratch still didn't want to slap leather, but it looked like he didn't have any choice.

Before the cowboy could raise his gun, though, Veronique moved like a striking snake. She plucked a small knife from a sheath strapped to her leg under the hem of the short dress and brought it up, driving the blade into the man's forearm. He bellowed as the cold steel penetrating his flesh forced his hand to open wide in reaction. His Colt thudded to the ground without being fired.

The cowboy didn't get a chance to do anything else. Professor Sarlat, who had managed to get back to his feet, had that heavy cane in his hands as he stepped up and swung it. The walking stick crashed into the back of the cowboy's head and knocked him forward. He took a single step before he pitched to the ground on his face and didn't move again.

"By God . . . that'll teach you . . . to manhandle a lady, you worm!" Sarlat told the cowboy breathlessly, although Scratch figured the hombre was unconscious and didn't hear the words.

Scratch was a little out of breath himself, the price of not being as young as he used to be. He rested a hand against the wagon to steady himself and drew in a couple of lungfuls of air. As the pulse hammering inside his head began to slow down a little, he asked, "Are you and Mademoiselle Ballantine all right, Professor?"

"A bit shaken up, but I'm sure we'll be fine," Sarlat said. "Eh, Veronique?"

She leaned down, grasped the handle of the knife that was still lodged in the cowboy's arm, and pulled the blade free none too gently.

"*Oui*, fine," she said, glaring at the unconscious man as if she wanted to do a little carving on him with that blade. "Now." Her expression softened as she looked at Scratch and added, "Thanks to M'sieu Morton."

"Seems to me that I've got you to thank for me not bein' shot, mademoiselle," Scratch told her.

"No, I'm certain you would have killed this pig yourself had I not intervened." She kicked the cowboy in the side, but with the soft slipper she wore for dancing, she probably didn't do much damage, Scratch thought. "But that would have caused more trouble for us, satisfying though it might have been."

Sarlat said, "The law doesn't look kindly on it whenever there's violence connected with our performance. Somehow, peace officers always tend to believe that any trouble is our fault."

"Well, I'm here to testify that you two ain't to blame for any of this, and I'm sure these other good folks will agree with that." Scratch turned a hard gaze on the crowd. "Ain't that right?"

He got nods and murmurs of agreement from several of the men.

Anyway, since there hadn't been any shooting, this ruckus might not even attract any attention from the marshal. Jonas Haltom had more pressing matters to attend to, like the prisoner he had locked up in the jail.

As that thought went through Scratch's mind, he looked around for his hat. Spotting it on the ground, he picked it up and dusted it off before settling it back on his head.

"I got to be goin'—" he began.

"But you haven't seen any of the performance," Sarlat protested. "Veronique was just about to dance."

She smiled at Scratch, and he felt the power of it right down to his toes.

"As much as I'd like to stay and watch that, there are other things I have to do," he said. "First, though . . ." Scratch looked at the crowd again. "Some of you fellas help me drag off these coyotes."

He could tell that none of the men really wanted to get involved, but his flinty stare made several of them grudgingly volunteer. The cowboy Scratch had kicked in the groin had passed out, too, so all three of them were unconscious as Scratch and the townies he pressed into service hauled them up to the bridge and dumped them there.

"Their horses are probably still on the other side of the creek," Scratch said. "When they come to, likely they'll stagger across there, mount up, and head for home."

"You don't know what you've let yourself in for, Morton," said one of the men who had helped Scratch. "That Fontaine crew is a rough bunch, each and every one of 'em. These three will have a man-sized grudge against you."

"If I worried about every no-account varmint who's got a grudge against me, I'd never get any sleep," Scratch said with a grin.

"Well, you'd better sleep with one eye open and a hand on your gun, if you know what I mean," the townsman warned.

"I always do, amigo," Scratch said. "I always do."

CHAPTER 16

Scratch left his horse with the elderly night hostler at Brantley's Livery Stable, then took his Winchester and ambled up the street toward the marshal's office.

Everything was still quiet around the jail. Scratch was glad to see that, although he was a little surprised by it.

Across the street was the Bear Creek Hotel, which had several rocking chairs on its porch where guests could sit. Even though Scratch wasn't staying at the hotel, he parked himself in one of those chairs where he could keep an eye on the jail. His rifle rested across his lap as he sat there.

The lamps in the hotel lobby had been blown out by now, except for a small one behind the desk, so the porch was mostly in shadow. That was the way Scratch wanted it. If anybody showed up to cause trouble, maybe they wouldn't notice he was there until it was too late.

The town quieted down more and more as time passed, although Scratch could still hear some noise coming from the other side of the creek. The saloons closed around midnight during the week like this, although they stayed open all night on Saturday.

He had been sitting on the hotel porch for about an hour when he heard the sudden clatter of a lot of hoofbeats on the bridge spanning Bear Creek. The sound made him come to his feet and draw back even farther into the shadows. He held the Winchester slanted across his chest. If those riders crossing the creek attacked the jail with the intent of taking Bo out and stringing him up, Scratch intended to give them some hot lead discouragement.

The possibility that he might be killed in a battle like that never crossed his mind. The only thing he thought about was protecting his best friend.

Instead of turning toward the jail, though, the horsebackers turned the other way when they reached the end of the bridge and headed south out of the settlement. Scratch figured they had to be the Fontaine crew, riding back to the Rafter F. That was the only group in town large enough to be leaving Bear Creek together after dark this way.

That meant either Danny Fontaine hadn't been able to stir them up into a lynching frenzy, or more likely Fontaine was just biding his time for some reason.

Scratch couldn't rule out the possibility of a trick

of some sort, either. The Rafter F hands might double back.

So he sat down again with the rifle across his lap and settled back to keep watch some more.

Despite what he had told Lauralee about not needing as much sleep as he would, Scratch found himself getting drowsy. Over the course of his adventurous life, he had found himself in many situations where his own hide, as well as that of Bo, depended on him staying alert. So he was confident that he wasn't going to fall asleep. His eyes went down to narrow slits, but he was still awake.

A while later, a jolt went through him, jerking him upright in the rocking chair. Scratch muttered a curse as he realized that he had indeed dozed off despite all his good intentions. He shook his head and yawned, and as he moved his hand to shift his grip on the rifle, he felt something hard in the pocket of his buckskin jacket.

Professor Sarlat's elixir, that was what it had to be. Scratch recalled slipping the bottle into his pocket earlier in the day, after he had helped out the professor and Veronique the first time. He took it out and hefted it in his hands.

Maybe there really was something to Sarlat's claims that the elixir was a restorative and cure-all. Scratch could use something like that right about now. Not only was he tired, he was also bruised and battered from the tussle with the three cowboys.

The professor's tonic might make him feel better, even if it was mostly booze.

Especially if it was mostly booze, Scratch thought with a grin.

Balancing the Winchester in his lap, he used both hands to hold the bottle and work the cork out of its neck. When he had the bottle open, he held it to his nose and sniffed the contents.

The elixir didn't smell as bad as he expected. He caught a definite tang of alcohol, but it was mixed with a fruity smell. Nothing that Scratch could really identify, though. He thought it smelled more like a mixture of several different fruits. Maybe a little bit of chili pepper, too. It was odd, but not unappealing.

"Only one way to find out how it tastes," he told himself out loud. He put the bottle to his lips, tipped it up, and took a sip.

The taste was as smooth as it could be, but Scratch was prepared to have the stuff go off in his mouth like a keg of blasting powder anyway. Instead it immediately began to glow with a comforting warmth that spread through him as he swallowed. He took another sip.

If anything, the effect got better with the second drink. It wasn't because of the alcohol in the tonic, either, Scratch thought. It was all the other ingredients, whatever they were, that made him feel so good. A third swallow convinced him of that.

He was going to have to ask Sarlat what was in there. The professor might not tell him. Scratch wouldn't blame him for being secretive. Once word of how wonderful this concoction was got around, it might be worth a fortune.

He took one more nip, then licked his lips and forced himself to replace the cork in the bottle. He knew that if he didn't, he'd sit here and drink the whole thing. That might not be a good idea. Just because it tasted great now and seemed to invigorate him, that didn't mean the effects would last.

But one thing he could be sure of: that was the best medicine show tonic he'd ever had. If the professor and Veronique stayed around Bear Creek for a few days, he'd have to stock up on the stuff, Scratch told himself.

Lauralee Parker showed up a little after midnight, wearing trousers and a man's coat and carrying a shotgun under her arm. Scratch told her he was fine and could stand guard by himself, but she insisted on sitting with him. That was just like her, and he knew he'd be wasting his breath to argue with her.

Besides, even though he wasn't dozing off anymore, he had to admit that he enjoyed the blonde's company. They talked for a long time, until Lauralee got sleepy. Scratch told her to go ahead and get a nap.

"I'm supposed to be here to spell you," she objected.

"I ain't all that tired. I'll catch a few winks later, after you do."

She didn't argue, and after a few minutes Scratch heard the deep, regular sound of her breathing as she leaned back in her rocking chair and slept. It was a nice sound, he thought.

Along toward morning, after Lauralee woke up, Scratch allowed himself to doze off again for a little while. Even though the professor's elixir had made him feel better, he couldn't do without sleep completely. When he woke up, the eastern sky was turning gray with the approach of dawn.

"Any trouble?" he asked Lauralee.

"Not a bit. The night was as quiet as could be. That's a relief, isn't it, Scratch?"

"Maybe," Scratch mused. "But it's sorta like waitin' for a storm to break, too."

They stood up and stretched. Lauralee said, "Why don't we get some breakfast before I go back to the Southern Belle?"

"That sounds like a good idea. I could use some coffee."

Although it wouldn't compare to the professor's elixir, Scratch thought.

The Red Top Café opened early. By the time Scratch and Lauralee finished eating and stepped back out into the street, the sun was just up.

"Do you think I should go and see Bo?" she asked.

"I reckon he'd like that."

Lauralee nodded and said, "I'll come by later in the day then, after I've had a chance to sleep a little more and freshen up."

"That ought to brighten his day more than anything else except gettin' out of that dang jail."

Lauralee waved farewell and headed back across the creek. Scratch went to the marshal's office and knocked on the door.

"Who's out there?" Haltom shouted from inside. Scratch couldn't be sure, but he thought the marshal sounded like he had just woken up.

"It's me, Scratch Morton, Marshal."

"You're by yourself?"

"Yeah."

Haltom unbarred the door. Scratch went in and nodded to the lawman, who tried but failed to suppress a prodigious yawn.

"I told you I wouldn't let anything happen to the prisoner," Haltom said when he'd finished the yawn.

"Yeah, I know it didn't, because I was sittin' right across the street with a rifle all night."

Haltom scowled.

"You didn't have to do that. You shouldn't be interfering with law business."

"The way I see it, I didn't interfere with anything."

"Well, next time do whatever you were doing somewhere else."

Scratch ignored that. He didn't figure Haltom had any legal reason to keep him from sitting on the hotel porch, as long as the hotel's owner didn't complain about it. As the marshal went over to the stove to stir up the fire and get some coffee heating, Scratch said, "I want to see Bo."

"Fine. Our breakfast ought to be here pretty soon."

"They were gettin' it ready at the Red Top when I left over there," Scratch agreed.

When Haltom had the fire in the stove burning to suit him, he unlocked the cell block door. Scratch left his rifle and gun belt on the marshal's desk, then went in and found Bo curled up in a thin blanket on the bunk, still sleeping.

"Well, that's a sight you don't see very often," Scratch said. "Bo Creel still abed after the sun's up."

Bo rolled over, pushed the blanket aside, and stood up to stretch. He grimaced as his bones popped and crackled a little.

"Reminds me why it's a good idea not to sleep on a jail cell bunk at our age," he said with a wry smile.

"That ain't a good idea at any age," Scratch said.

Bo took hold of the bars and asked, "Any trouble last night?"

"Nope, and I got to admit that I'm a mite surprised. I figured that Fontaine kid would try to stir up somethin'. The whole town's in such a state, it wouldn't have taken much."

"Well, be thankful for small favors, I suppose."

"Oh, I am, I am," Scratch assured his friend.

The cell block door was open, so he heard someone else knock on the front door of the marshal's office. Scratch stepped over to the opening so he could look into the office as Haltom called to the visitor, "Who's that?"

"It's Judge Buchanan, Jonas. Open up."

Haltom didn't argue or ask the judge if he was alone. He unbarred the door and opened it himself this time.

Judge Clarence Buchanan was a heavyset man in his fifties with graying brown hair. His ample belly stretched the material of the tweed suit he wore. He looked over at the open cell block door and said in evident surprise, "Scratch Morton."

"Howdy, Judge," Scratch said. "Wish I could say it's good to see you again."

Buchanan frowned and asked, "Did you ever appear before me in court?"

"Nope. You were still just practicin' law the last time Bo and me came through these parts. We heard you'd been appointed justice of the peace, though."

"Hmmph. As I recall, you two have had your share of run-ins with the law . . . although nothing anywhere near as serious as the crimes for which your friend is now locked up."

"Which he didn't do," Scratch said sharply.

"According to you. I think we all know that you'd lie to protect him."

"I don't have to lie. It's the truth . . . and I'm workin' on gettin' the proof of what I said."

"Proof is what the law deals in, all right." Buchanan turned to the marshal and went on, "To that end, Jonas, I'll hold a hearing this morning to consider evidence in this case and determine whether the prisoner should be charged with two counts of murder. Ten o'clock in the town hall."

Haltom nodded and said, "All right, Your Honor. I'll have Creel there."

"Hold on a minute," Scratch said. "Are you still the only lawyer in town, Judge?"

"I am," Buchanan admitted.

"Then how in blazes is Bo gonna get a fair trial if the judge is the only lawyer around here?"

Scratch couldn't keep the anger out of his voice as he asked the question. Buchanan glared at him and said, "Creel doesn't need a lawyer. This is a hearing, not a trial. The trial will take place in Hallettsville, and he can get a lawyer then. All I'm going to determine is if there's sufficient evidence to warrant the charges."

"Sounds like you've already made up your mind about that," Scratch snapped. He knew he wasn't doing Bo any good by arguing with Clarence Buchanan, but the old blowhard had always rubbed him the wrong way.

The justice of the peace looked at Haltom and said again, "Ten o'clock."

"We'll be there," Haltom said.

On his way out of the marshal's office, Buchanan paused and looked back at Scratch.

"If you're so worried about your friend having legal representation," he said, "why don't *you* act as his lawyer?"

"Me?" Scratch said. "I don't know anything about the law."

"Except how to break it now and then, eh?" Buchanan asked with a sneer. He went out, pulling the door closed behind him.

Haltom looked at Scratch and just shook his head.

Scratch sighed and stepped back into the cell block. He said, "Bo, I reckon I might've made things a mite worse."

"I heard the conversation," Bo said, smiling. "And for what it's worth, that pompous old goat puts a burr under my saddle, too." He paused. "But you know, maybe you acting as my lawyer isn't such a bad idea."

"It's a *terrible* idea!" Scratch exclaimed.

"Who else is on my side?" Bo asked.

"Lauralee Parker, for one."

"You saw Lauralee?"

"Yeah." Scratch didn't explain that she had helped him stand guard all night. "She told me to tell you that she's comin' by to visit you later today."

Bo smiled and said, "It'll be good to see her again. Has she changed much?"

"Not a hair, except maybe she's a little prettier now than she was the last time we were here."

"Hard to believe that's possible."

"You'll see for yourself after a while. In the meantime . . ."

"What is it, Scratch?" Bo asked when his friend's voice trailed off.

"I've done some pokin' around about this case . . . and nothin' I've found out is any good."

CHAPTER 17

Scratch spent a few minutes telling his old friend about his conversation with Barney Dunn at the Southern Belle.

"He spins a convincin' yarn," Scratch admitted, "and it's hard to get around that picture he drew lookin' so much like you, Bo."

"Maybe we crossed trails with him somewhere else," Bo suggested. "You said he came to Texas from back East somewhere, but there's no telling where he might have gone in between here and there. We could have met him in Kansas or Missouri or just about anywhere."

Scratch scraped a thumbnail along his jaw and frowned in thought as he considered that possibility.

"Yeah, I reckon so," he said dubiously. "The problem is, I don't recall ever meetin' him before, and I've got a pretty good memory for faces."

"Someone could have pointed us out to him and told him who we are." Bo shook his head and raised an objection to his own theory. "But even if that were the case, how in blazes could he have known that he would need to draw a picture of me some-day, so he could frame me for a murder?"

"Yeah, that ain't very likely, is it?"

"The only answer that makes sense," Bo said, "is that Dunn really saw someone who looks just like me killing that poor girl."

"To do that, the varmint would have to be your twin brother!" Scratch said. "You don't have a twin, do you?"

"You've met all my brothers. There's some family resemblance, sure, but no one would ever mistake one of us for any of the others." Bo sighed. "This is almost enough to make me believe in the old stories about doppelgangers."

"Double what?" Scratch asked with a frown.

"Doppelgangers. It's a German word, means 'double walker.' Comes from the idea that every-body has an identical double they don't know about somewhere in the world."

"You mean somewhere there's a fella who looks the same as me?" Scratch asked. "In New York or Europe or some such?"

"That's the idea," Bo said.

Scratch shook his head.

"Nope, can't be true," he declared. "I'm a Texan, and the notion that there could be another me some-wheres else just ain't possible."

"You weren't born in Texas and neither was I," Bo pointed out.

"That don't matter. This is where I was destined to end up."

"Maybe the same thing is true of my doppel-ganger."

Scratch frowned and said, "Well, yeah, if you look at it like that . . . but the whole thing still seems pretty far-fetched to me."

"The old stories say that it's bad luck to see your own doppelganger," Bo mused. "Some of them even claim that if you see your double, it means you're going to die."

Those words made a chill go through Scratch. The way he saw it, if they *weren't* able to turn up Bo's double, he was liable to die . . . swinging from a gallows or a hanging tree for the murders of those two saloon girls.

Bo's breakfast arrived shortly after that, along with a meal for Marshal Haltom. Bo didn't have much appetite, but he forced himself to eat because he knew he needed to keep his strength up. With the situation like it was, there was no telling when trouble might erupt.

Bo found himself feeling sorry for Scratch. He could tell that his old friend was struggling with this. Scratch was plenty smart and had good instincts, but he wasn't built for pondering and working out puzzles. He was more the sort who just bulled ahead until he was past whatever obstacle had popped up in his path.

Unfortunately, such dogged determination might not be enough in this case. There was a mystery to be solved, and until it was, Bo was going to be in trouble.

After breakfast, Marshal Haltom came into the cell block carrying his shotgun.

"All right, Morton, clear out," he ordered. "It's time to take Creel over to the town hall for that hearing."

"Whether it's official or not, you might as well consider me a deputy," Scratch said, "because I'm goin' with you to make sure Bo stays safe."

"You think I can't deliver a prisoner to a hearing?" Clearly, the lawman was offended by the suggestion.

"Reckon you probably can. I'm just not takin' any chances, that's all."

"I don't guess I can stop you from walking in that direction," Haltom admitted. "I'm warning you, though, stay out of my way and don't try anything." He gestured with the shotgun. "Go on out in the office."

Scratch left the cell block. Haltom unlocked Bo's cell and backed off, leveling the scattergun at the prisoner.

"Come on out of there now," the marshal said.

"I hope you're being careful with that Greener,

Marshal," Bo said as he swung the door open. "And I sure hope it doesn't have a hair trigger."

"As long as you behave yourself, you won't have any reason to find out."

Bo left the cell, moving deliberately and keeping his hands in plain sight. As he turned toward the office, Haltom fell in behind him. Bo could almost feel the shotgun's twin barrels prodding him in the back, even though the lawman didn't actually touch him with them. The threat of that double load of buckshot so close behind him was impossible to ignore, though.

When he stepped into the office, he saw that Scratch had already buckled on the Remington revolvers and had a Winchester tucked under his arm. The door was still unbarred from the visit of the waitress from the café who had brought breakfast for Bo and the marshal.

A pair of handcuffs lay on the desk. Haltom nodded toward them and said, "Put those on yourself, Creel."

"That's not necessary, Marshal. I respect the law. I'm not going to try to escape."

"I don't care. Anybody charged with crimes as serious as you are isn't going into court without wearing the cuffs. Now put 'em on."

Bo sighed and snapped the steel cuffs around his wrists. It was a little awkward, but he managed. At least his hands were in front of him, he thought, so it wasn't too uncomfortable.

Haltom said to Scratch, "You might as well make yourself useful, Morton. Open the door."

Scratch nodded. He opened the door and stepped out onto the boardwalk, rifle held at the ready now as he turned his head and scanned the street in both directions for any signs of trouble. Bo saw Scratch's head swivel back and forth and knew what his old friend was doing.

"Looks all right, Marshal," Scratch reported.

"Blast it, you're not my deputy," Haltom snapped. "If I want any information from you, I'll ask for it."

"You make it mighty hard to cut you any slack, Marshal."

"Yeah, I'll lose sleep over that opinion, too," Haltom said with a mocking sneer. "Keep moving, Creel. You know where the town hall is."

"If it hasn't moved in the past ten years, I do," Bo said.

"It's still in the same place. You take a step in any other direction and I'll blow a hole in you."

Word must have gotten around town about the hearing, Bo thought as he started walking up the street toward the town hall. The boardwalks were crowded, and more people stared out the windows of the buildings as the little procession passed. He spotted a few friendly faces, but most of the expressions were either hostile or blankly curious.

Scratch walked in front, still watchful, with Bo behind him and Marshal Haltom bringing up the rear.

The town hall was a large frame building that stood by itself. Instead of the boardwalk that fronted the businesses along the street, it had a separate front porch, and attached to the awning over that porch was a sign that read BEAR CREEK TOWN HALL & COMMUNITY CENTER. Covered dish suppers were held there several times a year, as were socials and dances. It was also the site of town meetings whenever the council wanted to discuss an issue with the citizens, and Judge Buchanan's justice of the peace court met there regularly.

That was the use it was being put to today. Bo expected the place would be packed as people came to see what the judge was going to do with him. He looked over his shoulder and saw that a crowd was already following him and Scratch and Marshal Haltom.

That crowd parted suddenly as the sound of hoofbeats filled the air. People moved aside hurriedly, some with angry shouts.

"Move on up there, Creel," Haltom ordered with a note of urgency in his voice. "Get inside, damn it!"

Hearing the commotion, Scratch swung around to see what was happening.

"Hold your fire, Morton!" Haltom said. He took one hand off the shotgun and used it to give Bo a shove. "Inside!"

Bo wished his hands were free. He didn't like the thought of trouble bearing down on him while he wasn't able to defend himself properly. But Scratch was here, and he knew he could depend on his old friend.

With Haltom prodding him from behind, Bo stumbled toward the porch steps. Scratch moved to the side so Bo could go past him.

"I'll cover you, pard," the silver-haired Texan said.

Bo went up the steps and stopped on the porch to turn around and see what was happening. Quite a hubbub was still going on in the street as a dozen riders reined to a halt in front of the town hall. Scratch and Haltom planted themselves on the porch between the newcomers and Bo.

"Hold it right there!" Haltom yelled at the men on horseback. He leveled the shotgun at them. Bo had to give the marshal some credit: Haltom obviously didn't like him and believed he was guilty, but despite that, the lawman didn't hesitate to put himself potentially in harm's way to protect his prisoner.

Bo recognized Danny Fontaine. The young firebrand sat his horse between a somewhat older, dark-haired man, and an hombre in his fifties with a gray, bristling mustache. The resemblance between the three of them made Bo believe he was looking at Ned Fontaine, the owner of the Rafter F, and his two sons.

Bo spotted several familiar faces among the

other riders, too, and knew they were some of the Fontaine crew.

The man Bo took to be Ned Fontaine said, "You don't need that shotgun, Marshal. We're not here looking for trouble. We're just come into town for the trial. We want to see that murderer get what's coming to him."

"It's not a trial, blast it," Haltom declared, echoing what Judge Buchanan had said earlier. "It's just a hearing to decide what's going to happen next."

"I'll tell you what ought to happen," the older of Fontaine's sons said. His name was Nick, Bo recalled. "That mad dog ought to be stretching rope."

"Yeah!" Danny agreed.

"That's not gonna happen!" Haltom roared. "Creel, get inside like I told you."

Scratch said, "Go ahead, Bo. These varmints ain't gonna bother you."

Danny sneered at the men on the porch and said, "That's mighty big talk for an old geezer like you, mister."

"I'm still spry enough to pull a trigger, boy," Scratch said in a low, menacing tone.

"Hold your fire," Haltom snapped. "Creel, go on."

Bo backed through the open doors into the town hall. From the corner of his eye he saw Judge Buchanan standing at the side of the room, looking worried.

"Now you, Morton," Haltom ordered.

With obvious reluctance, Scratch backed through the doorway. Bo could still see the Fontaines sitting on their horses. The patriarch started to dismount.

"What do you think you're doing?" Haltom said.

"We're going to attend the hearing," Fontaine replied. "You can't stop us. This is a public proceeding. I know the law."

"I'll just bet you do. But you and your men don't live in the town. Citizens ought to get first crack at the seats."

Fontaine smiled thinly.

"I don't see or hear anybody objecting to us attending," he said.

That was true enough, Bo thought. The Fontaines had the citizens of Bear Creek so thoroughly buffaloed that nobody was going to speak up and deny them anything they wanted.

"Leave your guns outside," Haltom ordered.

For a second Bo thought Fontaine was going to argue with the marshal, but then the man let out a cold laugh and said, "Fine. You heard the man, boys. Hang your guns on your saddles."

He started unbuckling his own gun belt to set an example.

Buchanan came over to Bo and said, "Take a seat at the table there in the front of the room, Creel. We'll get underway shortly."

Bo did what the judge told him. Scratch stood at one end of the table while Haltom took up a position at the other. In a low voice, Haltom said to

Scratch, "If anybody asks, I deputized you. That's why you've still got your guns."

"I wouldn't have the job on a bet if it was official," Scratch said, "but I'll play along." He paused. "It must get under your skin, Marshal, havin' to defend somebody you think is guilty."

"I go by the book," Haltom said grimly. "And the book says nobody interferes with the legal process."

Ned Fontaine, his sons, and the men of his crew he had brought with him all filed into the town hall and took seats on the rows of benches that were arranged for court proceedings. Some of the townspeople managed to get seats, too, and others stood along the walls. The room was full, just as Bo expected.

Judge Buchanan went behind another table in front of the one where Bo sat. He took a seat there, pulled a big, gold, turnip watch from his pocket, and opened it to check the time. It must have been ten o'clock, because Buchanan put the watch away, picked up a gavel, and banged it on the table.

"This court's now in session," he growled.

CHAPTER 18

When the spectators had quieted down, the judge went on, "We're here to determine whether the defendant, Bo Creel, should be held over and delivered to the county seat for trial in the matter of two murders, namely those of Rose Delavan and Sally Gilbert. Since this is a hearing and not a formal trial, I'll conduct it informally. Marshal, what evidence do we have to consider in this case?"

Judge Buchanan was bound to already know the answer to that question, thought Bo, but informal or not, certain procedures had to be followed.

Marshal Haltom turned to face the judge and said, "There are a couple of witnesses, Your Honor, and one piece of physical evidence, a sketch drawn by one of those witnesses."

"Are the witnesses here in court?"

"They are, Your Honor."

Bo had already spotted Lauralee Parker sitting among the spectators, and he assumed the little man next to Lauralee was probably Barney Dunn. He didn't know who the other witness might be.

Scratch had sure been right about one thing: Lauralee was just as pretty, if not prettier, than she had been the last time Bo had seen her. Judging by the amount she appeared to have aged, he would have said no more than a year or two had passed since then, rather than ten.

"Call the first witness, then," Buchanan ordered.

"Step up here, Dunn," the marshal said.

The man sitting next to Lauralee got to his feet, confirming Bo's guess as to his identity. With a nervous look on his round, red face, he came forward. Judge Buchanan pushed a Bible across the table toward him and said, "Put your hand on that. You swear to tell the truth, the whole truth, and nothing but the truth?"

Barney Dunn rested his hand on the Bible and said, "I do, Your Honor."

Buchanan nodded toward a chair at the end of the table and ordered, "Sit down."

When Dunn was seated, the judge went on, "I'll handle the questioning. State your name and occupation."

"It's, uh, Barney Dunn, sir. I work at the Southern Belle Saloon as a bartender."

"Very well, Mr. Dunn, tell us what you know about this case."

Dunn licked his lips and began, "Well, uh, a couple of weeks ago, it had gotten pretty late one night and the saloon was almost empty, and I needed to, uh, answer the call of nature, you know what I mean?"

"You don't have to go into great detail about that part of the story," Buchanan said. "Continue."

"Since there was another bartender on duty and we weren't busy at all, I figured it would be all right to step out back into the alley and, uh, tend to what needed tending to. But when I got out there I heard something going on, sort of a scuffling sound, you know, like somebody was fighting. And then there was this other sound . . ." Dunn had to stop and draw a shaky breath before he could go on. "Have you ever been in a butcher shop, Judge, and heard somebody cutting meat with a cleaver? That's what it sounded like. So I, uh, struck a match to see what was going on."

Buchanan interrupted the bartender to ask, "You didn't flee when it was obvious there was some sort of trouble?"

"That's just it, Your Honor. It wasn't that obvious. I never expected what I wound up seeing. I was just curious." Dunn shook his head and added, "Now I wish I had run the other way as soon as I heard the racket."

"If you had, the killer might not have ever been caught."

That comment from the judge didn't sound very impartial, Bo thought.

"Go on," Buchanan said.

Dunn took another deep breath and said, "When

the match flared up, I saw a guy in the alley bending over what looked like a pile of old clothes at first. But then I realized it was . . . it was a body. I recognized the dress, because I'd seen Rose wearing it earlier that evening. Rose was a hefty gal, you know, but in a good way. Really healthy. She could take care of herself, too. But this guy, he'd done something awful to her. He had a big knife in his hand and he . . ." Dunn gulped. "He was using it to chop her up, like she was a side of meat or something."

The town hall was hushed with horror. It remained that way for several seconds after Dunn stopped talking before Judge Buchanan cleared his throat and said, "Go on, Mr. Dunn."

Obviously having to force the words out, Dunn said, "When the match lit, the guy . . . the guy turned around. I got a good look at his face. And then he swung that knife at *me*. I tell you, Judge, I could just about see my own head flyin' off my shoulders. I moved faster than I ever have in my life. I jumped back, and the knife barely missed me. I dropped the match and made a run for the back door of the saloon. The guy was right behind me. I heard his feet hitting the ground. But I guess I was so scared I ran like the wind. I got back inside before he could catch me."

Again silence hung over the room until Judge Buchanan leaned forward and said heavily, "You've testified that you got a good look at the face of the man in the alley, Mr. Dunn. Do you see him in this courtroom?"

Dunn glanced apprehensively at Bo.

"Yeah," he said, his voice not much more than a whisper. "That's him sitting over there at that other table. The one called Bo Creel."

Bo felt almost like he was trapped in a nightmare from which there was no escape. He knew he hadn't killed Rose Delavan or the other saloon girl who had met a grisly fate at the hands of the Bear Creek Butcher. That was absolutely certain. And yet Barney Dunn seemed utterly convinced of the truth of what he was saying.

"What happened after that?" the judge asked.

"The saloon was empty. The customers had all left. Miss Parker, the owner, was upstairs, and the other bartender was out on the boardwalk in front smoking a cigar before he started cleaning up. Thank God the guy didn't chase me in there, because he still might've killed me before I could get anybody to help. But I yelled for the other bartender and grabbed a sawed-off shotgun we keep under the bar in case of trouble. Some other men heard me yelling and they came in to see what was going on, too. We got a lantern and we all went back out into the alley. Poor Rose looked even worse in that better light."

"The killer was gone?"

Dunn nodded and said, "Yeah. There was no sign of him. But one of the guys asked me what he'd looked like, and when I started describing him, somebody said that sounded like Bo Creel. I didn't know who that was, but they told me he was somebody who used to live around here. Later, after we went back into the saloon, I made a sketch of the guy I saw. Several of the men said it looked just like Creel."

Buchanan looked over at Marshal Haltom and asked, "That drawing is the piece of physical evidence you mentioned, Marshal?"

"That's right, Your Honor," Haltom said. He reached to an inside pocket of his coat and drew out the folded piece of paper to hand over to the judge. "Here it is."

Buchanan unfolded the paper, spread it on the table, stared down at it for a long moment, and grunted. He looked up and his eyes bored into Bo's face, then he checked the sketch again before pushing it away.

"Do you have anything else to add?" he asked Dunn.

"No, sir, that's the whole story. All I know of it, anyway."

"All right, you're excused. Who's your other witness, Marshal?"

"That would be Dr. Kenneth Perkins," Haltom said.

Dunn went back to his seat next to Lauralee. A tall, slender, gray-haired man whom Bo recognized as Doc Perkins took the chair at the end of the judge's table after being sworn in.

"What do you have to contribute to this hearing, Doctor?" Buchanan asked.

"Marshal Haltom thought I should testify since I examined the bodies of both victims," Perkins answered. "I can confirm that the injuries to both Rose Delavan and Sally Gilbert were inflicted with a large, heavy-bladed knife, and based on the similarities of those injuries, it's my opinion that the same man was responsible for both attacks. In addition, I can testify that each of the women had a broken neck and severe bruising around the throat. I think the murderer choked them to death and broke their necks, then used the knife on them."

"Good Lord," muttered Buchanan. "That's awful."

"I have one more thing to add, Your Honor," Perkins said.

Buchanan waved a hand.

"Go ahead."

"I've seen that drawing Mr. Dunn made, and I agree that it looks very much like Bo Creel. But it's also my opinion, having known Bo and his family for many years, that he isn't capable of committing these crimes."

That simple declaration brought an outburst of surprised reaction from the spectators. Several of the Rafter F men yelled angrily.

Bo looked at Perkins and smiled faintly. Even

though it might not do any good, he was glad that the old doctor still believed in him.

Judge Buchanan snatched up his gavel and banged it on the table.

"Settle down! Settle down!" he shouted. "By God, this is a courtroom, not the street! We'll have some decorum here, or you can all clear out!"

It took several minutes for the room to get quiet again. When it did, the judge said, "I didn't ask you for an opinion on that, Doctor. That's not for you to decide."

"It all seems like part of the same case to me, Your Honor," Perkins said.

Buchanan glared.

"Anything else?" he asked curtly.

The doctor shook his head.

"I've said my piece."

"The witness is excused, then." Buchanan looked at Haltom as Doc Perkins went back to his seat. "Anything else, Marshal?"

"No, that's it, Your Honor."

Buchanan looked at Bo with narrowed eyes and said, "Stand up, Mr. Creel."

That sounded ominously like he was about to be sentenced, thought Bo as he got to his feet. And in a way, he supposed he was.

"Do you have anything to say for yourself?" Buchanan asked.

"Only that I'm not guilty, Your Honor," Bo answered quietly.

That brought hooting and catcalls from the Fontaine men. Danny Fontaine shouted, "He's guilty as hell!"

Buchanan smacked the gavel down and roared, "Quiet!" When the noise had settled down, he glared at Bo. "You're saying that you didn't kill those women?"

"That's exactly what I'm saying, Your Honor."

"Then how do you explain everything we've heard here today?" Buchanan pointed the gavel at Barney Dunn's sketch. "How do you explain that?"

Bo shook his head and said, "I can't. All I know is that I didn't do those terrible things."

"That'll be up to a jury to decide. I'm remanding you to the custody of the Lavaca County sheriff and charging you with two counts of murder. You'll be taken to Hallettsville as soon as transportation can be arranged and held there until such time as you can stand trial for those crimes."

Bo heard the sighs of relief that came from some of the spectators. As much as it pained him, he realized that most of the citizens of Bear Creek believed he was the killer. They were glad he was locked up, and they wanted him to stay that way.

Haltom said, "I can take Creel to Hallettsville today, Your Honor—"

Buchanan interrupted him, saying, "No, I want you to send word to the sheriff there and ask him to send a wagon and some deputies for the prisoner. Preferably at least half a dozen."

"But, Judge, I can handle this—"

"No," Buchanan broke again, his voice firm. "This case has stirred up the whole countryside. It needs to be resolved. I'm taking no chances on the prisoner escaping while he's being transported to the county seat. This is no reflection on your abilities, Marshal, simply a precaution."

"Yes, sir," Haltom said, but Bo could tell from the way the marshal's jaw was clenched that Haltom did indeed take it as a reflection on his abilities. "You know it'll likely be tomorrow before those deputies can get here with a wagon, don't you?"

"Creel can spend one more night in jail here."

"Fine," Haltom said with a nod.

Out among the spectators, Ned Fontaine stood up and said, "Wait just a minute. You're sending Creel to Hallettsville, Your Honor?"

"That's right, Mr. Fontaine."

"But it's *not* right," Fontaine said. He looked around at the other people in the room. "Creel killed two of our own. We shouldn't have to send him off to the county seat to be tried for that! He should face justice right here in Bear Creek!"

Loud, angry shouts of agreement came from his sons and the men who had ridden into the settlement with him. That didn't surprise Bo, but he felt a touch of disappointment when he realized that a number of the citizens were joining in. Those were people who knew him, or at least knew his family, and they were calling for his head.

"We can have a trial right here and now, damn it!" Fontaine went on. "All we need is a judge and a jury! We've got a judge, and I know there are more than twelve men in this room who'd be willing to serve on a jury."

Buchanan and Haltom exchanged glances, and Bo could tell that both men were worried. A demonstration like this could get out of hand in a hurry. Even though the Rafter F men had left their gun belts outside, some of them could have snuck hideout pistols into the town hall.

Scratch edged closer to Bo and said in a low voice, "If all hell breaks loose, partner, you grab one of these Remingtons of mine. I know you can use it, even with your hands cuffed like that."

Bo knew that, too. But he didn't want to have to shoot anybody, least of all somebody he might have grown up with, just because Fontaine was stirring everybody up until they were loco.

"I know what you're thinkin'," Scratch went on, "and I feel the same way, but I'll be damned if I'll let anybody string you up, Bo."

Buchanan got to his feet and hammered on the table with his gavel as he shouted for quiet. The Fontaines kept up their demand for a trial, with some of the townspeople joining in. As the crowd surged forward, Bo stood up and turned to face them.

"Stop it!" he told them in a loud voice. "I know a lot of you folks. You don't really want to do this!"

The angry yells just increased in volume.

"That's enough, by God!" Marshal Haltom said. The shotgun in his hands came up so that both barrels pointed squarely at the crowd. Haltom thumbed the hammers back, first one and then the other. Even though that ominous clicking sound couldn't be heard over the chaos in the town hall, just the sight of those twin black muzzles was enough to make the shouting abruptly come to a dead stop.

"There's not going to be a trial here today!" Haltom's angry voice cut through the sudden silence.

"Maybe there doesn't need to be one," Ned Fontaine said. His tone was just as ominous as the marshal's was. "We all know Creel's guilty. A trial would just be a waste of time. There are plenty of good cottonwood trees along the creek that'll do just fine for a hanging!"

CHAPTER 19

It seemed likely that violence was going to break out at any second. If it did, innocent people were going to be hurt. The buckshot in Marshal Haltom's scattergun wouldn't discriminate. It would cut down anybody who got in its way.

Bo knew that, and even though he didn't want to die, he had to wonder if it would be better to let Fontaine have his way. He would be trading his life for the lives of Bear Creek's citizens that might be lost otherwise . . .

Then Scratch leveled his Winchester at Ned Fontaine and said in a voice that cracked through all the hubbub, "You got two seconds to call off your dogs, Fontaine, or I'm puttin' a bullet through your brain! One! T—"

"Hold on, hold on!" Fontaine called. Stunned silence again spread rapidly through the room. The rancher went on, "Marshal, you heard that man threaten to kill me. I demand that you arrest him!"

"The only reason he threatened to kill you is because he beat me to it," Haltom snapped. "You're out of line here, Fontaine. Judge, is the hearing over?"

"It is," Buchanan said. He smacked the gavel down on the table. "Court's adjourned!"

Haltom squinted over the barrels of his shotgun and said, "So this isn't a public proceeding anymore, and you're trespassing on property the town owns, Fontaine. Take your men and get out now, or I won't be responsible for what happens."

Some of the townspeople were starting to move toward the doors, obviously unwilling to stay there and possibly find themselves in the line of fire. Fontaine must have sensed that his support was slipping. He glared at Haltom and said, "You're making a mistake by siding with that murderer, Marshal."

"A jury will determine whether or not he's a murderer. Now git!"

"You'll be sorry you talked to me that way."

"I'm sorry you even came into town today." Haltom gestured with the shotgun's barrel. "Go on, get out of here, you and the whole Rafter F bunch."

The spectators were making it a regular exodus now as they left the town hall. The lynch mob fever had broken. Scratch had shattered it with his well-aimed rifle and his coldly voiced threat. The townspeople had realized that if they kept it up, there was a good chance some of them would die.

"This isn't over," Fontaine warned ominously.

"The hell it isn't," Haltom shot back.

Bo could tell that Fontaine didn't want to let the marshal get the last word in, but there really wasn't anything left to say. Fontaine turned and stalked toward the door, followed by his sons, both of whom glowered darkly at Bo before they turned away. The Rafter F punchers filed out behind them.

The courtroom emptied in a matter of moments except for Bo, Scratch, Marshal Haltom, and Judge Buchanan. The judge slumped back in his chair and heaved a sigh. Beads of sweat stood out on his beefy face.

"That was a near thing," he said.

"I don't reckon Fontaine knows just how tight my finger was on the trigger," Scratch said. "Wouldn't have taken but a hair more pressure to put a bullet through that rattlesnake brain of his."

Haltom said, "I'm glad you didn't shoot. Innocent folks would have gotten hurt if any gunplay broke out." He shrugged. "I'd have risked it, though, to keep anybody from taking a prisoner away from me."

"Do you have a man you can trust to send to Hallettsville for the sheriff?" Buchanan asked.

Haltom frowned in thought. He looked at Scratch, who shook his head without hesitation.

"Forget it," the silver-haired Texan said. "I ain't helpin' what strikes me as one of those, what do you call 'em, miscarriages of justice. Besides, everybody in this room knows good and well that just because Fontaine and his bunch left, that don't mean they're through with this. I plan on bein' here when they make their move."

"You think they'll try again to raise a lynch mob?" the judge asked worriedly.

"It wouldn't surprise me a bit," Scratch said.

"Or me, either," Haltom agreed. "I'll send Rusty Gardner for the sheriff, Judge. He's young, but he's said something to me several times about how he'd like to be a deputy someday. I reckon this is his chance."

"Is he trustworthy?"

"I believe he is."

"Very well, then," Buchanan said. "He needs to stress to the sheriff that it's imperative the prisoner be taken to the county seat as soon as possible."

"I'll write a note to send with Rusty," Haltom said.

Bo was annoyed that they were talking about him like he wasn't right there in the town hall with them, but he supposed that didn't really matter now. It was a lot more important that they were going to put him on trial for something he hadn't done.

"Judge, can I say something?" he asked.

Buchanan frowned at him.

"You had a chance to speak during the hearing, Mr. Creel."

"I know that, but I've been thinking . . . If I did kill those girls, the way everybody seems to believe I did, would Scratch and I have ridden into town as bold as brass, right out in the open, the way we did? Isn't that enough to tell you right there that we didn't have any idea what's been going on around here?"

The judge's frown deepened.

"That's a good argument," he admitted. "Your lawyer can make it during your trial. And by that time, if you've been telling the truth about working for Judge Parker when the crimes were committed, you may have proof of that, as well. In that case, I'm sure a competent attorney will have no problem convincing a jury to render a verdict of not guilty."

"And for that matter," Marshal Haltom added, "you'll probably be just as safe in the jail at Hallettsville as you would be here. Maybe safer."

The lawman was probably right about that, Bo realized. Still, the thought of continuing to be locked up made his skin crawl. After all those years of riding free with Scratch, Bo didn't like being behind bars.

"All right," he said. "I'll cooperate. Just don't expect me to be too enthusiastic about it."

"I don't care if you're enthusiastic," Haltom said, "as long as you don't try to escape. Come on. Let's get you back to jail."

Since the possibility of an ambush existed, even on a walk as short as the one from the town hall back to the jail, Scratch went first to scout the town while Haltom wrote the note to send to the sheriff in Hallettsville.

A lot of people were still on the boardwalks, and most of them were looking toward the town hall, but Scratch didn't see any signs of threatening behavior.

"If you are looking for those men who hate your friend, M'sieu Scratch, they have all gone across the creek to guzzle down the cheap rotgut."

The husky, alluring female voice made Scratch look behind him. Veronique Ballantine stood there, wearing a demure dress and shading herself with a parasol. She looked as lovely as ever.

Scratch tugged on the brim of his hat and said, "Howdy, mam'selle. Were you at the hearing? I didn't see you or the professor in the town hall."

Veronique shook her head and said, "No, but we were just outside. We heard what was going on, and like everyone else we heard what those men were saying when they left. I believe they were urging the townspeople to violence against your friend."

"Darned right they were," Scratch said grimly. "They want to string him up."

"Because he is guilty of those terrible crimes we have heard about?"

"That's part of it, I reckon," Scratch admitted. "But the real reason the Fontaines keep tryin' to stir things up is because they were already feudin' with

Bo's family. This is just an excuse for them to make things hard for the Creels."

"That is despicable behavior."

Scratch grunted and said, "Yep. You won't get no argument from me about that."

"Come to the wagon later," Veronique suggested. "Professor Sarlat and I will be glad to see you."

"Much obliged. I'll stop by if I get a chance."

Right now he was more worried about getting Bo safely back to the jail. Since everything looked clear at the moment, he said "so long" to the beautiful medicine show entertainer and hurried back to the town hall. Marshal Haltom was waiting in the doorway, the shotgun in his hands.

"I just sent that rider to Hallettsville," the lawman said. "He ought to be back tonight with the sheriff's reply."

Scratch nodded and said, "I don't see any sign of an ambush right now."

Haltom turned his head to look back into the town hall and nodded curtly.

"Let's go, Creel," he ordered Bo.

The walk back to the jail drew a lot of unfriendly stares from the townspeople, but that was all. Scratch was relieved when they reached the jail, but that relief didn't last long.

He knew the building wouldn't stand up to a determined assault from a large group of men, and he had a hunch that was exactly what the Fontaines were working up to on the other side of the creek. They would have all day to keep the liquor flowing freely for anyone who wanted to get drunk and listen to the venom they would be spewing.

When Bo was locked up in his cell, Scratch followed Haltom into the office and said, "The judge should've let us take Bo to Hallettsville today. The Fontaines are liable to be on your doorstep with a lynch mob tonight."

"No, the judge was right," Haltom said glumly. "If I'd tried to take Creel to the county seat by himself, he might've made a break for it. And don't waste your breath saying that you would have gone along to help. You know good and well you'd have knocked me on the head the first chance you got and took off with Creel."

Scratch couldn't exactly deny that. The thought had definitely crossed his mind.

"So what are we left with?" he demanded. "You can't hold this jail by yourself, and you know it. I might be able to round up a few old friends who'd pitch in and help, but not enough to make a difference against a hundred liquored-up varmints with a hang rope."

Haltom had the bleak, fatalistic look of a man who knew he had probably been sentenced to death. He said, "I'll do the job I was hired to do, and if it doesn't work out, then that's just too bad."

"You'll gun down townspeople if they break in here? Your own friends?"

"If they're breaking the law, I sure as hell will," the marshal insisted.

Scratch wasn't sure he believed Haltom, though. The man was probably sincere in what he said, but when the time came that he was looking over the Greener's barrels at people he saw on the street every day, he might not be able to pull the triggers . . . especially in defense of a man he believed to be a cold-blooded and particularly brutal killer of women.

There was no getting around it, thought Scratch. So far he had gone along with what Bo wanted because he respected his trail partner's wishes. Bo was a law-abiding man.

But sometimes the law was just flat-out wrong, and to abide by it would be the same thing as committing suicide. In a case like that, Scratch had to do what he knew was right.

"Where are you going?" Haltom asked as Scratch started toward the door.

"Nothin's gonna happen while it's light," Scratch replied. "I'll be back later."

"Better be careful when you come around. My trigger finger's liable to be a mite nervous."

Scratch didn't doubt it.

He stepped out of the marshal's office and closed the door behind him. The bar scraped into place in its brackets on the other side of the door. Scratch turned toward the bridge.

He wanted to get the lay of the land while he made his plans. He knew now that he was going to have to bust Bo out of that jail, come hell or high water, and he had the rest of the day to figure out exactly how he was going to do it.

CHAPTER 20

Scratch circled the jail, looking it over. The windows in the cells were too small for anybody to go through, but if the bars were pulled out of their frame, say with a rope tied to a couple of horses, enough of the wall might bust out around the opening to let a prisoner crawl through it. The window in the marshal's office was bigger, but Haltom would be waiting on the other side of it with a double load of buckshot in his scattergun.

There wasn't a back door. The front door could be busted down, but only with some time and effort.

Unfortunately, the building was constructed of lumber, which meant it would burn. That might be the tack the lynch mob would take. Even though most frontier towns lived in mortal fear of fire, Fontaine might risk it since he could have men with buckets of water standing by to keep the flames from spreading. Once the jail was on fire, Haltom would have no choice but to come out and bring Bo with him.

Scratch didn't mean to let the situation get that far. As soon as it was dark, he was going to fetch his horse and Bo's mount from the stable and jerk that cell window out of the wall. He could fire one of the Remingtons through the opening to keep Marshal Haltom back while Bo scrambled out.

A jailbreak like that would make them outlaws and fugitives, Scratch thought glumly. Even though they had both been locked up before, those had all been misunderstandings that had been cleared up before things deteriorated this badly. They had never stepped completely over the law's line, just sort of edged a toe over it now and then, always in a good cause.

But saving Bo's life was a good cause, too, Scratch told himself. He was convinced that if he didn't get Bo out of that jail, his old friend wouldn't survive the night.

With that decision made, he walked along the street toward the public well and the medicine show wagon. He was aware that some people were sending hostile glances in his direction, but he ignored them. Everybody in Bear Creek knew by now that he and Bo were friends and that he believed Bo was innocent. The only ones who were likely to start any trouble, though, were across the creek in the saloons.

Professor Sarlat, looking as splendid as ever in

his top hat and swallowtail coat, was brushing his horses, which were picketed near the wagon where they could graze on the grass growing under some oak trees. He greeted Scratch with a smile.

"Good day to you, Mr. Morton," the professor said. "How are you?"

"Middlin'," Scratch said. "I reckon I feel better than I expected to, considerin' that ruckus I was in last night and the fact that I didn't get much sleep."

"Ah," Sarlat said with a sly grin. "You partook of my miraculous elixir, didn't you?"

"If by partook you mean I guzzled down half of it, yeah, that's about right," Scratch admitted with a chuckle. He patted his jacket pocket where the brown glass bottle still resided. "That's powerful good stuff."

"Powerful is indeed the right word. My elixir is unmatched in its potency."

"It helped me get through the night while I was guardin' the jail, that's for sure."

Sarlat's face grew solemn as he said, "Veronique and I have heard about your friend's plight. I wish there was something we could do to help."

"Don't worry about that," Scratch said. "Bo ain't gonna be in jail much longer."

"Yes, I know. The sheriff is supposed to travel from the county seat tomorrow and transport him to the jail over there, isn't that correct?"

"Yeah, but it may not come to that."

As soon as Scratch said that, he realized he

might have made a mistake. The professor had to be pretty smart, or else he wouldn't be a professor. It was possible he might figure out what Scratch meant by that comment.

Sarlat gave Scratch a shrewd look and said, "It sounds as if you might be planning something, my friend."

"Look, Professor, just forget I said anything, all right? If I've got somethin' in mind, and I ain't sayin' that I do, it ain't anythin' you need to be concerned about."

"You've come to our assistance twice. If there's anything we can do to assist you, Veronique and I would be more than happy to do it. I'm confident that I speak for her, as well." Sarlat smiled. "She seems a bit smitten with you, I must say."

"Oh, I don't reckon that's right," Scratch said. "I figured the two of you . . ."

"No, indeed. I know that people in our profession—traveling entertainers, as it were—don't have the best reputation when it comes to such things, but I assure you, the lovely lady and I are business associates, that's all."

"Well, it don't really matter, since I'm probably old enough to be her grandpappy."

"Yes, but that doesn't mean she's not fond of you." Sarlat stroked his goatee and frowned in thought. "Speaking hypothetically, if someone were to try to arrange for a prisoner to escape from jail, that goal would be easier to attain if there were some sort of distraction taking place at the same time, wouldn't it?"

Scratch's eyes narrowed.

"Yeah, I suppose it would, if I follow what you're sayin'," he replied. "But whoever provided that distraction would be puttin' themselves in a bad spot."

"Not if it appeared that the whole thing was sheer coincidence. Especially considering that it's our job to attract attention, after all."

"People would still suspect that you were tryin' to help me."

"They might suspect, but they wouldn't be able to prove anything." Sarlat chuckled. "We appear to have left the realm of the hypothetical. If you intend to break your friend out of jail, Scratch, Veronique and I can help. Tell me what time you intend to make your move, and we'll do something to attract the attention of the entire town."

Scratch hesitated. It was possible that the professor was trying to trick him into admitting that he planned to bust Bo out of jail. If he did, Sarlat might try to sell him out to the marshal . . . or worse, to the Fontaines.

Sarlat and Veronique had no reason to want to help the Rafter F bunch, though, Scratch reminded himself. After those two run-ins with Fontaine's punchers, they were more likely to want to cause trouble for the rancher and his men. Because of that, Scratch's instincts told him that Sarlat could be trusted.

"If anything was to happen tonight," he said, "I reckon it'd probably be as soon as it's good and dark."

"Excellent. I'll remember that."

"And if there was to be some sort of hoo-raw out in the street just about then, it sure might come in handy."

The professor laid a finger alongside his nose and nodded.

"I take your meaning, sir," he said with a smile.

"Just be careful," Scratch said. "I don't want anything bad happenin' to you and the lady, and I know Bo wouldn't, either."

"Don't worry. No one will suspect a thing."

Scratch wasn't sure about that, but it wouldn't hurt to draw attention away from the jail. He was confident that he could deal with Marshal Haltom, but he didn't want the townspeople to interfere with his plan.

Scratch put out his hand and said, "I may not see you again, Professor, and in case I don't, I want you to know it's been a pleasure meetin' you and Miss Veronique."

Sarlat shook hands with him.

"Veronique will be disappointed if she doesn't get to say farewell to you," the professor said. "I suppose if your plan is successful, you'll have to leave the vicinity as quickly as possible."

"It'll be downright rapid," Scratch said.

* * *

His belly reminded him that it was time to eat, no matter what else was going on, so after leaving the medicine show wagon he headed for the café to get some lunch.

Folks in the Red Top gave him some dirty looks, but Scratch ignored them. He had never worried that much about other people's opinion of him, as long as he knew he was in the right, like he did now.

After he had eaten, he continued to follow his instincts and headed for the bridge. A smart man kept up with what his enemies were doing, and right now most of those enemies were on the other side of the creek.

Scratch walked across the bridge, went to the Southern Belle, and pushed the batwings aside. He had heard a lot of noise coming from the saloon as he approached, but it fell silent as he entered.

The unfriendly looks he had gotten from the townspeople earlier were nothing compared to the glares directed at him now. The tables were full and men stood two-deep at the bar, and it seemed like every hombre in the place was looking at Scratch like he was lower than a pile of buffalo droppings.

Some of them, maybe even most of them, were drunk already. Scratch could tell that by looking at them.

But three men who sat at one of the rear tables clearly weren't drunk. Ned Fontaine and his two sons had glasses of whiskey in front of them, but they must have been nursing the drinks along for quite a while.

That right there was enough to tell Scratch that they were planning something and wanted to keep clear heads while they urged the rest of the men in the saloon to keep drinking. All the drunken cowboys and townies were weapons for the Fontaines to use as they saw fit.

The only really friendly face in the saloon belonged to Lauralee Parker, who came out from behind the bar and went to meet Scratch. That seemed to break the spell. The crowd went back to talking and tossing down booze.

Lauralee took Scratch's hand and said, "Come with me." She led him toward the empty table in the back that was always reserved for her and her guests.

To get there they had to pass fairly close to the table where the Fontaines were sitting. Nick leaned back in his chair and said, "I don't know why you'd want to associate with a worthless old saddle tramp like that, Lauralee."

Still holding on to Scratch's hand, she turned her head sharply to glower at Nick and said, "Who I associate with is none of your business, Nick Fontaine."

"Maybe it will be one of these days," Nick drawled with an arrogant smirk on his face.

"You're even dumber than you look if you think

there's any chance in hell of that," Lauralee snapped. "Come on, Scratch."

When they were seated at her table, Scratch said, "You might not want to get the Fontaines too mad at you. A lot of your business probably comes from them and their punchers."

"You think I care about that? I've got a good mind to tell them to get out right now and take their drinking elsewhere."

Scratch shook his head.

"Don't do that," he told her. "You're probably makin' some good money today, and somebody ought to get somethin' out of this mess."

"But Bo—"

"Bo would tell you the same thing if he was here."

Lauralee leaned toward him and lowered her voice.

"You know good and well why Ned Fontaine keeps buying the drinks. He wants the whole bunch so drunk they'll do whatever he tells them. They'll charge the jail and go after Bo, even with the marshal and his shotgun waiting for them."

"And if everything works out," Scratch said, "Bo won't still be there for them to try it."

Lauralee's blue eyes widened as she realized what he meant.

"You're going to break him out!"

"As soon as it's dark," Scratch agreed with a slight nod. "Then we'll light a shuck out of Bear Creek."

"But you'll be fugitives. You'll have to run from the law from now on."

"Maybe not. I'm hopin' we can get Judge Parker up in Fort Smith to lend us a hand and clear our names. There may still be some trouble over the jailbreak, but once folks realize that Bo's innocent and the only way to save him from bein' lynched was to get him out of there, I reckon there's a chance any other charges will be dropped."

"You're risking a lot," Lauralee said.

"Yeah, but I'd rather do that than risk Bo's life."

"I can't argue with that." She paused. "What can I do to help?"

"Nothin'," Scratch replied. "Just don't say anythin' about it to anybody."

"You know I won't. I'd like to do more than that, though."

Scratch smiled.

"Just have your bartenders keep pourin' drinks. Maybe some of those fellas will get so drunk they'll pass out, and then they can't be part of any lynch mob."

"You know, that's an idea," Lauralee said. "I could have them slip something into the whiskey—"

Scratch stopped her by shaking his head.

"That'd be liable to come back on you," he said. "And you've got to live here and stay in business. I'm tellin' you, it's help enough just knowin' that we've still got a few friends here in town."

"All right," she said in grudging acceptance.

"But if you need anything, you know where to come."

"I sure do."

They talked for a few minutes more, then Scratch said he had to be going. The men in the saloon were ignoring him now, but he knew that wouldn't last if he walked all the way through the crowded room again.

"Think I'll slip out the back," he told Lauralee.

"All right. Remember what I told you about coming to see me if I can help."

"I ain't likely to forget it."

Scratch got to his feet and moved over to a door in the back of the room, beside the stage. It opened into a short corridor with another door at the far end. He knew that one let out into the alley behind the saloon.

The alley where somebody who looked just like Bo had killed Rose Delavan, Scratch reminded himself. So far he hadn't taken a look at the place. Maybe it was time he did.

He eased the door closed behind him and went along the corridor to the other door. As he stepped out into the alley, the usual smells of trash and animal droppings made him wrinkle his nose.

He looked around. On the other side of the alley stood an old storage shed with a bunch of empty barrels in it. To the left of the shed was an outhouse, to the right a stretch of empty ground with a few trees and bushes growing on it.

Scratch hadn't known Rose, but he thought this was a particularly bleak and squalid place for anybody to die. He studied the ground, not knowing what he expected to see. In the weeks since Rose's death, all the blood that had been spilled would have soaked into the ground. If it had rained any since then, that would have finished washing away any traces of the murder.

"I thought I saw you slip out the back door like the yellow dog you are."

The harsh voice made Scratch's head snap around. Two men had just come around the corner of the building. He recognized them instantly as two of the varmints he had clashed with at the medicine show wagon the night before.

A footstep from the other direction made him glance that way. The third member of that ugly trio had just come around the other corner. They had him boxed in between them.

The man who had spoken sneered and went on, "You didn't think we were gonna let you get away with what you did last night, did you, old-timer?"

"No, polecats like you always come around to stink everythin' up again," Scratch snapped.

The spokesman for the three Rafter F hands was walking a little funny as they came closer. His face twisted with hate.

"We're gonna make you sorry you were ever born," he blustered.

For a moment Scratch considered reaching for his

guns. He knew he was fast enough to clear leather with both Remingtons, and he could shoot in two directions at once.

But gunplay would draw the attention of the men boozing it up in the saloon, and he knew without a doubt which side they would be on. Anyway, if he killed these men, the marshal would probably lock him up for it, and then he couldn't do a blasted thing to help Bo.

No, this had to be settled without guns if possible, and against three younger men experienced in brawling, it wasn't likely that he would come out on top. His chances would be better, though, if he could rattle them some, make them rush their attack.

"You're the one I kicked in the family jewels, ain't you?" he asked the spokesman with a mocking grin. "Well, it don't really matter, I guess, since no gal would ever have anything to do with an ugly son of a bitch like you, not even a Dodge City whore."

The cowboy's face contorted even more, and Scratch knew his gibe had gone home. The man said, "I'm gonna kill you, you old bastard. Get him!"

All three cowboys rushed at Scratch, fists poised to beat him within an inch of his life, or maybe even all the way into the grave.

CHAPTER 21

Since there was only one man attacking him from behind, Scratch twisted around and lunged in that direction, going in low and ducking under the roundhouse punch the cowboy swung at his head. He hooked a fist into the man's belly and then grabbed the front of his shirt to haul him around and fling him at the other two.

They collided, and one of the men lost his balance and fell down, nearly upsetting the other two. That gave Scratch time to whirl around and break into a run.

Retreating in the face of trouble rubbed Scratch the wrong way, but sometimes it was the smart thing to do. After all, Sam Houston had retreated from Santa Anna's army during the Runaway Scrape, until it was time to turn and make a valiant stand at San Jacinto. That had worked out all right, even against overwhelming odds.

Scratch didn't actually try to run away. He wasn't

that fleet of foot. Instead he dashed over to the shed and put his back against one of the big barrels stacked up there. With his back protected, they couldn't come at him from all directions at once.

In fact, they weren't even smart enough to coordinate their attack. One man rushed him alone. Scratch ducked a punch and drove a fist into the cowboy's belly. His other hand lifted in an uppercut that caught the man under the chin and snapped his head back. Scratch kicked him in the knee, causing the man's leg to collapse and dump him in the dirt of the alley. That put him in the way of the other two and slowed them down again.

Scratch reached up and caught hold of one of the barrels stacked atop other barrels. He heaved against it and toppled it forward. Even though the barrel was empty, it still weighed quite a bit, and when it landed on top of the man Scratch had just knocked down, the hombre let out a pained grunt. Scratch kicked the barrel and sent it rolling into the legs of the other two.

One of them stumbled and fell over it. The whole thing would have been comical if Scratch hadn't been fighting for his life.

The third man was able to get around the barrel. He windmilled punches at Scratch, and the silver-haired Texan couldn't block all of them. A hard fist crashed against his jaw and forced him back into the barrels again.

That collision knocked another barrel off the

stack, but this time it toppled onto Scratch and drove him to his knees. One of the men on the ground tackled him. Scratch wound up on his back with the man on top of him, pummeling away at him.

The man still on his feet crowded in, yelling, "Get out of the way! I'll stomp the old bastard!"

He aimed a kick at Scratch's head. Scratch grabbed the shirtfront of the man on top of him and hauled hard, yanking that man's head in the way of that kick, which had gone too far to stop. His companion's boot thudded solidly into the man's head.

That impact made the man's eyes roll up in their sockets. Scratch shoved him aside and rolled in the other direction. He came up on one knee and flung up his hands to catch a second kick aimed in his direction. A quick heave sent the man flying over backward.

So far luck and his unexpected ferocity had carried him through. Even though he had clashed with them the night before, the three men probably had underestimated Scratch's rough-and-tumble abilities, due to his age and the fact that they had him outnumbered three to one.

That advantage couldn't last, though, and Scratch knew it. He scrambled to his feet and prepared to make a run for it again. This time he would try to get away while his three opponents were all still on the ground.

He hadn't made it very far when one of the men launched after him in a diving tackle that caught him around the knees. Scratch pitched forward as the man jerked his legs out from under him. He hit the hard-packed dirt with stunning force and wasn't able to move for a couple of seconds.

That was long enough to be his undoing. The other two men caught up, and then all three of them went to work on him with hammering punches and thudding kicks. Scratch tried to fight them off, but it was no use. Whether he wanted any gunplay or not, he no longer had a choice.

When he reached for one of the Remingtons, his hand slapped an empty holster. The revolver had fallen out during the ruckus.

His left-hand Remington was still in its holster, but his move had given away what he was trying to do. As he reached for it, one of the men yelled, "Look out! He's goin' for his gun!"

A booted foot came down hard on Scratch's left wrist, pinning that arm to the ground before he could close his hand around the Remington's ivory grips. He tried to reach across his body with his right hand, but another kick slammed into that shoulder, making his whole right arm go numb.

Fury roared through him like a grizzly bear. Some of it was directed at himself. He shouldn't have come across the creek today. It would have been better for him to stay on the other side of the stream so he could help Bo. If he didn't get away, his oldest and best friend might not have a chance . . .

With that thought fueling him, Scratch surged up from the ground. His right arm still wouldn't work, but he swung a punch with his left that knocked one of the men back and gave him a narrow opening.

It wasn't enough. Something hard, probably a gun butt, landed on the back of his head. It was like an explosion going off inside his skull. Red rockets erupted behind Scratch's eyes, but the glare was washed out almost instantly by an inexorable tide of blackness.

Scratch didn't feel himself hit the ground. He was already out cold.

He fully expected the three cowboys to carry through on their threat to stomp him to death, so he was more than a little surprised—but gratified—to wake up an unknown amount of time later.

Consciousness came back to him slowly, bringing with it a great deal of pain. An imp straight out of Hades seemed to be pounding an anvil inside his skull, and every muscle and bone in his body ached to the point that moving was simply inconceivable.

But he had to move. Bo still needed his help. It might not be too late to help his friend.

At least, Scratch *hoped* it wasn't too late . . .

He was lying on what he thought was the ground.

With an effort, he tried to get his hands underneath him and lever himself to his feet. That effort failed because his arms wouldn't move. His wrists weren't tied, but somebody had looped a rope around his torso several times, making it impossible for him to lift his arms.

Scratch bit back a groan. He wouldn't allow himself to give in to despair. At least he could open his eyes and take stock of his surroundings.

His eyelids seemed to weigh a ton, but after a while he succeeding in raising them. It was so dark around him that at first he thought his eyes were still closed. Then, when he was sure they weren't, he experienced a moment of near-panic when he thought he might be blind.

Light began to seep into his vision here and there, assuring him that he could still see after all. As his eyes adjusted to the gloom, he realized that he was inside some sort of structure, but it was open to the air because he could feel a slight breeze against his face.

That breeze carried a mixture of foul odors with it. He had smelled that particular stink before, he thought. His brain struggled to identify it, and after a few moments he realized it was the smell of the alley behind the Southern Belle Saloon where the three cowboys from the Rafter F had jumped him.

He wasn't just lying out in the open in the alley, though. Large dark shapes loomed around him. Tied up the way he was, he couldn't stand up or move his arms, but he was able to roll onto his side and lift his head to get a better look around.

Somebody had dragged him into that shed, he finally figured out. He was lying behind those empty barrels. The ones he had knocked down had been stacked up again. Anybody walking by in the alley wouldn't be able to see him.

Not that there was much reason for anybody who might help him to be back here, he thought bitterly. But his captors had taken that precaution anyway.

The darkness told him it was night. He heard a low hum of noise that he thought came from the saloon across the alley. Men were in there talking and laughing and drinking. Were they still working themselves up to form a lynch mob, egged on by the Fontaines . . . or had they already done their dirty work and returned to celebrate?

Was Bo's lifeless body already dangling from the limb of a tree?

Scratch had to find out, and he couldn't do that if he was stuck here, tied up in the darkness like a pig on its way to market.

He wasn't thinking anymore about how bad he hurt from the beating he had taken. All his thoughts were concentrated on finding a way out of this predicament. He rolled over again, thinking that if he could work his way over to the wall of the shed, he might be able to find a nail head sticking out that he could use to work at the ropes binding him.

Before he reached the wall, he stopped because

he had felt something hard in his pocket as he rolled over it. He could move the fingers of his right hand enough to reach the object, and as he explored its shape he realized it was the bottle of elixir Professor Sarlat had given him. Scratch was a little surprised it hadn't fallen out during the fight.

The cork *had* come out of the neck, though. His jacket was still damp where the liquid that was left had leaked out.

That was all right, he thought. In fact, it might make what he had in mind a little easier.

Straining with the effort, he managed to get his fingers in the pocket and grasp the bottle. He worked it loose and dropped it on the ground. Then he wriggled his body backward until he could touch the bottle with his foot. He lifted his leg and brought the back of his boot heel down on the bottle as hard as he could. It took two tries, but then he was rewarded by the sound of glass breaking.

Scratch twisted and rolled until he had worked his way back around to where he could fumble on the ground and find the pieces of the broken bottle. He got hold of the largest fragment, ignoring the way it sliced tiny cuts in his fingertips, and turned his wrist until he was able to rest the sharp edge against the lowest turn of the rope around his torso. He started sawing at it.

Cutting through the ropes this way was going to take time, he knew, but he didn't have a choice. This was the only way he could get free.

The rope was a tough lasso, and it stubbornly resisted his efforts. Blood seeping from the cuts made his fingers slick and threatened his grip on the broken glass.

But after long minutes that seemed even longer, the strands began to part. When the first loop gave way, that allowed his hand and wrist to move a little more freely. He could get better leverage and could saw harder on the next loop.

His progress was slow but steady. He didn't allow himself to think about what might have already happened but instead focused all his attention on what he was doing. Eventually his forearm was free. He was able to get hold of the rope and start unwinding it until it all came loose. Pain shot through his arms when he moved them, but he welcomed those pins and needles, knowing that they meant the blood was flowing and his muscles were working again. Now that he was able to brace himself, he clambered to his feet and stood there swaying slightly for a moment as he breathed hard from the strain and effort.

The sound of voices approaching made him stiffen.

"—think we should have gone ahead and stomped the guts out of him."

That was the voice of one of the men who'd attacked him. Another man chuckled and said, "Aw, you're still just mad because the old pelican kicked you in the *cojones*."

"Well, hell, wouldn't you be?"

"It's like he said, you don't actually *need* 'em—"

"Shut up. Let's just get him and drag him out, like the boss said. Anyway, I reckon it'll be pretty entertaining to make the son of a bitch watch while his friend's strung up."

Those words sent a thrill of excitement shooting through Scratch. So they hadn't broken into the jail and lynched Bo yet!

From the sound of it, though, that atrocity wasn't far off. These men had been sent to get him so he could be forced to witness the lynching. That would be a particularly cruel turn of fate.

But it wasn't going to happen, Scratch vowed. He heard the men's footsteps as they approached the shed. Listening intently, he waited until they were right on the other side of the stacked-up barrels, still talking but not expecting any trouble since they thought he was still tied up.

Then he lunged forward, spreading his arms wide to send two of the barrels toppling forward as he crashed through the barrier.

CHAPTER 22

The two men were taken by surprise as the barrels tumbled down on top of them and knocked them to the ground. One of them started to yell in alarm.

Scratch shut him up with a hard kick to the jaw that resulted in the sharp crack of bone breaking. The man writhed on the ground and moaned thickly. Scratch didn't feel a bit bad about breaking the varmint's jaw.

The other man clawed at the gun on his hip as he scrambled up onto one knee. Scratch put a hand on one of the barrels and vaulted over it to crash into the Rafter F man. Both of them went down. Scratch grabbed the wrist of the man's gun hand and smashed it against the ground. The revolver flew out of the man's fingers and slid across the dirt.

It wasn't quite as dark in the alley as it had been under the shed. A little light from the moon and stars penetrated back here, and those rays struck silvery glints from the ivory handle of the gun the man had just dropped. Scratch caught a glimpse of that and recognized it as one of his Remingtons.

"Steal a man's guns, will you?" he grated as he smashed a fist into the man's face.

Scratch hit him twice more, as fast and hard as he could. The man went limp. Scratch had knocked him out.

The man with the broken jaw was still lying on the ground, whimpering. All the fight had been knocked out of him. Scratch scooped up the Remington, reversed it, and struck with the butt, knocking the man unconscious just to be sure he wouldn't cause any more trouble.

Scratch went back to the other man and found his second revolver stuck behind the hombre's belt. He felt a little better about things with the Remingtons filling his hands. He slid the weapons back into their holsters where they belonged.

There was no time to waste. Going by what the two men had been saying as they walked up to the shed, the mob was about ready to start across the creek and head for the jail. If he was going to get Bo out of there, it had to be now.

Scratch ran along the alley, cut through the gap between two buildings, and reached the street that ran between the array of saloons and gambling dens. At the end of that street to his right was the bridge over Bear Creek. He glanced to his left, toward the Southern Belle.

Men began to emerge from the saloon, talking in loud, drunken voices. Scratch caught a couple of words—"killer" and "rope"—and that was enough to tell him that time was up. The lynch mob wasn't waiting for the two men who'd gone to get him.

He raced toward the bridge, staying to the shadows as much as he could in hopes that the mob wouldn't spot him and speed up their assault on the jail. They weren't moving very fast at the moment, he saw when he glanced over his shoulder, probably because some of them were so full of rotgut whiskey that they weren't very steady on their feet.

When he reached the bridge he pounded across the planks. As he turned toward the jail he saw that the medicine show wagon had been moved and was parked in front of the café now, directly across from the marshal's office. Veronique Ballantine sat on the lowered tailgate. When she spotted him, she slid off the gate and called, "M'sieu Scratch! Professor, M'sieu Scratch is here!"

Sarlat stuck his head out the door at the back of the wagon and said, "It's about time! We thought you had abandoned your plan, my friend."

Scratch stumbled to a halt. He was out of breath from running, and as he tried to drag air into his lungs, he said, "The lynch mob's . . . on its way. They'll be here . . . in a few minutes."

"We'll have a show ready for them, you can count on that," Sarlat promised. "Now go! Help your friend!"

Scratch jerked his head in a nod and turned toward the livery stable. He had to get his and Bo's horses ready to ride so they could make their getaway from Bear Creek.

He had just reached the stable when a sudden rataplan of hoofbeats made him pause and look along the street to the south. A group of riders was entering town, and as they passed through a rectangle of light coming from the window of a building, Scratch recognized the man in the lead.

John Creel's rugged face and the white hair under his black Stetson were unmistakable. Just behind him rode Bo's brothers and several of the Star C hands.

The Creels had come to town, but for what reason, Scratch had no idea.

He didn't have a chance to ask them, because at that moment the mob reached the western end of the bridge and spilled into the street, blocking the path of the horsebackers. John Creel had to haul back suddenly on his reins, forcing his companions to do likewise.

Somebody yelled, "Hey, it's that damn murderer's kinfolks!"

"They must've come to bust him outta jail!" another man shouted. "We gotta stop 'em!"

The men closest to the Creels lunged at them, reaching up with clawing hands to grab them and try to drag them out of their saddles. John Creel barked a curse and kicked out at the men attacking him. In a matter of heartbeats the street was a roiling mass of confusion as the two groups battled.

And if that wasn't enough, at that moment a red rocket rose into the night sky above Bear Creek, trailing sparks along its arching path until it burst in an explosion of garish brilliance that lit up the street.

Scratch saw that the rocket had come from the vicinity of the medicine show wagon and knew that Professor Sarlat had delivered on his promise to provide a distraction that would draw the attention of the whole town.

It probably would have, too, if not for the riot already going on at the foot of the bridge between the lynch mob and the bunch from the Star C.

Scratch turned and plunged into the livery stable, rushing past the startled hostler who wore an expression of amazement on his elderly face. The commotion continued outside as Scratch threw saddles on the two horses and cinched them in place.

"You didn't see me tonight," he snapped at the hostler. "Got that, amigo?"

The slack-jawed old-timer just stared.

It didn't really matter, thought Scratch. Once things settled down, everybody in town would know who was responsible for breaking Bo out of jail. He was the only one in these parts who would attempt such a brazen thing, and besides, Marshal Haltom would probably recognize him.

That couldn't be helped. Scratch knew he couldn't count on the Creels being able to stop the lynch mob.

He swung up onto his horse and galloped out through the barn's double doors, leading Bo's mount behind him. A glance up the street toward the jail revealed that the rocket hadn't been the only part of the distraction staged by the professor and Veronique. Sarlat was playing his accordion animatedly, and Veronique whirled and capered on the wagon's tailgate.

She wasn't just dancing, though.

She was taking her clothes off while she was doing it.

Scratch only caught a glimpse of what was going on, but that was enough to make him wish he could have sat back and enjoyed the show. As it was, anybody from the lynch mob who broke away from the riot and headed for the jail would no doubt be stopped in their tracks by the sight of Veronique's nearly nude loveliness.

At the corner, Scratch reined the horses into a sharp turn that sent them thundering along the passage between buildings. When they came out at the rear, he turned again, this time toward the back of the jail.

He hoped none of Bo's family was hurt bad in the melee, but at the moment he didn't have time to check on them. As he rode, he took the lasso loose from his saddle and shook out an end of it.

He circled the jail and came up alongside the window of Bo's cell.

"Bo!" he called softly but urgently. "Bo, you hear me?"

"What the hell!" Bo exclaimed as he stuck his face up to the little window and grasped the bars. "Scratch, what do you think you're doing? What's going on out there? It sounds like the Battle of San Jacinto all over again!"

"No, but it's in a good cause, just like that ruckus was," Scratch said as he held out the end of the rope and passed it through the window between the bars. "Grab that and tie it around the bars!"

"No! I'm not going to let you turn yourself into an outlaw—"

"That racket is comin' from a lynch mob, Bo. Your pa and brothers are holdin' 'em back for now, but I don't reckon it'll last. You got to get out of here, or you'll be swingin' from a cottonwood branch before you know it!"

"Pa and the boys came to help me?" Bo asked, sounding surprised.

Scratch didn't actually know why the Creels had shown up in Bear Creek when they did, but he figured Bo might cooperate more if he thought they had come to rescue him.

"That's right," Scratch said. "And you can't let what they're doin' be all for nothin'."

Bo made up his mind. He grasped the rope, pulled it farther into the cell, and began looping it around the bars. At the same time, Scratch dallied it around his saddle horn and then leaned over to secure the other end of the rope to the horn on Bo's saddle.

"Ready?" he called tensely.

"Ready!" came Bo's reply.

Scratch turned the horses and urged them away from the jail. The rope snapped taut behind them. Scratch heard it groan as the tension grew tighter and tighter.

Somewhere in the jail, Marshal Haltom yelled, "Hey! Creel! What're you—"

The bars tore out of the window with a crash of masonry, the squeal of nails pulling loose, and the splintering of boards. As Scratch had hoped, some of the wall had come out along with the bars, leaving a hole big enough—maybe—for Bo to clamber through.

"Come on!" he cried as he tore the rope loose from the saddles and let it drop, not caring if he recovered it.

"Creel! Stop or I'll shoot!"

That was the marshal again. Scratch shouted, "Bo, get down!" and unleathered one of the Remingtons. Bo's head disappeared from the ragged opening in the wall. Scratch fired two swift shots through the dark hole. The muzzle flashes lit up the night.

"Now!" he called to Bo.

Bo hauled himself up and through the busted-out window. Scratch caught a glimpse of movement behind his friend and yelled, "Down!" as he pulled the horses aside. Bo dived forward, spilling through the opening, just as Haltom cut loose with the Greener.

Most of the buckshot hit the wall inside the cell. The balls that came through the opening whistled off harmlessly into the night. Scratch fired twice more, aiming high. He wasn't trying to kill the lawman. He just wanted Haltom ducking for cover.

Bo rolled over and came up on his feet. He lunged toward the horses, got a foot in the stirrup, and swung up onto his mount. Scratch tossed him the reins.

"Let's get out of here!"

"Right behind you, partner!" Bo said.

Leaning forward in their saddles to make themselves smaller targets, they kicked their horses into a gallop and raced away from the jail into the darkness.

CHAPTER 23

Bo's pulse hammered in his head. Emotions warred inside him as he rode next to Scratch.

First among them was relief at being out of that jail. Despite his insistence on abiding by the law and trusting in the legal process, he hated being behind bars with every fiber of his being.

He was also gratified that his father and brothers had come to Bear Creek to help him. His father and Hank must have been able to convince Riley and Cooper that he was innocent, or at least that he shouldn't be taken out and strung up from a tree.

But he was worried, too, about what Scratch had given up to help him. They were fugitives now, both of them, and it was possible they might be on the run from the law for the rest of their lives. That was no way for a man to live.

That thought filled Bo with more determination than ever. He would find the real Bear Creek Butcher and clear his name. That was the only chance he and

Scratch had to avoid being tagged permanently as outlaws.

They didn't slow their horses until the settlement was a mile behind them. As they pulled the mounts back to a walk, Scratch said, "That was mighty close. Another five minutes and it might've been too late to get you out of there."

"You were cutting it pretty close, all right," Bo agreed. "But I didn't really expect you to throw your own life away like this."

"Aw, hell, Bo, you know better than that. What would you have done if it was me locked up in that jail with a lynch mob comin' up the street?"

Bo had to chuckle, despite the seriousness of the situation.

"Well, when you put it like that, I suppose I would have done the same thing," he admitted.

"Dang right you would have. We've had each other's back for more'n forty years now. It's too late for a couple of old codgers like us to change our ways."

"I suppose you're right. Which means you probably know what we're going to do next."

"Find out who really killed those poor gals?"

"That's right," Bo said. "And we're going to start by going back to Bear Creek."

Even in the darkness, Bo could tell that Scratch was staring over at him incredulously. For a long moment, the silver-haired Texan didn't make any reply. Then he finally said, "I must be losin' my hearin' in my old age. I would've swore I just heard you say you want to go back to Bear Creek."

"That's what I said."

"The place where damned near the whole town thinks you're a cold-blooded murderer and wants to string you up to the nearest tree? That place?"

"That's where the answers are," Bo said. "We won't find out who killed those women anywhere else."

Scratch was quiet again. Bo knew his partner was smart enough to understand that was their only possible course of action. But understanding it didn't mean Scratch had to like it.

"You're right," Scratch said at last. "I reckon I thought we'd hole up somewhere and let all the trouble die down a mite, then go back and see what we could root out."

"That's just what they'll expect us to do, at least the ones who don't think we'll keep running all the way to Mexico. The only way we can really take them by surprise is to double back tonight."

"Whoever killed those gals won't be expectin' that, will they?" Scratch mused.

"That's right."

Scratch nodded and said, "I'm with you, then. You reckon the marshal's already puttin' together a posse?"

"I'd be shocked if he's not," Bo said. "He won't have any shortage of volunteers, either. Every man in the mob that almost stormed the jail will be willing to come along."

"Every man who ain't too drunk to ride, you mean," Scratch said with a chuckle. "Ned Fontaine primed 'em with plenty of liquid courage ever since that hearin' this morning."

"Marshal Haltom would have done his best to keep them from lynching me, but after that jailbreak I doubt if he'll be so worried about my welfare."

"You mean if they spot us, they'll be shootin' to kill," Scratch said.

"That's right."

"Well, we'll just have to make sure they don't spot us." Scratch looked around. They were in thickly wooded hills west of town. "Why don't we cut back to the north? They probably won't expect us to go that way. We can hit the Bastrop road and come back in from that direction."

"Sounds like a good idea to me," Bo said.

"What'll we do when we get there?"

Bo thought about that for a moment before he said, "I want to talk to Barney Dunn."

"The bartender?"

"He's the one who identified me in court."

"And he sounded mighty sincere about it, too," Scratch pointed out. "Even if we got our hands on him and forced him to change his story, nobody would believe it now."

"I don't want him to change his story. I just don't think he's told all of it yet."

"I talked to him, Bo. He seemed pretty convinced that the fella he saw that night looked like you."

"Maybe he saw something else important and doesn't even realize it. Somehow, he's got to have the answers we're looking for."

"We'll talk to him, then," Scratch agreed, but he sounded a little dubious about the hope that it would do any good.

Steering by the stars, they turned and headed north. The path they followed wound through the hills. They stuck mostly to the trees, since the shadows were black and thick underneath the branches and made it less likely that a posse or anyone else would spot them.

"If the marshal was smart," Scratch said, "he'd wait until mornin' to set out. Nobody but a Comanche or an Apache can track worth a damn at night."

"Haltom's smart enough," Bo said. "But emotions are running too high in town right now. Even if he knows he'd be more likely to find us by waiting until morning, he'll come after us tonight. The mob wouldn't have it any different, and the marshal's on the same side as them now."

"Everybody's out to get Bo Creel, eh?"

"That's about the size of it," Bo agreed with a dry fatalism in his voice. "I don't think I have any friends left back there in Bear Creek."

"That's not true. Lauralee still believes you're innocent, and she claims some of the other folks do, too. There's just not enough of 'em to make themselves heard over the bunch that's yellin' for your head."

"And there are my pa and my brothers, too," Bo mused.

"Bo . . . there's somethin' I reckon I ought to tell you."

Scratch sounded troubled by whatever was on his mind, so Bo said, "Go ahead. I'm listening."

"I didn't send for John and your brothers. I reckon it was just pure luck they showed up when they did. Maybe they did come into town to help you, like you thought. I just don't know, one way or the other."

Bo had to think about that for a moment. Finally he said, "Well, I guess we'll probably find out sooner or later, if we live long enough. In the meantime, I'll just be glad that they rode in right then."

"Nothin' wrong with that," Scratch agreed.

After a while they came to a road that headed northwest and southeast. Both men knew it was the road running from Bastrop to Bear Creek. They turned back to the southeast, toward the settlement.

No one else appeared to be abroad in these parts tonight. The road was deserted except for the two riders. They kept their eyes and ears open, knowing that if they encountered anyone else they would need to get off the road and into the trees in hopes that they wouldn't be seen.

"Bo, I've been thinkin'," Scratch said quietly. "About the Bear Creek Butcher."

"What about him?"

"Well, we know he ain't you—"

"I appreciate the vote of confidence," Bo said, smiling in the darkness.

Scratch went on, "And right now, there really ain't no tellin' who he really is. But no matter who he turns out to be . . . why in blazes would anybody do what he did? Why strangle those gals and then chop 'em up like that?"

"The obvious answer is because he's loco."

"How could anybody be that crazy?"

Bo shook his head and said, "We don't really have any way of knowing that, either. Something goes wrong inside, in somebody's heart or brain or both, and they turn poison mean. They just want to hurt other people. We've run into hombres who were kill-crazy before."

"Yeah, but they were usually outlaws. They were after loot, and they'd gun down anybody who got in their way. Those saloon girls didn't have anything to steal except their lives."

"I guess that was enough for the Butcher," Bo said.

Scratch's questions made him think, though. Sure, anybody who saw the results of the Butcher's actions would think he was a madman. That was the only reasonable conclusion to draw.

But maybe there was something more to it than that, Bo mused. Some motivation nobody had seen yet. Determining whether or not that was true might go a long way toward helping them figure out who the murderer really was.

Eventually lights came into view up ahead. The two Texans reined to a halt.

"That'll be the settlement," Scratch said. "We don't want to ride right down the street to the bridge. We'd better go ahead and cross over the creek so we can come up behind the saloons."

Bo nodded in agreement.

"We ought to be pretty close to Dogleg Ford. You think we can find it in the dark?"

"Sure we can. Hell, we ought to know every foot of this country, as much as we traipsed all over it when we were kids."

True to Scratch's prediction, they located Dogleg Ford without much trouble. Where the creek took the sharp bend that gave the ford its name, it shallowed down over a gravel bed that provided solid footing for the horses. Bo and Scratch rode across with their mounts' hooves kicking up small splashes in the water.

When they were on the eastern bank, they followed the stream south, not stopping until they were about a quarter of a mile from the cluster of lights that marked the location of the saloons. Bo and Scratch sat their saddles under a cottonwood tree that threw a lot of shadows from its spreading branches.

"Can't just waltz in there and grab Dunn," Scratch commented quietly. "There'll still be too many folks around for that."

"The saloon will close around midnight," Bo said. "We'll wait until then and slip up on foot to see where he goes. You don't happen to know where he lives, do you?"

"Nope, and I never thought to ask Lauralee about it."

"That's all right. We'll wait until we get him alone somewhere, then grab him and ask some questions. He's got to have seen something else, maybe even something he's forgotten about, that will give us a clue."

And if they couldn't come up with anything by questioning the bartender, thought Bo, then he and Scratch would just have to dodge the law long enough to get confirmation from Judge Parker and Marshal Brubaker that they were nowhere near Bear Creek when the killings took place. Whether or not that would get them off the hook for the jail-break, Bo didn't know. He suspected they would wind up having to pay for the damage to the jail, at the very least.

But paying a fine was a far cry from swinging from a cottonwood branch at the end of a hang rope.

Having to wait for the Southern Belle to close gave their horses a chance to rest. While they were doing that, Scratch told Bo about the things he had been doing, including the way he'd been knocked out and captured by some of the Rafter F hands.

"Sounds like Fontaine will do just about anything to gain an advantage over the Star C," Bo commented.

"Yeah, and those hombres had a personal grudge against me, too," Scratch said. He told Bo about Professor Sarlat and Veronique and how he had stepped in when the Rafter F punchers were harassing the couple from the medicine show.

The silver-haired Texan licked his lips and said, "I sure wish I had a bottle of that elixir right about now. It's mighty potent stuff, Bo."

"You know it's bound to be mostly alcohol," Bo pointed out.

"Oh, it's got booze in it, I reckon, but it's a lot more than that."

"Yeah, opium, maybe."

"You'll see," Scratch insisted. "When this mess is cleared up, I'll get a bottle and you can try it. Then you'll understand what I'm talkin' about."

Bo said, "I have to admit, I'm looking forward to meeting the two of them. The professor sounds like a character, and that girl Veronique . . . well, you make her sound pretty interesting."

"Oh, she's interestin', all right," Scratch said. "Interestin' enough to plumb take your breath away." He explained about the rocket and the impromptu striptease that had followed it. "Those two know how to catch an hombre's eye, that's for sure."

"By those two, you mean the professor and the girl?"

Scratch thought about it for a moment and replied, "Yeah, I guess you could say that."

The faint tinkling of piano music drifted through the night air from several of the saloons. It tapered off as the hour grew late. Some of the lamps were blown out.

"Come on," Bo said. "We need to get closer."

They led their horses and approached the row of saloons on foot. Scratch led the way to the back of the shed where he had been held prisoner earlier in the day.

"We can leave the horses here," Scratch whispered. "Nobody'll have any reason to bother 'em."

Bo agreed with that plan. They tied their reins to one of the posts that held up the shed's rear wall and were about to cross the alley so they could slip through the thick shadows next to the saloon when the back door opened. Bo and Scratch drew back, crouching next to the shed.

A figure appeared in the doorway and paused, turning back slightly to say, "Good night, Miss Lauralee. You sure you don't need me anymore?"

Lauralee's voice came from somewhere inside the saloon.

"No, Barney, that's all right," she said. "It's been a long day. You go on home and get some rest."

"Yes, ma'am."

Barney Dunn closed the saloon's rear door behind him.

"That's him," Scratch breathed as he leaned close to Bo's ear.

"I know. I saw him at the hearing. We'll follow him."

Dunn ambled along the alley with his hands stuck in his pockets. He didn't seem disturbed by the fact that this was where he had witnessed a brutal murder and nearly been killed himself. He whistled a sprightly tune under his breath as if he didn't have a care in the world.

That was sort of odd, thought Bo. And it made him more eager than ever to ask the bartender some questions.

They allowed Dunn to get a short lead on them, then followed with the stealth that had saved their lives on many occasions in the past. In addition to the saloons, gambling dens, and bawdy houses on this side of the creek, there were also a number of small cabins where the people who worked in those establishments lived. Bo figured that Barney Dunn was headed for one of those dwellings.

He was about to tap Scratch on the shoulder and indicate with hand signals that they should go ahead and grab the bartender, when Dunn abruptly veered off his course and headed for a dilapidated old barn. Maybe that was where he had his bunk, Bo thought.

Some instinct made him hesitate before jumping Dunn, though. He whispered to Scratch, "Go back and get the horses. Be as quiet about it as you can."

"You reckon Dunn lives in that barn?"

"Maybe. Or maybe he's got a horse of his own in there."

Bo waited next to the thick trunk of a post oak while Scratch hurried back to the shed to fetch their horses. He watched as Barney Dunn went into the barn. A dim glow from inside told him that Dunn had lit a candle or a lamp.

The light burned only for a few minutes, though, before it went out again. Dunn might have turned in for the night.

Thudding hoofbeats told Bo that wasn't the case. Dunn rode out of the barn on horseback, swaying and bouncing in the saddle even though his mount wasn't going very fast. The Easterner clearly wasn't an experienced rider, but he was able to stay in the saddle as he turned the horse and headed east. He was out of sight, vanishing into the night, by the time Scratch returned with their horses.

"What happened?" he asked Bo.

"Dunn saddled up a horse and rode out." Bo pointed. "That way."

Scratch bit back a curse.

"You let him get away?"

Bo smiled and said, "Not so's you'd notice. We can catch up to him and trail him without any trouble."

"Ah," Scratch said in understanding. "You want to see where he's going."

"That's right," Bo said as he swung up into the saddle. "It may not have anything to do with those killings, but I figure it won't hurt to find out for sure."

Scratch muttered agreement, and the two of them set out on the trail of the suddenly mysterious bartender.

CHAPTER 24

Bo figured that as much trouble as their quarry had been having just staying mounted and keeping the horse moving, Dunn wouldn't be paying much attention to anything going on behind him. Even so, he and Scratch were careful not to get too close to the man they were trailing. Once they were near enough to hear Dunn's horse, they hung back so he wouldn't notice them.

"Where do you reckon he's goin'?" Scratch quietly asked.

"I don't have any idea," Bo replied honestly. "As far as I know, Dunn's just a bartender. He shouldn't have any reason to be wandering around the country-side like this, unless maybe he has a place out here where he's been living."

"He don't strike me as the sort who'd live in the country."

"Me, neither," Bo agreed. "He can't be going very far, though. If he is, he'll be mighty sore by the time he gets there, the way he was bouncing in the saddle."

After a mile or so, the trail entered a long, narrow valley between a couple of wooded hills. Bo spotted a light and pointed it out to Scratch.

"Looks like there's some sort of cabin up ahead," he said. "Could be we were wrong about Dunn living out here."

"Not even a dude like him would have gone off and left a lantern burnin'," Scratch said. "You reckon he's got somebody stayin' with him?"

"We're about to find out. We'd better get down and go the rest of the way on foot."

They dismounted and left the horses behind, tied this time to a scrubby mesquite. Bo took along Scratch's Winchester since his Colt was back in Bear Creek, locked up in a drawer in Marshal Haltom's desk.

Silvery illumination from the moon and stars washed over the landscape and revealed a log cabin, the rear of which butted up against one of the hillsides. Smoke curled from the stone chimney at one end of the cabin. The door hung open, letting light from inside spill out.

Someone was definitely home.

Bo and Scratch knelt behind some brush and watched as Barney Dunn rode up to the cabin. The bartender hauled back on the horse's reins and said, "Whoa. Whoa, I tell you."

The horse stopped. Dunn dismounted awkwardly.

As he tied the reins to a post driven into the ground, he called, "Jake? Jake, are you in there? You know you're not supposed to have the door open like that!"

Bo and Scratch glanced at each other. Scratch whispered, "Who's Jake?"

Bo shook his head. He was certain that name hadn't come up in any connection since he and Scratch had been back here in their old stomping grounds.

A tall, broad-shouldered figure appeared in the doorway. With the light behind the man, Bo and Scratch couldn't make out any more details about him. The man said, "Hello, Barney. I'm sorry about the door. It got smoky . . . inside the cabin. I had to . . . open the door to let some of the smoke out."

The man spoke in a slow, halting way, as if his brain didn't work very fast.

Dunn grunted and said, "That's all right, I guess, Jake. But don't let it happen again. You know you have to do what we tell you, because we're just lookin' out for you."

"I know, Barney," the man called Jake said. "I'm glad you look out for me. I'm too dumb to . . . look out for myself."

"Yeah, yeah, just go on back inside. The others'll be here soon."

"Good. I always get lonely . . . when I'm left here by myself."

Scratch leaned closer to Bo and whispered, "That hombre sounds like he's got the brain of a kid, even though he's a grown man. Somethin' about him is familiar, too."

"Yeah, I was just thinking the same thing," Bo replied, equally quiet. An unaccountable chill went through him as he looked at the man in the doorway.

Jake started to turn and go back into the cabin the way Dunn had told him to. He stopped to look back at the bartender and announced, "I saw a deer today, Barney. It came up . . . almost right to the cabin."

The way Jake was standing now, light from inside the cabin played over part of his face. Bo and Scratch still couldn't get a good look at him, but a shiver went through Bo anyway. He felt like he had seen Jake before, like he ought to know who the man was.

Then Dunn stepped through the door, shooing Jake ahead of him, and closed it behind him.

After a moment Scratch said, "Somethin' mighty strange is goin' on here, Bo. Who is that fella? And who are the others that Dunn said somethin' about?"

"I don't know. I want to get closer before they show up, though. I want a better look at that hombre Jake."

"Are you thinkin'—"

"I just want a better look at him, that's all," Bo said, his voice holding a grim edge.

They worked their way closer to the cabin,

staying behind cover as much as possible. A glow falling on the hillside behind the cabin told Bo there was a window back there. With a gesture, he pointed that out to Scratch, who motioned that they ought to circle around. Bo nodded.

The shutters were closed over the window, they found when they got there, but there were big enough cracks around the ill-fitting panels to let out quite a bit of light. Those same gaps would allow Bo and Scratch to look inside the cabin.

Bo moved to one side of the window, Scratch to the other. Scratch took off his cream-colored Stetson so it would be easier for him to put his eye to one of the cracks. Bo's black hat was back at the Star C, he supposed. He had left it there the day Marshal Haltom had arrested him.

Bo leaned forward, resting one hand against the cabin's rough log wall to brace himself. He squinted through the gap next to the shutter. The angle and narrowness of the opening didn't allow him to see everything inside the cabin, but he could see a table where Barney Dunn sat. The bartender had his back to the window. Bo couldn't see Jake.

"You want some . . . coffee, Barney?" the man asked. He was off to Bo's left somewhere, near the fireplace.

"Yeah, that'd be good, thanks," Dunn replied.

"What's going on . . . in town?"

Dunn chuckled.

"Oh, all kinds of fireworks, and I mean that

literally. Although I suppose you don't understand what I mean by that, do you?"

"I know what fireworks are. I think . . . I saw some once . . . somewhere. Is it . . . the Fourth of July?"

"What? No, no, it's not the Fourth of July. But that didn't stop a rocket from going up anyway."

Jake said, "I wish I could have . . . seen it."

"It was better you were right here, where nobody could hurt you. But you'll be goin' back into town soon, I promise. Maybe tonight. The boss ain't told me all the details yet."

The boss?

Bo had a strong hunch that Dunn wasn't talking about Lauralee Parker, his employer at the Southern Belle. With every moment that passed, Bo felt more certain that he'd been right to be a little suspicious about Barney Dunn. The bartender seemed to be involved in some sort of mysterious scheme. Bo wanted to find out more.

On the other side of the window, Scratch's breath suddenly hissed between his teeth in a surprised reaction that the silver-haired Texan wasn't able to suppress completely. Bo didn't think the sound was loud enough to be heard inside the cabin, but it alarmed him. Scratch must have seen something that shocked him.

A second later, Bo knew what it was, because he saw the same thing. The man called Jake came into view, carrying a cup of coffee that he placed on the table in front of Dunn. The light from the lantern that also sat on the table cast his features in sharp relief.

Jake was a dead ringer for Bo Creel.

It wasn't exactly like looking in a mirror, because in a mirror the details would be reversed. But even so, Bo knew he was looking at his exact double. His twin brother, if he had had one. His doppelganger. And one more thing . . .

The man who had to be the Bear Creek Butcher.

That was how Dunn had been able to describe Bo right down to a T, and how he had been able to draw that sketch and capture Bo's appearance so accurately, too. Dunn knew the killer, and as comfortable in each other's company as they appeared to be, that whole story about how the Bear Creek Butcher had almost cut off the bartender's head had to be a lie.

But why? Who was Jake, and why was someone using him to frame Bo for murder?

And why would someone with as simple a mind as Jake seemed to have killed those saloon girls in the first place?

Questions that had seemed to have no answer had now been resolved, but other, even more baffling questions had taken their place. Bo felt almost as stunned as if someone had walloped him in the head.

Inside the cabin, Jake sat down across from

Dunn and said, "I hope we leave soon. I don't . . . like it here much."

"Don't worry about that," Dunn said. "You just do what you're told, and everything will be all right."

"I always do what I'm told. Especially what my pa tells me to do."

"And your pa told you to do whatever *I* tell you. You see how that works?"

"Yeah, I guess."

Dunn sipped his coffee and said, "Everything's goin' just like it's supposed to. Pretty soon we're gonna be rich. Although I guess money doesn't mean a whole lot to somebody like you, huh?"

"I like money," Jake said. "Coins are shiny and pretty. I like to stack them up and build towers out of them."

"So do I, kid," Dunn replied with a laugh. "So do I. But it ain't because they're shiny and pretty. I like 'em because of everything you can buy with 'em."

Jake shook his head and said, "My pa buys me everything I need."

It was odd hearing Dunn refer to Jake as a kid, thought Bo, because Jake was definitely older than the bartender. His dark brown hair had gray strands in it, much like Bo's. The two of them appeared to be about the same age.

Because of Jake's childlike attitude, though, it

made sense that anyone who was around him would start to think of him as a kid, in spite of his actual age.

Bo reached over, tapped Scratch on the shoulder, and motioned with his head that they should back away from the cabin. They withdrew a short distance, far enough away that they could talk in whispers without having to worry about being overheard by the two men inside the cabin.

"What in the Sam Hill is goin' on here, Bo?" Scratch demanded in amazement. "Is that one of them, what did you call 'em, doublegangers? Because that fella Jake is your double, that's for damn sure!"

"I don't have any explanation for it," Bo said. He couldn't keep the amazement out of his own voice. "He really does look just like me."

"And that means he's got to be the Bear Creek Butcher. Nothin' else makes sense." Scratch took off his hat and ran his fingers through his hair in obvious confusion. He went on, "But that don't make sense, either. Why would anybody as simple and harmless as that hombre seems to be ever want to hurt those saloon gals?"

The question was the same one Bo had asked himself a moment earlier, and a theory had suggested itself to him.

"I can think of one reason," Bo said. As he spoke another chill ran through him, this time at the sheer evil of the idea he was contemplating. "Jake might have hurt those girls . . . if his father told him to."

"Son of a . . ." Scratch fell silent, no doubt struck by the horror of what Bo was suggesting. After a moment he said, "A fella would have to be a damn monster to make somebody who was simpleminded do that."

"Yeah, that's about how I feel, too."

"So what do we do now? Grab Dunn and Jake and take 'em back to Bear Creek? We can show people that you ain't guilty because there's somebody who looks just like you."

"If we do that, we're liable to tip off whoever is behind this. He'd probably light a shuck and leave Dunn and Jake to take the blame." Bo's voice hardened as he went on, "I don't want him to get away with what he's done. I want to find out what this is all about, too."

"So for now we wait?" Scratch asked.

"Yeah, I think—" Bo stopped short and held up a hand. "Listen."

Scratch tilted his head and listened intently, as did Bo. After a moment Scratch said quietly, "Horses. Sounds like several of 'em."

"Dunn told Jake the boss was going to be here later," Bo said. "I've got a hunch that boss is Jake's father." His hands tightened on the rifle he carried. "I want to get a look at him."

"And then we round up the whole bunch," Scratch said.

"And then we round up the whole bunch," Bo agreed grimly.

CHAPTER 25

The hoofbeats of the approaching horses grew louder as the two Texans worked their way back to the cabin. Scratch was still dumbfounded that Bo could have such an exact double, but there was no denying the evidence of his own eyes. He had seen the man for himself.

He didn't know what he would do if he ever ran into his own doubleganger. He hoped it would never happen, though.

Another sound mixed in with the hoofbeats. Scratch recognized it as the squeaking of wagon wheels as they turned on their axles. That meant the horses were probably a team pulling the vehicle.

Back at the cabin's rear window, Scratch resumed the position he'd been in before with his eye pressed to one of the gaps around the shutters. He held his hat in his left hand and rested his right hand on the butt of the Remington on that side, ready to draw the revolver as soon as Bo indicated that they should make their move.

Inside the cabin, Dunn and Jake must have heard the wagon approaching, too. Dunn took another drink of his coffee and stood up.

"That'll be the boss," he said.

"Good," Jake said. "I miss Pa when he's not here."

It still made a shiver run down Scratch's back-bone when he saw and heard Jake. It was just like looking at Bo, and their voices were similar, too, but then the childlike words came out of Jake's mouth and Scratch was reminded of just how truly different they were. Jake had an air of innocence that made it almost impossible to believe he could have committed those crimes, but there was no other explanation.

If the situation bothered Scratch as much as it did, he couldn't imagine what it made Bo feel like.

The hoofbeats stopped. Scratch heard a murmur of voices but couldn't make out the words. He pressed his eye closer to the gap and waited for the door to open.

He wasn't prepared for what he saw when it did.

Professor Thaddeus Sarlat stepped into the cabin, and close behind him came the beautiful Veronique.

Scratch clenched his jaw tight. He had to do that to keep a curse from erupting out of his mouth.

"Pa!" Jake said. He went to Sarlat and put his

arms around him in a clumsy hug. "I'm so happy you're back."

Sarlat patted Jake on the shoulder and said, "Yes, yes, we told you we'd return, didn't we?"

Jake hugged Veronique, too, but there was nothing about it that was reminiscent of the way a man hugged a beautiful woman. Scratch halfway expected him to call her "Mama," but at least he didn't do that.

"Everything on schedule, boss?" Dunn asked.

Sarlat nodded and said, "Yes, perfectly. Veronique and I will take Jake back to town now, just to make sure everything is wrapped up according to our plan."

"What about me?"

"You can stay here if you like," Sarlat told the bartender. "Or you can go back to Bear Creek. It's up to you." He smiled thinly. "After tonight, though, you may not want to be around there anymore."

"You're right about that," Dunn said. "I'm gonna take my share and go back East where things are civilized. Or maybe to New Orleans." He leered at Veronique. "That's where you're from, ain't it?"

"Oui," she said. The icy tone of her voice told Scratch that she didn't particularly care for Dunn. That was no surprise. The bartender was pretty weasel-like.

Scratch's brain was spinning as he tried to make sense of the things he was hearing. He had felt a genuine liking for the professor and Veronique. They had been willing to pitch in and help him rescue Bo from the jail in Bear Creek.

And yet it was undeniable that the two of them were mixed up in something pretty sinister. Scratch just couldn't figure out exactly what it was.

Maybe Bo could, he told himself. Bo was good at figuring things out.

"Come along, Jake," Sarlat said as he put a hand on Jake's arm.

"Are we going . . . to town again?" Jake asked.

"That's right."

"Are you gonna have me . . . do something again?"

"One more time, Jake," Sarlat said, his voice gentle but persuasive. "That's all. Then you won't have to help me with my job anymore."

"I don't mind . . . too much. I always like to do . . . what you tell me to do."

Blood roared inside Scratch's head. That son of a bitch. Sarlat was one hell of an actor, pretending to be just a medicine show professor when obviously he was something much worse.

Veronique was part of it, too. Scratch hated to think that someone so lovely could also be so evil, but this wasn't the first time he and Bo had run into a woman who was just as villainous as any of the men around her.

He looked over at Bo, expecting his friend to

signal that they should make their move and get the drop on the people in the cabin. It would be easy enough to do. Bo could knock the rickety shutters aside with the rifle butt while Scratch kicked in the door and covered them with his Remingtons.

Instead, Bo motioned for Scratch to follow him and started to fade back away from the cabin. Scratch didn't understand that, but he went along with what Bo wanted, knowing that in the long run Bo's hunches were always worth playing.

When they were back up the hill in the trees where they wouldn't be heard, Bo stopped and said, "I reckon from the way you described them, that must be Professor Sarlat and Mademoiselle Ballantine."

"Yeah," Scratch said, "but I swear, Bo, I thought they were good folks. They helped me pull off that jailbreak tonight."

"For some reason they must have wanted me out of jail. I don't know how that fits in with their plan, but it's bound to."

"I guess. This whole business has thrown me for a loop. I reckon it must be even worse for you, knowin' that somebody who looks just like you really is a killer."

"If you want to call him that," Bo said. "As far as I'm concerned, Sarlat's the real killer. Jake's just the tool he's been using to commit his crimes."

"Yeah, that's the way I figure it, too. How come we're not down there roundin' 'em up?"

"Because even though we know now who's behind this, we still don't know what it's all about. And I want to find out."

"How do you figure we'll go about doin' that?" Scratch asked.

"You follow the wagon back to town and keep an eye on those three. Maybe Sarlat will give away what the rest of his plan is. Just make sure Jake doesn't hurt anyone else."

Scratch nodded and said, "What'll you be doin'?"

"I'm going to grab Barney Dunn, just like we planned, and question him. We're not as much in the dark as we were, since we know he's been working with the people responsible for the deaths of those women." Bo's voice hardened even more. "I think I can convince Dunn to talk."

Scratch let out a grim chuckle.

"I'll just bet you can," he said.

Down below, Sarlat was on the wagon seat. Veronique led Jake to the door in the back of the wagon, and both of them went inside the enclosed rear of the vehicle. Sarlat hauled on the reins, turned the team around, and started toward Bear Creek.

"I'll get after 'em," Scratch said. "You'll head for Bear Creek with Dunn after you're finished palaverin' with him?"

"That's right. Be careful, Scratch. Don't trust anybody."

"After what I've seen tonight," Scratch said, "I don't intend to."

Scratch slipped away into the darkness to get his horse and go after the medicine show wagon. Bo headed down the hill toward the cabin. The horse Barney Dunn had ridden out there was still tied up in front of the ramshackle building and the lantern still burned inside, so Bo knew the bartender was there.

Not for long, though. As Bo crouched off to the side behind some brush, Dunn appeared in the doorway. He paused to stretch next to a stack of firewood with an ax leaning against it, putting his hands in the small of his back and arching it. He seemed reluctant to get back onto the horse, and having seen the way the man rode, Bo could understand why.

After a moment, Dunn sighed and headed toward his mount, probably intending to unsaddle it since he had indicated that he was going to stay at the cabin rather than returning to Bear Creek.

Bo straightened, stepped out of concealment, and leveled the rifle at the bartender.

"Hold it right there, Dunn," Bo ordered in a hard, flat voice.

Dunn jerked in surprise and stepped back.

"What the hell! Who—" He stopped short and gulped as Bo came closer. "Jake! What are you doin' back here? You scared me, kid. Put that gun down before you hurt some—"

Dunn stopped again, this time because his jaw hung slack and open in astonishment as he realized who he was facing.

"Creel," he choked out.

"That's right," Bo said.

"But . . . but . . . you should be long gone by now! You broke out of jail! You've got a posse chasing you!"

Bo shook his head.

"I don't plan on spending the rest of my life on the run," he said. "I want answers, and you've got them, Dunn."

"Don't shoot me. Please." Dunn held out his hands toward Bo as he pleaded. "I'm sorry I said all that in court. I had to. I . . . I had to tell the judge what I saw—"

"Don't waste your breath," Bo interrupted him. "We both know good and well you never saw me in that alley. You saw Jake."

Even in the darkness, Bo could see how Dunn's eyes bugged out in shock.

"You . . . you know about Jake?"

"You just mentioned him, remember? I know he looks just like me. I know that he thinks he's Professor Sarlat's son and will do anything the professor tells him to do, even when he knows it's wrong. But he's not Sarlat's son, is he?"

Dunn seemed to be too scared to follow what Bo was saying. He moaned and covered his face with his hands.

"Don't kill me," he said, his voice muffled. "I didn't know so many people were gonna be hurt . . . I was just trying to make enough money to get back East . . ."

"Come on," Bo said. "If you don't want to answer my questions here, we'll just go back to Bear Creek. You can spill the whole story there."

He kept the rifle pointed at Dunn with one hand while he walked over to the bartender's horse and reached for the reins with the other. He took his eyes off of Dunn only for a second, but that was long enough for the man's frantic fear to prompt him into trying a desperate move.

Dunn's hand shot out with surprising speed, closed around the ax handle, and swept it up. He swung the double-bitted tool at Bo's head. Bo saw the movement from the corner of his eye and barely had time to jerk the rifle barrel up to block the ax.

Ax and rifle came together with a jarring impact that knocked the Winchester from Bo's hand. The ax glanced off, though, and kept going to hit the cabin wall instead of burying itself in Bo's skull. The blade stuck in the wood as Dunn tried to pull it back.

Bo charged at Dunn, but the bartender jerked the

ax free and swung it in a backhand slash. Bo had to dive to the ground to avoid it. He rolled and crashed into Dunn's legs. With a yell of alarm, the bartender dropped the ax and went down.

Terror and desperation made him slippery as an eel as Bo tried to grab him. Dunn writhed away and scrambled after the rifle Bo had dropped. Bo could have grabbed the ax as he went after Dunn, but he wanted the bartender alive. Dunn wouldn't be able to answer any questions if he was dead.

Bo tackled him just as Dunn reached the Winchester. Dunn squealed like a pig and lashed out with both feet. One of them caught Bo on the side of the head and knocked him to the side with stars exploding inside his skull. He shook that off and surged to his feet.

Dunn made it up first, though, and darted to the horse, jerking the reins free from the post and grabbing at the saddle. Spooked by the ruckus, the horse shied away just as Dunn got one foot in the stirrup and tried to haul himself onto the animal's back. As the horse leaped, Dunn fell back and yelled.

That was just about the worst thing he could have done. The horse bolted, taking off through the darkness.

And Dunn's foot was twisted and still hung up in the stirrup.

"No!" Bo shouted. He lunged after the horse in an attempt to grab the dangling reins and bring it under control. Dunn started screaming as he was dragged along the rough ground. That just made the horse stampede more. Bo had no chance of catching it.

He continued to run after it, though, as Dunn kept shrieking in pain and terror. Those shrieks ended abruptly after a few seconds, and Bo knew that wasn't good. He followed the pounding hoofbeats until they stopped, as well.

When he came out into a clearing a minute later, he saw that the runaway horse had come to a halt. Dunn's foot had finally slipped out of the stirrup, and with that unaccustomed weight gone, the horse had calmed down some. It danced skittishly away from a dark shape lying motionless in the grass.

Bo trotted over to the limp figure and dropped to one knee beside Dunn. The bartender lay facedown. Bo grasped his shoulders and rolled him onto his back. As he did, he saw how loose Dunn's head was on his shoulders.

Marshal Haltom hadn't taken away Bo's matches. Bo fished the little tin from his pocket, took out one of the matches, and snapped it to life with a flick of his thumbnail. As the match flared up, its garish light revealed exactly what Bo had been afraid he would see.

Dunn's neck was twisted at an unnatural angle. It must have broken one of the times that Dunn slammed against the ground while being dragged by the horse. The bartender's eyes were wide open and stared sightlessly.

Whatever secrets Barney Dunn knew, he would never tell them now.

CHAPTER 26

Following the medicine show wagon back to Bear Creek wasn't difficult. Scratch could have gotten ahead of Sarlat and his two companions if he'd wanted to, but Bo had said to follow them and try to find out exactly what they were up to, so that's what Scratch was going to do.

Since they were east of the creek, the red-light district of the settlement was the first thing they came to. Most of the buildings were dark, Scratch saw as he approached. The saloons and gambling dens were closed down for the night. The two bawdy houses were still open, with lights burning in their parlors and in some of the rooms.

The wagon came to a stop in front of the Southern Belle. About a hundred yards behind, Scratch reined in and swung down from his saddle. He led his horse into a thick patch of shadow next to one of the buildings and watched intently as Professor Sarlat climbed off the seat and went to the back of the vehicle to open the door.

Veronique and Jake got out. Scratch was too far away to hear if anything was said among the three of them, but Sarlat and Veronique seemed to know what they were doing. Veronique stepped up onto the driver's box, sat down, and took up the reins. She got the team moving again.

That left Sarlat and Jake standing on the board-walk in front of the Southern Belle.

A chill went through Scratch. The professor couldn't be up to anything good, and as far as Scratch knew, Lauralee Parker lived alone on the second floor of the saloon. If Sarlat had brought the simpleminded Jake back into town to commit an-other murder . . .

Well, it wasn't hard to figure out who the profes-sor's intended victim was.

Scratch left his horse with the reins dangling, knowing the animal wouldn't go far, and hurried toward the saloon as Sarlat and Jake disappeared into the darkness of the passage beside the building. Their goal had to be the back door, where it would be easier to break in without anyone noticing them. Once they were inside, they could go up the stairs to the second floor, along the balcony to Lauralee's quarters, and inside, where she would be sleeping peacefully as Sarlat pressed a knife into Jake's hand and told him what to do.

Scratch gave a little shake of his head to get that

grisly image out of his brain. That wasn't going to happen, he told himself, because he was going to get there in time to stop it.

He cut across to the alley before he got to the Southern Belle, hoping to get the drop on Sarlat and Jake before they could get inside. But as far as he could see in the gloom behind the buildings, he was too late. No one was moving around the saloon's back door, and when he got there he saw that it was already open.

Scratch bit back a curse and jerked both Remingtons from their holsters as he darted inside. He still didn't know what Sarlat's master plan was, and he didn't really consider Jake to blame for what he was about to do, but none of that mattered anymore.

To save Lauralee's life, Scratch would ventilate both of the varmints if he had to and then try to sort everything out later.

The door from the hallway into the saloon's main room was open, too. Scratch hurried through it and turned toward the stairs. His eyes scanned the balcony. He wished it wasn't so dark in here.

His breath hissed between his teeth as he spotted a couple of dark figures skulking toward Lauralee's room. With Bo no longer in jail, if she was found murdered and hacked to pieces with a knife, he would be blamed for her death. Scratch had no doubt of that. And then everybody who was left in town would join in the effort to hunt Bo down and kill him like he was a mad dog.

And Bear Creek would be empty.

"Son of a bitch," Scratch said under his breath as he started up the stairs. He realized he had stumbled over something important in his thinking. He didn't have a handle on all the details, but a clearer picture was starting to form.

He reached the landing in time to see the two figures disappear. They were in Lauralee's room! Scratch ran along the balcony, no longer trying to be stealthy in his pursuit. There was no time for that.

Suddenly, a dark shape loomed up and crashed into him. The impact sent Scratch careening toward the railing along the edge of the balcony. Fists hammered into him. He knew he was fighting Jake. Sarlat had heard him coming.

They hit the balcony railing. It sagged and nails squealed in the wood, although it didn't give way. Scratch slashed at Jake's head with one of the Remingtons, but Jake ducked under the blow. Scratch didn't want to kill the hombre, but Jake might not give him a choice in the matter.

Jake's left hand closed around Scratch's throat. His right sledged into Scratch's body again and again.

Scratch reversed the right-hand Remington and smashed the butt against Jake's head. Jake couldn't avoid the blow this time. His fingers slipped away from Scratch's throat and he started to slide down. His weight still pinned Scratch against the railing, though. Scratch shoved him away.

A whisper of sound warned Scratch. He crouched as the blade of a large knife zipped through the air just above his head, knocking his hat off. If he hadn't moved when he did, the knife would cut his throat all the way to the bone. It might have even taken his head off.

Since the half-stunned Jake was still tangled around Scratch's feet, that had to be Sarlat attacking him with the knife. Anticipating a backhanded stroke, Scratch thrust up his revolver to protect his face. Sparks flew as knife and gun barrel came together with the ring of metal against metal.

Jake recovered enough to wrap his arms around Scratch's legs and heave. Scratch had no chance to save his balance. He went over, landing on the carpet runner laid along the balcony.

A flicker of shadows above him prompted him to roll to the side. The knife came down only inches from his ear and thudded into the floor. Scratch lifted his leg and kicked up with it, feeling his boot heel strike something solid. Sarlat flew backward and crashed into the wall.

Light flared up, blinding Scratch for a second. The only thing that saved him was that Sarlat and Jake were taken by surprise just as much as he was. They squinted and held up their hands to block some of the glare.

As Scratch's eyes began to adjust he saw Lauralee standing in the door of her room, wearing a long white nightdress, holding a lamp in one hand and an old pistol in the other. She saw Scratch and what must have appeared to her eyes to be Bo sprawled on the balcony, and she exclaimed, "What in the world!"

Scratch didn't have time to warn her or to stop Sarlat. The professor was too close to Lauralee to risk a shot. He grabbed her, looping an arm tightly around her while with his other hand he held the knife to her throat.

"Drop the gun, my dear," he ordered. "Otherwise I'll have no choice but to cut that pretty throat of yours."

Lauralee couldn't even gasp in surprise with the razor-sharp blade so close to her throat.

"Let her go, Professor," Scratch said. "If you don't, I'll kill you."

Sarlat's thin lips curved in a cold smile.

"I don't think so, Mr. Morton," he said. "You won't risk a shot. Even if you inflicted a mortal wound on me, you couldn't stop me from cutting her throat. And once I did that, there would be no saving her. She would bleed to death in a matter of seconds."

"Take it easy," Scratch said. "Ain't no need for anybody to die here."

"On the contrary, I'm afraid it's imperative." Sarlat paused. "But perhaps it's not necessary that that unfortunate outcome take place right away. Give Jake your guns."

Jake had pushed himself to a sitting position. He

shook his head vehemently and said, "I don't like guns, Pa. They're too . . . loud."

"He's not your pa," Scratch snapped. "You don't have to do what he says, Jake."

"Yeah, he . . . is. He's always been . . . my pa."

"The guns," Sarlat urged.

With obvious reluctance, Jake held out his hands.

"You gotta . . . give 'em to me, mister. Pa says so."

Scratch knew he wasn't going to win this argument. Not with Lauralee's life hanging by a thread. But if he gave up his guns, what chance would either of them have?

Sarlat pressed harder with the knife. Lauralee whimpered in pain as the blade cut into the soft flesh of her neck and a thin trickle of crimson welled from the wound.

"All right, damn it!" Scratch burst out. "Don't hurt her anymore." He held the Remingtons out to Jake, who took them and scooted several feet away before he stood up.

Footsteps sounded downstairs. Veronique called up, "Professor! Are you all right? Someone was following you! I saw him when I looked back from the wagon."

"Come up, my dear," Sarlat told her. "Everything is under control."

Veronique came up the stairs quickly, pausing at the landing to exclaim in surprise in her native tongue.

"M'sieu Morton!" she said. "That was you I saw following the professor?"

"You shouldn't be mixed up in all this, Mademoiselle Ballantine," Scratch told her heavily. "Turn around and go get help now, and maybe things will work out better for you."

Veronique let out a skeptical breath and shook her head. She said, "After all the things I have been a part of, m'sieu, there is nothing left for me but to continue as the professor's assistant."

"You never seemed to mind spending your share of the money we made," Sarlat said dryly.

Scratch said, "This ain't dancin' around and hawkin' some cure-all tonic. This is murder, Veronique, plain and simple."

If he couldn't get through to her, his and Lauralee's last chance for survival might slip away.

The redhead smiled sadly and shook her head again.

"I like you, M'sieu Morton, but there is nothing I can do for you," she said. "Professor, what do you want me to do?"

"First of all, take those guns from Jake. I wouldn't want the young fellow to hurt himself with them."

Veronique did so, and the way she handled the heavy Remingtons told Scratch she had used guns before.

"Is the wagon parked by the well?" Sarlat asked.

"Oui, just as before."

"Go back and get it. Bring it around behind the building."

A puzzled frown creased Veronique's forehead.

"I do not understand."

"I'm taking Morton and Miss Parker with me," the professor explained. "You know how nimbly I think on my feet, my dear. This will be even better than our original plan. Instead of having Miss Parker's body be discovered to finish clearing out the town, she'll be kidnapped. Kidnapped by the Butcher of Bear Creek!" Sarlat laughed. "I'll be counting on you to create such a sense of hysteria that everyone who's not already with the posse will rush out to look for this blond angel of the barroom."

"I can do that," Veronique said, nodding. "But where will you be?"

"I'll take the two of them back to the cabin and hold them there until Ramsey and his men have had a chance to finish their work. We'll all rendezvous there tomorrow and split up the loot, then go our separate ways until next time, as usual."

"What about me? I'm usually with you."

"I'm sure you'll have no trouble stealing a horse and getting back to the cabin. Just make sure that you don't lead anyone there."

As Sarlat talked, the whole thing continued making more sense to Scratch, but the bad part about that was that there was nothing he could do at the moment to stop it. He had to play along for the time being and hope he got a chance to turn the tables on the professor.

He could hope, as well, that Bo might show up. That would change things around in a hurry.

Veronique sighed and nodded. She said, "I hope you know what you are doing, Professor."

"I always do, don't I?" he asked with a smirk.

With that, he drew the knife sharply across Lauralee's throat.

CHAPTER 27

Scratch yelled furiously and started to surge to his feet, but Veronique pointed both pistols at him and eared back the hammers. He might have gotten up anyway, despite the threat of the Remingtons, but then he saw that the cut on Lauralee's neck wasn't deep enough to be fatal, although it was bleeding quite a bit.

"Be careful, Mr. Morton," Sarlat warned. "I can still kill her in the blink of an eye."

"What'd you hurt her for?" Scratch demanded.

"To create the proper atmosphere. Look how the blood is dripping on her nightdress. Keep him covered, Veronique."

Lauralee appeared to be stunned by what had happened. She whimpered in pain and shock as Sarlat took the knife away from her throat long enough to grasp the neckline of her nightdress. With an ugly ripping sound, he split the dress down the front and yanked the ruined garment off of her. He held it to her neck, being sure to get plenty of the crimson blood smeared on it. Once he had done that, he tossed the bloody dress back into Lauralee's room.

"Setting the stage, so to speak," Sarlat said. "When the townspeople see that, they'll know that something terrible has befallen this poor young woman, and they'll rush right out to find her and help her if they can. Of course, they won't find her."

"And by the time they get back to Bear Creek," Scratch said, "the whole town will have been looted by your outlaw pards, that fella Ramsey and his gang you talked about."

Sarlat looked surprised.

"You're more intelligent than I gave you credit for, my friend," he said. "Veronique, give me one of the guns."

The redhead handed over one of Scratch's Remingtons.

"Now go fetch the wagon, as we discussed. Be as discreet about it as you can."

"Oui, Professor," she said. She hurried along the balcony.

Sarlat gave Lauralee a push and told her, "Sit down by your friend."

Scratch kept his eyes averted from her nude body as she stumbled across the balcony and sat down beside him. He took off his bandanna and held it out to her, saying, "Tie that around your neck until the bleedin' stops." Without asking Sarlat's permission, he took off his buckskin jacket as well and draped it around Lauralee's bare shoulders. She was slender enough that it would provide her at least a semblance of decency.

"You can get up now, Jake," Sarlat told the look-alike.

Jake climbed to his feet and shook his head.

"I don't like this, Pa," he said. "I don't like all this we're doin'."

"You know I'm always looking out for your best interests, son," Sarlat told him in a soothing voice. "I would never do anything if it wasn't best for you."

"I know, but . . . you hurt that pretty lady."

"Sometimes pretty ladies have to be hurt. We've talked about that."

"I know, I just . . ." Jake ran the fingers of both hands through his hair and looked like a frightened rabbit, like he wanted to just bolt and find himself a nice deep hole to crawl into. "I wish things weren't like this."

"Everything will be fine," Sarlat assured him.

Lauralee seemed to be getting over the shock of being captured and then having her throat nicked like that. She looked up at Sarlat, and with some of the customary fire back in her voice she said, "How can you tell him those things? How can you take advantage of him that way?"

Sarlat sneered at her.

"You don't know anything about it," he said. "Jake here wouldn't even be alive today if it weren't for me. I saved him, by God! He owes his life to me."

Scratch said, "What kind of a life is it, bein' turned into a killer and a monster when anybody can see that ain't what he naturally is?"

Sarlat's face darkened with anger as he thrust the Remington toward the prisoners.

"I remind you, I don't necessarily have to keep either of you alive, so you had better just be quiet."

"Who is he?" Lauralee asked. "I know good and well he's not Bo Creel. I can see that now, even though he looks just like Bo."

"That's none of your business, either," Sarlat snapped.

He didn't say anything else. Lauralee hunkered closer to Scratch, wrapped in his buckskin jacket. Even though she continued glaring at the professor, Scratch could feel her trembling slightly from fear. He didn't blame her. He wasn't exactly fearless himself. Thaddeus Sarlat's friendly exterior had fooled him for a while, but Scratch could see now that the professor was pure evil.

A few minutes later they heard rapid footsteps on the stairs. Veronique appeared at the landing. She said a little breathlessly, "The wagon is behind the building, Professor, as you asked."

"Excellent work, my dear. I know I can always count on you." Sarlat gestured at Scratch and Lauralee with the Remington he held. "On your feet, both of you."

"Do we cooperate with him?" Lauralee asked Scratch.

"We ain't got no choice right now," the silver-haired Texan told her.

Sarlat chuckled and said, "I know what you're trying to do. You think you'll play along with me for the time being and wait for a chance to take me by surprise. I can assure you, Mr. Morton, that's not going to happen."

"You'll get what you got comin' to you," Scratch said, his eyes narrowing with anger as he climbed to his feet. He extended a hand to Lauralee to help her up. "Whether it's me or Bo or somebody else, sooner or later somebody'll be handin' you your needin's."

"Well, until that time I intend to enjoy the fruits of my labors. Let's go."

With Sarlat and Veronique both covering them, Scratch and Lauralee went along the balcony and down the stairs. Jake brought up the rear of the grim little procession.

Scratch's jacket wrapped all the way around Lauralee's slender frame with plenty to spare and came down to the middle of her thighs, so she was somewhat decently covered, anyway. The bandanna tied around her neck seemed to have stopped the bleeding from the cut.

"Out the back," Sarlat ordered. "Veronique, go first and keep them covered from that direction."

Veronique backed out the door and used both hands to steady the Remington she held as she leveled the revolver at the prisoners. They stepped out into the alley. The medicine show wagon was parked nearby. Its door hung open.

Scratch looked inside the darkened wagon, and his skin crawled. The sensation that if they got in there, they would never get out alive caused his stomach to clench.

"You can't afford to shoot us," he said. "The town may be half empty, but there are still plenty of folks who would come to see what all the ruckus was about."

"There may be some truth to that," Sarlat admitted. "Jake, come here."

Jake shuffled his feet reluctantly, but he came up beside Sarlat.

The professor held out the bloody knife toward him.

"Take that and go cut the woman," Sarlat ordered. "Keep cutting her until I tell you to stop." He smirked at Scratch. "A knife is silent, you see."

"It won't be if I scream," Lauralee said shakily.

"Which you won't be able to do if Jake finishes the job of cutting your throat."

Jake hadn't taken the knife from the professor. As he hesitated, Sarlat shook the weapon at him. "Do as I say, Jake! I'm your father."

Jake still hung back. The confrontation between "father" and "son" was distracting Sarlat, Scratch could tell, and he realized this might be his only chance to make a move.

Before he could do anything, though, Veronique acted with the same speed and athletic grace that made her such a good dancer. She stepped up behind Scratch and smashed the Remington she held against the back of his head. The blow took him by surprise and drove him to one knee.

Snarling, Sarlat stepped toward him and swung the other revolver. It crashed into Scratch's head and stretched him out in the dirt of the alley. He tasted that dirt in his mouth for a second before he passed out . . .

If despair had a taste, that would be it, he thought as everything faded away.

Getting knocked out twice in less than twenty-four hours must have addled his brain. When he woke up, Scratch would have sworn that he heard angels singing.

No, it wasn't a song, he realized after a moment.

But it *was* a woman's voice, and her words had an almost lullaby-like sound as she repeated, "Please don't be dead, please don't be dead."

"I ain't," Scratch said in a raspy whisper as he forced his eyes open. "Nobody who's dead would hurt this much."

Lauralee Parker leaned over him, and the firelight playing over her features made her beautiful despite the lines of strain visible on her face. Maybe he'd been right the first time, thought Scratch. Maybe he *had* heard an angel.

"You're alive," she said in obvious relief.

"Yeah," Scratch said. He tried to move his arms and found that he couldn't. He was tied up again, this time with the bonds around his wrists, holding his arms behind his back. "Help me sit up."

Lauralee looked at someone else.

"Go ahead," Professor Sarlat said. "I hardly think Mr. Morton represents much of a threat anymore."

You go ahead and believe that, old son, Scratch thought. *When I get loose, you'll find out different in a hell of a hurry.*

Lauralee put an arm around Scratch's shoulders and lifted him to a sitting position. He saw that they were on the floor inside the cabin, leaning against the wall not far from the fireplace. He felt the warmth from the crackling flames on his face. A bubble of sap popped every now and then as the chunks of firewood burned.

Sarlat sat at the table, but his chair was turned so that he could stretch his legs out in front of him in an indolent pose, crossed at the ankles. Jake was in the chair on the other side of the table, still looking upset.

Sarlat went on, "By now the lovely Veronique will have used her considerable talents as a thespian to discover that poor Miss Parker has been dragged out of her bed, brutally assaulted, and kidnapped by none other than the Butcher of Bear Creek, plunging the town into a frenzy. She will have sent the remaining men on the proverbial wild goose chase by loudly proclaiming that she saw the miscreant fleeing with his captive to the west. They'll beat the hills in that direction all night in a vain quest to rescue the fair damsel."

Scratch said coldly, "I ain't sure I've ever run into an hombre as much in love with the sound of his own voice as you, Sarlat."

"You're merely jealous of my erudition, old boy."

"You can take your erudition, whatever that is, and stick it up your—"

Sarlat reached over and put his hand on the ivory butt of the Remington that lay on the table beside him.

"Need I remind you that I don't actually need you alive any longer, either of you?" he said.

"Then why are we still alive?" Scratch asked.

Sarlat glanced at Jake, making Scratch wonder if

Jake had pleaded for their lives. Clearly, Sarlat had manipulated Jake into committing terrible acts of violence in the past, but Jake seemed to be getting a little balky about that, from what Scratch had seen and heard tonight.

"Jake, why don't you go out and see about the horses?" the professor suggested.

"They're fine," Jake said sullenly.

"I'm sure they are, but you know you like them, and they like you. There's no reason you shouldn't enjoy each other's company. Just don't wander off, all right? Stay near the cabin."

For a moment Jake looked like he might argue some more, but then he put his hands on the table and pushed himself to his feet.

"I like the horses," he said. "They're nice. And they like me."

"Of course they do." Sarlat smiled indulgently. "Go on now."

Jake left the cabin. Sarlat turned his attention back to Scratch and Lauralee.

"I thought you might like to hear the truth about who Jake really is and what we're doing here," he said.

"In other words, you want to gloat," Scratch snapped.

"Why complain, if it keeps you alive a while longer?"

He had a point there, Scratch supposed. And

there was no denying that he was curious as all get-out about Jake's true identity and what had brought them all here together around Bear Creek.

Besides, Bo was out there on the loose somewhere. One of the first things Scratch had noticed when he regained consciousness was that Barney Dunn was gone. He had no doubt that Bo had followed the bartender, but depending on what had happened, Bo might show up here again at any time. That would make a big difference.

"All right," Scratch said. "If you've got a yarn to spin, go ahead and spin it."

"Where should I begin?" Sarlat asked, still smirking. "With the most obvious question, I suppose. Just who is Jake?" The professor sat up straighter in his chair, clearly enjoying himself. "The answer is simple. Jake is your friend Bo Creel's twin brother."

CHAPTER 28

For a long moment, Scratch could only stare at Sarlat. Finally he said, "Now I know for sure that you're loco. Bo doesn't have a twin brother. Never did."

"Not that he knows about," Sarlat insisted. "The story goes back many, many years, my friend—"

"I ain't your friend."

"You'd be wise not to interrupt me again," Sarlat said, his eyes narrowing in anger. "Listening to this story is keeping you alive, after all."

Lauralee said, "Go ahead, mister. I'd like to know what you're talking about. I've known Bo for years, and I never heard him say anything about a twin brother, only the younger ones who live on the Star C."

"As I said, Creel isn't aware of any of this. It all happened when he was too young to remember it. How old do you think I am?"

The question took Scratch by surprise. He

frowned and said, "About as old as me, I reckon. Maybe a little older."

"If you're roughly the same age as your friend, then I'm more than twenty years older," Sarlat said. "I attribute my youthful appearance to many years of consuming the same tonic that I sell from my wagon. It revives and restores the body."

Scratch found that hard to believe, but he didn't argue with Sarlat. As good as that tonic had made him feel, maybe the professor was right . . . about that, anyway.

"At any rate," Sarlat continued, "as a young man I actually was a medical doctor. I practiced in Arkansas. In those days, Texas was still part of Mexico, and American settlers from Tennessee who were bound for Texas often passed through the area where I lived. One day such a family of would-be colonists sought me out. A man, his wife, and their twin, infant sons, one of whom was very ill with a terrible fever. The child was doomed, in my opinion. There was no way he could recover. When I broke the news to the poor parents, the mother was horribly distraught, as you can imagine. She told her husband that she couldn't bear to watch one of her sons die. In the spirit of generosity, I offered to care for the boy until he passed on and then see that he was properly laid to rest. In an attempt to make the best of these tragic circumstances, the father agreed, and the family moved on."

"I don't believe it," Scratch said, unable to hold

the reaction in any longer. "John Creel never would've done such a thing. He wouldn't have abandoned his own flesh and blood."

"He did," Sarlat insisted. "He did it to spare his wife's feelings and blunt the pain of her loss. The Creels left their son Jake with me and moved on to Texas with the other boy, your friend Bo. Before they drove off in their wagon, I heard Creel tell his wife that they would never speak of Jake again. Bo would be raised never knowing that he'd had a brother." Sarlat shrugged. "I think that perhaps Mrs. Creel wasn't very stable, emotionally or mentally, and that was the only way her husband thought he could prevent her from suffering a complete breakdown."

"What an awful thing she must have gone through," Lauralee said. "She must have thought about that lost child every day for the rest of her life."

Sarlat said, "I have no way of knowing about that. What I do know is that Jake stubbornly clung to life for several days, and then something miraculous occurred. The fever broke, and he began to recover."

"How come you didn't send word to his folks, so they could come back and get him?" Scratch asked.

"How was I going to find them? They'd gone off to the wilds of Texas. And I'll admit, I was perhaps a bit selfish in the decision I reached. I had no wife, no prospects for children. And I became quite fond of Jake right away. It didn't seem *that* bad for me to keep him and raise him as my own."

"Was he . . . was he always like he is now?" Lauralee asked.

Sarlat nodded solemnly.

"Yes. The high fever must have damaged his brain. It wasn't apparent at first because he was so young, but as he grew older I began to see signs that something was wrong. Learning was a great struggle for him, and he never was able to grasp some of the things that normal children could. I asked myself sometimes if it was possible that Jake was being punished for my sins, but then I realized that I had done nothing wrong. I simply tried to help his family in the only way I could."

Scratch's voice was hard as flint as he said, "Until you turned him into a killer."

"That came much later," Sarlat snapped. "Jake had as normal a childhood as I could give him. He grew into a young man. We would have stayed there and lived out our lives, but then . . . an elderly patient of mine died, and some money that belonged to him went missing—"

"You mean you stole it."

"I told you about interrupting me. Don't try my patience, Morton."

Lauralee said, "Go on with the story, Professor. We're listening."

Sarlat smoothed a hand down his frock coat and said, "Very well. That incident raised questions about me and some of the other patients I'd been unable to save, and with all the suspicion and speculation swirling about, I thought it might be best if Jake and I left and made a fresh start somewhere else."

In other words, they'd gotten out of town one jump ahead of a mob once folks figured out that Sarlat was filching his patients' money and letting them die . . . or maybe even easing them out of this world and into the next. Scratch wouldn't put that past the varmint for a second.

"I decided to put my medical abilities to good use," Sarlat went on, "and started selling the elixir I'd developed for my own use. We did that for a number of years, traveling around mostly in the South. I feel like I was actually doing good work, helping people with my elixir."

"Why didn't you just keep sellin' it?" Scratch asked. "You must've made decent money at it."

"Decent, yes, but I always felt that I could do better."

"Where did that French girl come from?" Lauralee wanted to know.

Sarlat smiled.

"Ah, the lovely Veronique," he said. "I first encountered her almost ten years ago in Louisiana. She was barely more than a child, but her mother, who was something of an opium fiend, had sold her to a house of ill repute in New Orleans. As you can imagine, she was quite popular with the degenerates there. I took pity on her. With Jake's help, I stole her. We took her out of there and gave her a new life."

"Travelin' with a medicine show," Scratch said.

"Which was infinitely better than the existence to which she was doomed if she had stayed where she was," Sarlat said, his voice hardening with anger. "I helped her, just like I helped Jake."

"Maybe you just wanted her for yourself."

Sarlat's face flushed even darker. He insisted, "I've never laid a lustful finger on the girl. You can ask her yourself if you don't believe me." He laughed coldly. "If you're still alive when she gets back here, that is."

Scratch didn't see any point in pressing the issue. He said, "How'd the rest of it come about? The killings and whatever else it is you've got in mind for Bear Creek?"

"The three of us fell in with a band of desperadoes. They would have just robbed us, killed Jake and myself, and had their sport with Veronique before murdering her, as well, if I hadn't come up with a way to make them into allies instead of enemies. Their leader is a man named Deuce Ramsey. Perhaps you've heard of him."

"No, but I don't know every two-bit owlhoot west of the Mississippi."

"Ramsey may be a two-bit owlhoot, as you put it,

but he also possesses a keen native cunning. He saw that the plan I put together could be successful. If we could come up with a way to leave a town defenseless, it would be easy for him and his men to ride in and clean out the banks, the stores, the saloons, and all the other business establishments. They could sack the town like vandals of old."

"And the easiest way to get all the men out of town was to lure 'em off on a wild goose chase after a crazy killer," Scratch guessed.

"Exactly. All it took in each town was a series of killings to stir up the population, and when the hysteria reached a peak, then a carefully selected confederate of mine, one of the locals who was trusted by the citizens, would find a way to send them all thundering off in a posse on the trail of the man who had been murdering their saloon girls and prostitutes."

"Barney?" Lauralee asked in amazement. "You're saying that Barney Dunn was working with you?"

Sarlat threw his head back and laughed in genuine amusement this time.

"Yes, Barney had you all fooled. I came into town several months ago in disguise and looked around, cultivating acquaintances until I found someone suitable to recruit for my plan. You may not realize this about him, Miss Parker, but Barney is a very greedy man. He's also desperate to return to his life in the East. He considers the frontier . . . uncivilized."

"I can't believe it," Lauralee muttered. "I always treated him decent. And then he goes and throws in with the likes of you."

"I'll allow that not-so-veiled insult to pass," Sarlat said. "Barney cooperated splendidly. He told the story I wanted him to tell with absolute conviction. His artistic ability was an unexpected bonus. Usually all people had to go by was a description of the killer. Barney provided them with visual evidence, as well."

"He drew a picture of Jake," Scratch said, "but then somebody said it looked just like Bo Creel." He frowned. "I don't get it. Did you come to Bear Creek knowin' that it was Bo's hometown?"

"That was sheer happenstance. The sort of turn of fate that most people would consider a wild coincidence. But what they fail to realize is just how much of everyone's life is coincidence. A man rides down one trail instead of another and is murdered by Indians or bandits. A man walks down a different street than he usually does, sees a woman, convinces himself he's in love with her, and pursues her until they're married, when all the time a much more suitable mate might have been just around the corner if he had taken his usual route. These things happen all the time. We call them destiny or fate or the hand of God, when all that's really happening is pure dumb luck!" Sarlat laughed again, obviously pleased with his speechifying. "So to answer your question, no, I had no idea this was where the Creel family ended up. The first I heard of it was when Barney, during one of our clandestine meetings, told me about how his drawing of Jake had been identified as Bo Creel. When I heard about that, the memories of what happened in Arkansas came back to me. The situation seemed far-fetched at first glance, but I knew it had to be true. And so I set out to take advantage of it. Let everyone think that Bo Creel, one of Bear Creek's wandering sons, had returned home and set out on a murderous rampage. My plan worked just as well that way as any other."

"Until Bo and me actually rode in and Bo got himself arrested. You couldn't have planned on that."

"That was an added complication," Sarlat admitted. "Again, the sort of coincidence that seems unbelievable on the face of it, even though such things happen all the time. As I said earlier, though, I can think quite well on my feet. In fact, sometimes it seems to me that my brain works even better than usual when I'm forced to improvise, as I was on this occasion. I was prepared to deal with your presence."

"Then Bo went and got himself locked up. You couldn't have that, because with the killer in jail, there wouldn't be a posse to go hellin' off after him. That's why you offered to help me bust him out."

"Indeed," Sarlat agreed with a nod. "With the way

that fellow Fontaine was stirring up the town, I knew most of the men would stampede out of Bear Creek on Bo Creel's trail if he got away. The arrival of Creel's family was simply a stroke of good fortune that made his escape even easier."

"You didn't arrange for 'em to show up when they did?" Scratch asked.

"I had nothing to do with it. But I didn't hesitate to take advantage of the development, either."

"That wasn't enough for you, though. There were still enough men in the settlement to put up a fight when your outlaw pards rode in. So you cooked up this deal with Lauralee to get rid of them, too."

Sarlat inclined his head in acknowledgment of Scratch's statement.

"There's one thing I don't understand. If you didn't know Bo lived around here, why did that bartender draw a picture of Jake? Why would you want him identified as the killer?" Scratch asked Sarlat.

"That was a misunderstanding. Jake had seen Barney drawing one day and he asked him to draw a picture of him. Barney had it at the bar working on it when someone saw it and thought he was drawing the killer and someone else identified it as Bo. After that it all snowballed, so Barney went along with the idea that the drawing was of the Butcher." Sarlat paused. "And now you know everything." He reached out and picked up the gun from the table beside him. "I bear you no ill will,

Mr. Morton, and none toward the lady, either. But now that you've heard my story, it serves no purpose to keep you alive. Regrettable, but true."

He pointed the Remington at them and pulled back the hammer. It made a sinister metallic ratcheting that sounded like death.

CHAPTER 29

Bitterly disappointed that he wasn't going to be able to question Barney Dunn, Bo loaded the bartender's body on Dunn's horse. There was nothing left for him to do except follow Scratch and the medicine show wagon back to Bear Creek. Bo fetched his own horse and set off toward the settlement, leading Dunn's mount with its grim burden.

He was only about halfway there when he heard hoofbeats in the night. They sounded like quite a few riders were coming toward him in the darkness, so he pulled off to the side and rode into a grove of oaks. The trees were putting on their spring growth, so the leaves cast thick shadows that concealed Bo, the two horses, and Dunn's body.

The riders were coming from the north, instead of from the settlement. Could the posse have circled around after all, Bo wondered, instead of continuing west like he and Scratch had expected?

As the men on horseback came closer, Bo began

hearing voices mixed in with the hoofbeats. His eyes narrowed in the darkness as he realized there was something familiar about them. After a moment he heard a raspy growl that he knew as well as his own voice, and when he did, he took a chance and heeled his horse into motion, riding out of the trees to intercept the men.

They reined in sharply and Bo heard startled exclamations, along with the unmistakable sound of guns being cocked. He called, "Hold your fire. It's me."

"Bo!" John Creel said. "Is that you?"

Bo walked his horse closer to the dozen or so riders.

"Yeah, it's me," he said again. "Good to see you again, Pa . . . even though I can't see you very well right now. I reckon that's the rest of the boys with you."

Bo's youngest brother, Hank, said, "We've been looking for you all night, Bo. We figured you were too smart to keep heading west, so we let the posse go on that way and circled back around here."

"Have you seen Scratch and that medicine show wagon from town?"

Riley said, "We haven't seen anybody. What medicine show wagon?"

"It doesn't matter now," Bo told him.

John said, "That looks like a carcass on that horse you're leadin', Bo. I'm glad to know it ain't Scratch. Who is it?"

"Barney Dunn, one of the bartenders from the Southern Belle."

"The one who identified you as the Bear Creek Butcher," Cooper said.

"Did you kill him?" Riley asked tightly.

"Blast it, you ought to know better than that," John snapped.

Bo said, "No, I didn't kill him. He was trying to get away from me and wound up being dragged by his horse. His neck broke. But that didn't happen until after Scratch and I found out he's been working with the folks who are really behind all this trouble."

"Who's that?" Hank asked, his voice eager.

"Professor Sarlat from the medicine show and his assistant. And one other man." Bo paused, and when he resumed, his voice was flat and hard. "Pa, I'm going to ask you a question, and I want an honest answer. Have I got a twin brother somewhere I don't know about?"

"What the hell kind of a—" John Creel began angrily, but then he stopped short and sighed. "You had a twin brother, Bo, but he died more than fifty years ago."

Those words struck Bo like a physical blow. He had spent his entire life never knowing that someone so close to him had even existed. It was a painful discovery, and the sense of loss that washed through him was powerful. He heard his brothers exclaim in surprise, too.

"How come none of us ever knew about this, Pa?" Riley demanded.

"Your mother didn't want to speak of it," John replied harshly. "She didn't want to hear anybody else talking about it, either. You know how she was. Any time there was something that might hurt her, she . . . she just sort of pretended that it didn't exist. So I got in the habit of doin' that, too, where the boy was concerned."

"You mean Jake?" Bo asked.

John stiffened in the saddle, and even in the dim light, Bo could tell that his father was staring at him in shock and amazement.

"How'd you know that was his name?" John asked after a few stunned seconds.

"Because he's still alive. I don't know what happened back then or why you were convinced he was dead, but he's not. He's alive, and he looks just like me." Bo hesitated. "But he's not right in the head. He's a grown man on the outside, but I think he's not much more than a little kid on the inside. That's why Sarlat's been able to tell him what to do, even when it meant hurting those saloon girls."

"My God." John Creel took off his black Stetson and passed a trembling hand over his face. "My God. It can't be. He was dyin'. The doctor in Arkansas told us he was, when we were on our way here to settle in Texas." John waved at his other sons. "None of these boys was born yet. There were just the two of you. Our firstborn. And . . . and poor little Jake was dyin' . . ."

Bo had never seen his father this shaken. John Creel had always been a rock, as sturdy and unchanging as a mountain. Obviously, though, this news had pierced him all the way to the heart.

Riley said, "I'm not making sense of any of this. But if you've seen this fella with your own eyes, Bo, I reckon we have to believe you. And that means you didn't kill those girls after all."

"I'm glad you can finally admit that," Bo said. "But if you still believed that, why did you come to town tonight to help Scratch break me out of jail?"

"We didn't come for that," Cooper said. "We found out about that hearing where Judge Buchanan said you had to be taken to Hallettsville to stand trial there. Nobody had the decency to let us know about it beforehand. Hank said we ought to go see you before they took you away. He talked us into it."

"Shamed them into it, is what he means," Hank put in. "I just said that no matter what you'd done, you were still our brother and we ought to stand by you. We wanted to find out if there was anything we could do to help . . . but by the time we got to Bear Creek, all hell was breaking loose."

Riley said, "I'm glad you got out of that jail when you did, Bo. You don't deserve to hang for something you didn't do. But what are you going to do now?"

"Scratch and I found the cabin Sarlat's been using as a hideout," Bo explained. "I don't know exactly what he's up to, but I think it's all coming to a head tonight. Scratch followed the medicine show wagon back to Bear Creek, while I tried to grab Dunn and ask him some questions. That didn't work out, though—" Bo inclined his head toward the corpse draped over the saddle of Dunn's horse. "So I was headed for the settlement to join up with Scratch again when I heard you fellas coming. I reckon now you know just as much as I do."

"I never saw a murkier mess in all my borned days," John said. "I reckon we'll all head for town and try to straighten it out."

Bo nodded, feeling warmth spread through him as he realized he was back with his family and they were on his side this time. He didn't know what they would find in Bear Creek, but he was confident that as long as they were together, the Creels could handle it.

One of the ranch hands took charge of leading the horse carrying Dunn's body. As they rode toward the settlement, John told Bo about what had happened in Arkansas, all those years ago. Bo could tell how difficult that was for his father, how painful those memories were, but as John said before he started the story: "You got a right to know."

Bo could tell, as well, that he wasn't the only one

listening intently. His brothers had a stake in this, too, because it involved their family, and Pete Hendry and the other Star C riders who had come along tonight were drawn in by John's explanation, too, by the simple human drama of the events the old cattleman was relating.

"So I'm thinkin'," John said as the tale drew to a close, "this medicine show professor you were talkin' about . . . what was his name again?"

"Sarlat," Bo said. "Thaddeus Sarlat."

John shook his head.

"That wasn't the doctor's name, up yonder in Arkansas, but I'll bet a hat it's the same fella. Has to be. An hombre low-down enough to keep somebody else's child like that wouldn't be bothered by changin' his name if it suited his purposes." John looked over at Bo. "You got to believe me, we never would've left Jake with him like that if he hadn't told us there was no chance the boy would live. I figured Jake wouldn't make it through the night, to tell you the truth, and I was afraid that when he passed, your ma might just give up and die, too, if she had to see it. So we ran out on him. Ain't no other way to look at it. And it's haunted me damn near every day since then. I swore to myself that I'd do the very best job I could raisin' the rest of you boys, to sort of make up for lettin' Jake down that way."

"You were trying to protect Ma," Bo said. "You

were doing the best you could at the time. I don't think you let anybody down."

"I appreciate the sentiment, son. But I'll wear my own scars."

Everyone did, Bo thought. That was the way of the world.

As they neared the settlement, Bo saw that a lot of lights were burning in windows. He said, "We'd better hold up a minute, Pa. Looks like something is going on in town."

"Maybe the posse's back," Riley suggested. "They could have realized they weren't going to catch you and Scratch."

"Could be," Bo said. "Why don't I go take a look? The rest of you stay here while I scout around."

"Are you sure that's smart?" Hank asked. "After all, you're the one they're looking for, Bo, not us."

"Although we sort of had to light a shuck in a hurry," Cooper added. "Ned Fontaine and his boys weren't too happy with us when we ruined their plans for a necktie party."

"I wanted to stay and shoot it out with the bastards," John rasped, "but they had us outnumbered too bad. Mark my words, there's a showdown comin' with the Fontaines, but it'll have to wait for another day."

Bo said, "So it might be just as dangerous for the rest of you to ride into town right now as it would be for me. I'm the one at the center of all this ruckus, even if it wasn't my idea, so I ought to run the risk."

"You got that Creel stubbornness in you, that's for sure," John said. "All right, go ahead, but we'll be close by. If you run into trouble, fire some shots and we'll come a-runnin'."

"Fine," Bo said. He heeled his horse into a trot toward the settlement, leaving the others waiting behind him in the dark.

Over the years, he and Scratch had been in many tight spots where their ability to move stealthily through the darkness without being detected was the only thing that had saved their lives. Bo put that skill to work now as he approached Bear Creek. When he was a couple of hundred yards away from the buildings on the eastern edge of town, he dismounted and left his horse there to move closer on foot.

Something was definitely going on. In addition to seeing more lights than should have been burning at this time of night, he heard loud, angry voices. He had no doubt that Sarlat and Veronique were responsible for whatever was happening, and it wouldn't have surprised him to find Scratch in the middle of it, too.

He slipped along the narrow passage between a couple of buildings and crouched at the corner of one of them where he risked a glance into the street. A large group of men stood in front of the Southern Belle. Some of them carried torches, and by their flickering light, Bo recognized many of the faces. They belonged to citizens of Bear Creek. Bo didn't see Marshal Haltom or any of the bunch from the Rafter F, though, so he guessed the men in this group were the ones who hadn't gone with the posse to chase after him and Scratch.

The beautiful redhead standing on the saloon's porch was familiar, too, although Bo had seen her only once. She was Veronique Ballantine, Professor Sarlat's assistant . . . and his partner in crime. She held up a hand and motioned for quiet, and when that didn't work she thrust something in the air above her head. Bo's hands tightened on the Winchester he held as he realized it was some sort of garment heavily stained with blood.

"This is all I found of poor Lauralee," Veronique said as the sight of the bloody dress shocked the men into silence. "M'sieu Creel must have eluded the posse and returned here to exact his vengeance on her for some reason unknown to me. But this time he has taken his victim's body with him! Perhaps she is still alive!"

Bo wanted to step out into the open and deny that awful charge, but he knew better than to risk it. The crowd was so worked up they wouldn't listen to any explanations from him, and a number of the men carried rifles and shotguns. Chances were that they would open up on him and blow him to pieces before he could say much of anything.

He felt cold and sick inside at the thought that

something had happened to Lauralee Parker. He had never known a sweeter, kinder young woman than her. The only conclusion he could draw was that Sarlat had brought Jake back here and forced him to kill Lauralee, then left Veronique behind to whip everybody who was left in town into a frenzy. But why go to that much trouble?

An answer suggested itself to Bo when Veronique went on, "I heard a horse going south just before I discovered that my friend Lauralee had vanished. Creel must be taking her to his family's ranch. It is probably too late to save her, my friends, but you must try."

A man in the crowd shouted, "The gal's right! Everybody get a horse and a gun! We're headed for the Star C!"

They wouldn't find anybody there except some of the hands who wouldn't have any idea what was going on, thought Bo. He hoped that nobody would get too itchy of a trigger finger and start shooting. Again he thought about revealing himself in the hope of heading off further trouble, but he knew he couldn't do that just yet.

Sarlat and Jake wouldn't have taken Lauralee to the Star C, that was for sure. More than likely they had headed back to that cabin east of town with her. That was where Bo and his family and the Star C punchers would go, too, in an attempt to catch up to Sarlat and bring him to justice.

But where in blazes was Scratch? He ought to be

around here somewhere, Bo told himself. He would wait a little longer, let the second posse of the night rush out of Bear Creek on a fool's errand, and then take a better look around the settlement for his partner.

Maybe he could nab Veronique, too. She might make a good bargaining chip if they had to lay siege to the cabin.

The group of townsmen split up, but it didn't take long for them to round up their horses and guns and get together again to gallop out of town to the south, more than three dozen men heading for the Star C. That probably didn't leave very many able-bodied men in the settlement, Bo thought as he watched from the eastern side of the creek, which must have been what Sarlat was after all along.

Bo had lost track of Veronique during the confusion of the new posse forming, but he assumed she was still around somewhere. The first place to look was the medicine show wagon. Once things had quieted down, he trotted across the bridge and swung into Main Street, which was now deserted.

Along the way he kept an eye out for Scratch and paused several times to give the call of a hoot owl, a signal that he and his trail partner used on occasion. So far there had been no response, no sign of Scratch, which was pretty worrisome.

Bo stopped as he realized the medicine show wagon wasn't parked next to the public well, where it had been earlier. He looked up and down the street and didn't see the vehicle anywhere.

But he heard the querulous voice of the elderly hostler at the livery stable as the old man called, "Hey, you can't . . . Come back here, dadgummit!"

A figure on horseback galloped out the front of the stable, where one of the big doors stood open. The rider turned to come toward Bo, who spotted long red hair flying in the wind. Veronique must have stolen a horse from the stable and was trying to get out of Bear Creek now that she had finished her work here, Bo thought.

He didn't want that to happen.

He drew back into the shadow of an alley mouth and waited in the darkness, timing his move until Veronique had almost reached him. Then he lunged out, reached up, and wrapped an arm around her to jerk her out of the saddle. She yelped in surprise and flailed at him as he swung her around and dropped her to the ground.

When she got a look at him, she exclaimed, "Jake!" then tried to scramble away as she realized her mistake. Bo leaned down and caught hold of her ankle. She kicked at him, but he blocked the blow with the rifle.

"Take it easy, miss," he told her. "I don't want to hurt you."

"Let me go!" she panted. "I'll scream! I'll tell everyone the Bear Creek Butcher has got me!"

"Who are you going to tell?" Bo asked. "The town's almost empty, at least as far as anybody who could help you goes. You sent them all away to look for me." He paused. "And for Lauralee Parker. So help me, if you people have hurt her—"

He stopped short as he heard something unexpected. It sounded almost like the rumble of distant thunder, but the sky was clear tonight. Those were hoofbeats, Bo thought, the hoofbeats of a dozen or more horses. A large group of riders was approaching the settlement, from the north this time so it couldn't be the bunch that had ridden out a few minutes earlier.

Veronique sneered up at him from the ground and said, "Now you will wish you had kept running."

The riders swept into town. Veronique leaped to her feet and ran. Bo let her go. He swung to face the newcomers, and as he did he saw moonlight reflecting from the barrels of their guns.

Now it all made sense. Those heavily armed strangers galloping toward him were outlaws, and they had to be working with Sarlat. The professor had orchestrated events so that the town was sitting there defenseless, with no one to stop them from coming in and cleaning it out.

No one, that is, except him . . . the man Bear Creek had turned on and declared a monster and a killer.

One of the raiders spotted him and yelled a warning. Guns began to roar. Muzzle flame split the night.

Holding the Winchester at his hip, Bo opened fire.

CHAPTER 30

He didn't stay where he was. He made too good a target out in the open. After cranking off four rounds as fast as he could work the rifle's lever, he turned and sprinted for the nearest cover, which was an alcove on the front of one of the buildings where the business's entrance was located.

Bo leaped onto the boardwalk and ducked into the opening, then thrust the Winchester's barrel around the corner and continued firing. His shots had caused the gang's charge to break up a little. Several of the riders milled around, obviously confused because they hadn't expected anybody to put up a fight.

There were at least two dozen of them, though, which meant the odds against Bo were overwhelming. He might manage to hold them off for a few minutes, but that was all.

It might be enough.

He traded shots with the outlaws, a fast exchange

of lead that sent splinters flying into the air as bullets chewed into the building's walls around Bo. He felt one of the sharp slivers sting his cheek but ignored the pain. He had to keep the raiders occupied for just a little longer . . .

John Creel and the crew from the Star C came boiling off the end of the bridge with guns blazing and smashed into the outlaws from the side. Instantly the street was a scene of chaos with revolvers roaring, horses smashing into each other, and men crying out as slugs tore into them. John and his sons and his ranch hands didn't have any way of knowing who they were fighting, but from the way the raiders had galloped in and started shooting up the town, they knew the men were up to no good.

Bo darted out of the alcove and raced toward the battle. He spotted his father as John Creel fought to keep his wheeling horse under control. At the same time, the gun in John's hand leaped and spat fire as he triggered at the outlaws.

Bo saw one of the raiders driving in behind his father and snapped the rifle to his shoulder. It cracked and sent a bullet ripping through the outlaw's body. The man flung his arms in the air and toppled loosely out of the saddle, landing in the limp sprawl that signified death.

John yanked his horse around, saw his oldest son, and shouted, "Bo!"

Then he jerked and sagged forward, and Bo knew he'd been hit.

"Pa!"

Bo moved even faster, racing to catch his father as John fell. He got an arm around John, whose weight drove Bo to one knee. One of the outlaws bore down on them.

Bo lifted the rifle and fired it one-handed, blowing the man backward out of the saddle. Then he dropped the Winchester and put both arms around his father.

"Pa, how bad are you hit?" he asked over the roar of gunfire.

"I'm all right, damn it!" John insisted. He had managed to hang on to his pistol. He pressed it into Bo's hand and went on, "Shoot some more of those sons of bitches!"

Bo did what his father told him, kneeling there and holding John up as he aimed the Colt and fired until the weapon was empty. His deadly accurate shots dropped several more of the raiders.

The shooting began to die out. The Star C crew had been outnumbered, but they had taken the outlaws completely by surprise and inflicted a great deal of damage in the opening seconds of the battle. They had the upper hand now, and the remaining outlaws started to surrender. The ones who didn't throw down their guns were blasted off their horses in short order.

Riley, Cooper, and Hank galloped over to Bo and

John. Bo's brothers threw themselves out of their saddles and rushed up.

"Pa!" Riley cried.

"How bad is he hurt?" Cooper asked.

John said, "I'm fine, blast it. Got a little graze in my side. Now one of you scoundrels help your old pappy up, why don't you?"

Hank and Cooper took hold of John's arms and lifted him to his feet. Riley pulled up his father's shirt to examine the wound and agreed that while it looked messy, it really wasn't that bad.

Pete Hendry came over and reported, "We've got five prisoners, boss. The rest of that bunch are either dead or hurt too bad to give us any trouble. Who are they, anyway?"

"Better ask Bo about that," John said. "This is his fandango."

"Well," Bo said, "I'm not exactly sure."

"Not sure!" Riley exclaimed. "Good Lord! We fight a pitched gun battle with a bunch of men and kill a lot of them, and you don't even know who they are? The law may be after all of us now, not just you!"

"I don't know exactly who they are," Bo went on, "but I'm pretty sure they were here to raid the town and clean out the bank and all the businesses."

"Pretty sure?" Cooper said.

"Give your brother the benefit of the doubt," John snapped. "Although not many folks around here have done that lately, including some of my own kinfolks, I'm ashamed to say!"

"Everybody just take it easy," Bo said. "Hank, see if you can patch up that wound in Pa's side. Were any of our men killed or badly wounded?"

Hendry said, "We've got a few ventilated, but not too bad. All of 'em can ride except one or two."

"Good," Bo said. "Because I know where we can find the answers to the rest of everybody's questions."

Scratch tensed his muscles, preparing to throw himself in front of Lauralee and shield her body with his own. He wasn't sure how much good that would do, but since she wasn't tied up, maybe it would give her a chance to make it to her feet. She could rush Sarlat and try to wrestle the gun away from him.

Before the professor could fire, Jake leaped up and said, "Pa, no! We don't need to kill anybody else!"

"You don't know what we need to do, Jake," Sarlat snapped. "Now sit down and be quiet. You don't have to hurt anyone. I'll take care of this."

"If I let you hurt them . . . it's the same thing as me doin' it," Jake insisted.

"That's enough! If you don't want to sit down,

then go outside. That might be better anyway. There's no need for you to see this."

With a sullen expression on his face, Jake started around the table toward the door. Sarlat had lowered the Remington slightly while he was talking to Jake, but now he raised it again.

Jake tackled him from behind.

The impact made Sarlat's arm jerk up, so when he pulled the trigger the bullet went into the cabin's roof. The gun's roar was deafeningly loud in the close quarters, but Scratch heard Jake cry, "No! Nobody else gets hurt!"

Sarlat screamed curses and writhed around, slashing at Jake with the gun barrel. The sight raked across Jake's cheek and left a bloody welt behind it.

"Get away from me!" Sarlat yelled. He chopped at Jake with the Remington. "Let go of me, you damned idiot!"

"Stop it, Pa!" Jake shouted right back at him. "Don't make me hurt you!"

Scratch and Lauralee watched in horrified fascination as Sarlat and his adopted son struggled, knowing that Jake was the only thing keeping them alive right now. Jake was taller and heavier and younger than Sarlat, despite the professor's so-called extra vitality from his elixir. Scratch could tell that it wouldn't take long for Jake to overpower Sarlat.

Then Sarlat jabbed the gun into Jake's body and pulled the trigger again.

The explosion was muffled. Jake staggered back, blood springing out on his shirt. He stared at Sarlat in disbelief and said in a hollow voice, "Pa . . . you hurt me."

"You've been giving me too much trouble lately, anyway," Sarlat snarled. "The last thing I need is an idiot with a conscience. It's time to move on—"

Jake righted himself and sprang toward Sarlat again. The professor screamed a curse and jerked the trigger twice more. The slugs pounded into Jake's body but couldn't stop him. He smashed into Sarlat and bent him back over the table as his fingers closed around the professor's throat.

Sarlat hammered at Jake with the gun, but nothing was going to budge Jake's fingers now. They were locked around Sarlat's throat like bands of iron. Scratch was barely breathing as he watched Sarlat's face turn purple and then blue. The professor's feet came up off the puncheon floor and kicked spasmodically. Finally, after a long, horrible couple of minutes that seemed even longer, Sarlat's body went limp. The Remington slipped from nerveless fingers and thudded to the floor.

Jake gave a slow, ponderous shake of his head and gazed down into the professor's wide, sightlessly staring eyes.

"Pa?" he whispered. "Are you gonna stop fightin' now, Pa? Are you gonna stop . . . hurtin' people . . ."

Jake tried to straighten up, but he collapsed onto the table next to the professor and then rolled off, falling on the floor. The front of his shirt was sodden with blood.

Lauralee buried her face against Scratch's shoulder and sobbed.

"He . . . he saved us," she got out.

"That he did," Scratch said in an awed voice. "I don't know if it makes up for all the bad things he done . . . but it's a start."

Normally he would have let Lauralee cry it out, but Bear Creek was still in danger from that raid by Deuce Ramsey's gang. After a few seconds Scratch went on, "You better untie me now, and we'll round up some horses so we can light a shuck for town."

With tears still running down her face, Lauralee nodded. She started to stand up.

That was when they heard the swift rataplan of hoofbeats coming from outside.

Bo kicked his horse into an even faster run when he heard the shots coming from somewhere up ahead. That was somewhere around the cabin where he hoped to find Scratch, he thought. The shots made him even more certain that his friend was there, and up to his neck in trouble, as usual.

Close behind Bo came the rest of his family, even John Creel, who had a makeshift bandage wrapped around his torso. They thundered up to the cabin. Bo was out of the saddle even before his horse stopped moving.

His father's Colt was in his hand, ready to roar, as he kicked the door open.

The sight that greeted him was totally unexpected. Scratch and Lauralee were sitting on the floor near the fireplace, apparently unhurt. From the way Scratch's arms were pulled back, Bo could tell that his wrists were tied up. For some reason, Lauralee was wearing Scratch's buckskin jacket, and that appeared to be all.

The really amazing sight, though, was Professor Thaddeus Sarlat's body lying on the table, his face a mottled blue, his tongue protruding, and his eyes bugged out. He was dead, beyond a doubt.

Lying on the floor beside the table was Jake, the front of his shirt soaked with blood where he had been shot several times. Jake . . .

Bo's brother.

"He saved us, Bo," Scratch said hoarsely. "Killed the professor and saved our lives."

Bo took an unsteady step forward and then went to a knee beside Jake. He set the gun on the floor and reached out to lift his brother's head and cradle it in his lap.

John Creel and his other sons crowded through

the doorway. John stopped short and groaned at the sight that met his eyes, a sound that held all the pain and grief in the world.

Bo thought Jake was dead, too, but Jake's eyes opened and he stared up at his brother.

"Wh-who . . . ?" he breathed, with a rattling sound to the words that told Bo there was no hope. "You look just like . . . me."

"I'm your brother, Jake," he said. "Your real brother. And your real pa is here, too, along with your other brothers." Bo could hardly force the words out. "Your family's here, Jake. Your family's come for you."

"I . . . I didn't know . . . I thought I was alone . . ."

"Not hardly," Bo said, almost overcome by emotion. "Pa, boys . . . come here."

They all crowded around. Riley had to hold John up. John grasped Jake's hand and held it tightly.

"Son," he said. "Son."

"You're my . . . pa? My real . . . pa?"

"I am. And I've missed you so much."

"I've done . . . some bad things, Pa. I hurt . . . those women. I never really . . . meant to. Pa . . . my other pa . . . said I had to."

John nodded as tears streamed down his rugged, leathery face.

"I know. It's not your fault, son. I . . . I know you've got a good heart. I can tell by lookin' at you."

Scratch said, "He saved our lives, Mr. Creel. That boy of yours, he saved our lives."

John bent and brushed his lips over Jake's forehead. He whispered, "I know. I know he's a good boy. He's a Creel." He looked over his shoulder at his other sons. "Say hello to your brother."

Riley and Cooper and Hank leaned in, all of them crying, too, and said hello to Jake. He looked around at them in wonderment and said, "I . . . I really do have a family."

"You sure do, Jake," Bo told him. He felt the spasm that ran through his brother's body, saw the end come in Jake's eyes. But Jake was smiling now. Smiling, and at peace . . .

After a long, solemn moment, Bo eased Jake's head to the floor. Gently, he closed his brother's eyes.

"We'll lay him to rest . . . next to his ma," John rasped.

Bo nodded.

"I think they'd both like that," he said.

He got to his feet and went over to the fireplace, where Lauralee was untying Scratch.

"Are you two all right?" Bo asked anxiously.

"Yeah," Scratch said as he flexed his hands to get some feeling back in them. "Lauralee's got a cut on her neck where Sarlat took a knife to her—"

"I'll be fine," she said. She put her arms around Bo and rested her head against his chest. At the same time, Scratch put a hand on Bo's shoulder.

The three of them stood together like that for a

long moment, looking at the man lying on the floor who had been more a victim of Thaddeus Sarlat's evil than any of them.

By the time both posses came dragging back into Bear Creek the next morning, having failed to find their quarry, the Creels, along with Scratch, Lauralee, and the Star C hands, were forted up inside the jail. Pete Hendry volunteered to go out with a white flag. He came back with Marshal Jonas Haltom, who looked back and forth in astonishment between Bo, who stood grimly beside the desk, and the bodies of Jake and Sarlat, which were stretched out on blankets on the floor.

"All right," Haltom finally said heavily. "Somebody better tell me exactly what's going on here."

Once he had heard the story, Haltom nodded and went to the door, where he called to one of the possemen to go and fetch Judge Buchanan. The heavyset justice of the peace arrived quickly, and he listened to the story, too.

"The conclusion is inescapable," Buchanan declared. He nodded at Jake and went on, "This man here committed the crimes for which you were blamed, Bo. I'm dropping those charges immediately and sending word of the truth to Hallettsville, as well."

"I appreciate that, Judge," Bo said. "Believe it or not, I don't like being on the wrong side of the law."

Haltom snorted and said, "You don't seem to mind taking it into your own hands, though."

"Only when we have to because of some mule-headed star packer," Scratch drawled.

Haltom glared, but he let that pass. He asked, "Where are the bodies of those outlaws? I didn't see them when we rode in."

"They're lined up in the livery stable," Bo explained. He jerked a thumb over his shoulder. "And the survivors are locked up in your cells that aren't missing bars in the window. We've been going through that stack of reward dodgers in your desk, and we found several of them. The leader's a man named Deuce Ramsey, who's wanted from here to Dakota Territory. He's in one of the cells with a busted shoulder, so he'll live to hang."

A faint smile tugged at Haltom's mouth as he said, "You know who's really going to be upset about this?"

John Creel said, "That low-down, skulkin' coyote Ned Fontaine and his boys?"

"That's right. Having been around that sorry bunch all night, I can't say that bothers me all that much, either." Haltom rubbed at his jaw. "What about Barney Dunn?"

"Already at the undertaker's," Bo said.

"Well, hell, you've cleaned up everything, haven't you? Everybody's accounted for."

Bo shook his head and said, "Not quite."

"What do you mean?"

Scratch said, "We never found hide nor hair of Veronique Ballantine. Nobody seems to have seen her after the shootin' started."

Haltom grunted and said, "I don't reckon one girl, even a redheaded medicine show gal, can cause that much trouble."

Bo and Scratch exchanged glances. They each hoped the marshal was right about that . . .

But neither of them would be surprised if one day their trail crossed that of Veronique Ballantine again.

J. A. Johnstone on William W. Johnstone
"When the Truth Becomes Legend"

William W. Johnstone was born in southern Missouri, the youngest of four children. He was raised with strong moral and family values by his minister father, and tutored by his schoolteacher mother. Despite this, he quit school at age fifteen.

"I have the highest respect for education," he says, "but such is the folly of youth, and wanting to see the world beyond the four walls and the blackboard."

True to this vow, Bill attempted to enlist in the French Foreign Legion ("I saw Gary Cooper in *Beau Geste* when I was a kid and I thought the French Foreign Legion would be fun") but was rejected, thankfully, for being underage. Instead, he joined a traveling carnival and did all kinds of odd jobs. It was listening to the veteran carny folk, some of whom had been on the circuit since the late 1800s, telling amazing tales about their experiences which planted the storytelling seed in Bill's imagination.

"They were honest people, despite the bad reputation traveling carny shows had back then," Bill remembers. "Of course, there were exceptions. There was one guy named Picky, who got that name because he was a master pickpocket. He could steal a man's socks right off his feet without him knowing. Believe me, Picky got us chased out of more than a few towns."

After a few months of this grueling existence, Bill returned home and finished high school. Next came stints as a deputy sheriff in the Tallulah, Louisiana, Sheriff's Department, followed by a hitch in the U.S. Army. Then he began a career in radio broadcasting at KTLD in Tallulah that would last sixteen years. It was here that he fine-tuned his storytelling skills. He turned to writing in 1970, but it wouldn't be until 1979 that his first novel, *The Devil's Kiss*, was published. Thus began the full-time writing career of William W. Johnstone. He wrote horror (*The Uninvited*), thrillers (*The Last of the Dog Team*), even a romance novel or two. Then, in February 1983, *Out of the Ashes* was published. Searching for his missing family in the aftermath of a post-apocalyptic America, rebel mercenary and patriot Ben Raines is united with the civilians of the Resistance forces and moves to the forefront of a revolution for the nation's future.

Out of the Ashes was a smash. The series would continue for the next twenty years, winning Bill three generations of fans all over the world. The series was often imitated but never duplicated. "We all tried to copy *The Ashes* series," said one publishing executive, "but Bill's uncanny ability, both then and now, to predict in which direction the political winds were blowing, brought a dead-on timeliness to the table no one else could capture." *The Ashes* series would end its run with more than thirty-four books and twenty million copies in print, making it one of the most successful men's action series in American book publishing. (*The Ashes* series also, Bill notes with a touch of pride, got him on the FBI's Watch List for its less than flattering portrayal of spineless politicians and the growing power of big government over our lives, among other things. "In that respect," says collaborator J. A. Johnstone, "Bill was years ahead of his time.")

Always steps ahead of the political curve, Bill's recent thrillers, written with J. A. Johnstone, include *Vengeance Is Mine, Invasion USA, Border War, Jackknife, Remember the Alamo, Home Invasion, Phoenix Rising, The Blood of Patriots, The Bleeding Edge,* and the upcoming *Suicide Mission.*

It is with the western, though, that Bill found his greatest success and propelled him onto both the *USA Today* and the *New York Times* bestseller lists.

Bill's western series, coauthored by J. A. Johnstone, include *The Mountain Man, Matt Jensen, the*

*Last Mountain Man, Preacher, The Family Jensen,
Luke Jensen Bounty Hunter, Eagles, MacCallister*
(an *Eagles* spin-off), *Sidewinders, The Brothers
O'Brien, Sixkiller, Blood Bond, The Last Gunfighter,*
and the upcoming new series *Flintlock* and *The
Trail West.* Coming in May 2013 is the hardcover
western *Butch Cassidy, The Lost Years*.

"The Western," Bill says, "is one of the few true
art forms that is one hundred percent American. I
liken the Western as America's version of England's
Arthurian legends, like the Knights of the Round
Table, or Robin Hood and his Merry Men. Starting
with the 1902 publication of *The Virginian* by
Owen Wister, and followed by the greats like Zane
Grey, Max Brand, Ernest Haycox, and of course
Louis L'Amour, the Western has helped to shape the
cultural landscape of America.

"I'm no goggle-eyed college academic, so when
my fans ask me why the Western is as popular now
as it was a century ago, I don't offer a 200-page
thesis. Instead, I can only offer this: The Western
is honest. In this great country, which is suffering
under the yoke of political correctness, the Western
harks back to an era when justice was sure and
swift. Steal a man's horse, rustle his cattle, rob a
bank, a stagecoach, or a train, you were hunted
down and fitted with a hangman's noose. One size
fits all.

"Sure, we Westerners are prone to a little embellish-
ment and exaggeration and, I admit it, occasionally

play a little fast and loose with the facts. But we do so for a very good reason—to enhance the enjoyment of readers.

"It was Owen Wister, in *The Virginian*, who first coined the phrase *'When you call me that, smile.'* Legend has it that Wister actually heard those words spoken by a deputy sheriff in Medicine Bow, Wyoming, when another poker player called him a son of a bitch.

"Did it really happen, or is it one of those myths that have passed down from one generation to the next? I honestly don't know. But there's a line in one of my favorite Westerns of all time, *The Man Who Shot Liberty Valance*, where the newspaper editor tells the young reporter, 'When the truth becomes legend, print the legend.'

"These are the words I live by."

Turn the page for an exciting preview!

*The Jensen clan is William W. Johnstone's epic
creation—godfearing pioneers bound by blood
on an untamed and beautiful land. Once more,
Preacher, Smoke, and Matt are reunited in a clash
of cultures and a brutal all-out fight for justice . . .*

HELL TO PAY

Smoke Jensen and his adopted son Matt are
cooling their heels in Colorado when they are
called to the Dakotas. Preacher, the legendary
mountain man, is in the midst of a vicious
struggle. Someone has kidnapped a proud Indian
chief's daughter and grandchild. When the
kidnapping turns to murder and Preacher vanishes
after clashing with a ruthless Union colonel
turned railroad king, Matt sets out to infiltrate the
colonel's gang of killers. Smoke seeks out the
only honest citizens in the crooked town of
Hammerhead. It will take brave men to blow
Hammerhead wide open and force the colonel and
his gunmen on a hard ride into a killing ground.

And the Family Jensen will make sure
there is hell to pay . . .

THE FAMILY JENSEN:
Hard Ride to Hell

From *USA TODAY* BESTSELLING AUTHORS
William W. Johnstone
with J. A. Johnstone

CHAPTER 1

The two men stood facing each other. One was red, the other white, but both were tall and lean, and the stiff, wary stance in which they held themselves belied their advanced years. They were both ready for trouble, and they didn't care who knew it.

Both wore buckskins, as well, and their faces were lined and leathery from long decades spent out in the weather. Silver and white streaked their hair.

The white man had a gun belt strapped around his waist, with a holstered Colt revolver riding on each hip. His thumbs were hooked in the belt close to each holster, and you could tell by looking at him that he was ready to hook and draw. Given the necessity, his hands would flash to the well-worn walnut butts of those guns with blinding speed, especially for a man of his age.

He wasn't the only one with a menacing attitude. The Indian had his hand near the tomahawk that was thrust behind the sash at his waist. To anyone watching, it would appear that both of these men were ready to try to kill each other.

Then a grin suddenly stretched across the whiskery face of the white man, and he said, "Two Bears, you old red heathen."

"Preacher, you pale-faced scoundrel," Two Bears replied. He smiled, too, and stepped forward. The two men clasped each other in a rough embrace and slapped each other on the back.

The large group of warriors standing nearby visibly relaxed at this display of affection between the two men. For the most part, the Assiniboine had been friendly with white men for many, many years. But even so, it wasn't that common for a white man to come riding boldly into their village as the one called Preacher had done.

Some of the men smiled now, because they had known all along what was coming. The legendary mountain man Preacher, who was famous—or in some cases infamous—from one end of the frontier to the other, had been friends with their chief, Two Bears, for more than three decades, and he had visited the village on occasion in the past.

The two men hadn't always been so cordial with each other. They had started out as rivals for the affections of the beautiful Assiniboine woman Raven's Wing. For Two Bears, that rivalry had escalated to the point of bitter hostility.

All that had been put aside when it became necessary for them to join forces to rescue Raven's

Wing from a group of brutal kidnappers and gunrunners.* Since that long-ago time when they were forced to become allies, they had gradually become friends as well.

Preacher stepped back and rested his hands on Two Bears's shoulders.

"I hear that Raven's Wing has passed," he said solemnly.

"Yes, last winter," Two Bears replied with an equally grave nod. "It was her time. She left this world peacefully, with a smile on her face."

"That's good to hear," Preacher said. "I never knew a finer lady."

"I miss her. Every time the sun rises or sets, every time the wind blows, every time I hear a wolf howl or see a bird soaring through the sky, I long to be with her again. But when the day is done and we are to be together again, we will be. This I know in my heart. Until then . . ." Two Bears smiled again. "Until then I can still see her in the fine strong sons she bore me, and the daughters who have given me grandchildren." He nodded toward a young woman standing nearby, who stood with an infant in her arms. "You remember my youngest daughter, Wild-flower?"

"I do," Preacher said, "although the last time I saw her, I reckon she wasn't much bigger'n that sprout with her."

*See the novel *Preacher's Fury*.

"My grandson," Two Bears said proudly. "Little Hawk."

Preacher took off his battered, floppy-brimmed felt hat and nodded politely to the woman.

"Wildflower," he said. "It's good to see you again." He looked at the boy. "And howdy to you, too, Little Hawk."

The baby didn't respond to Preacher, of course, but he watched the mountain man with huge, dark eyes.

"He has not seen that many white men in his life," Two Bears said. "You look strange, even to one so young."

Preacher snorted and said, "If it wasn't for this beard of mine, I'd look just about as much like an Injun as any of you do."

Two Bears half-turned and motioned to one of the lodges.

"Come. We will go to my lodge and smoke a pipe and talk. I would know what brings you to our village, Preacher."

"Horse, the same as usual," Preacher said as he jerked a thumb over his shoulder toward the big gray stallion that stood with his reins dangling. A large, wolflike cur sat on his haunches next to the stallion.

"How many horses called Horse and dogs called Dog have you had in your life, Preacher?" Two Bears asked with amusement sparkling in his eyes.

"Too many to count, I reckon," Preacher replied.

"But I figure if a name works just fine once, there ain't no reason it won't work again."

"How do you keep finding them?"

"It ain't so much me findin' them as it is them findin' me. Somehow they just show up. I'd call it fate, if I believed in such a thing."

"You do not believe in fate?"

"I believe in hot lead and cold steel," Preacher said. "Anything beyond that's just a guess."

Preacher didn't have any goal in visiting the Assiniboine village other than visiting an old friend. He had been drifting around the frontier for more than fifty years now, most of the time without any plan other than seeing what was on the far side of the hill.

When he had first set out from his folks' farm as a boy, the West had been a huge, relatively empty place, populated only by scattered bands of Indians and a handful of white fur trappers. At that time less than ten years had gone by since Lewis and Clark returned from their epic, history-changing journey up the Missouri River to the Pacific.

During the decades since then, Preacher had seen the West's population grow tremendously. Rail lines criss-crossed the country, and there were cities, towns, and settlements almost everywhere. Civilization had come to the frontier.

Much of the time, Preacher wasn't a hundred percent sure if that was a good thing or not.

But there was no taking it back, no returning things to the way they used to be, and besides, if not for the great westward expansion that had fundamentally changed the face of the nation, he never would have met the two fine young men he had come to consider his sons: Smoke and Matt Jensen.

It had been a while since Preacher had seen Smoke and Matt. He assumed that Smoke was down in Colorado, on his ranch called the Sugarloaf near the town of Big Rock. Once wrongly branded an outlaw, Smoke Jensen was perhaps the fastest man with a gun to ever walk the West. Most of the time he didn't go looking for trouble, but it seemed to find him anyway, despite all his best intentions to live a peaceful life on his ranch with his beautiful, spirited wife, Sally.

There was no telling where Matt was. He could be anywhere from the Rio Grande to the Canadian border. He and Smoke weren't brothers by blood. The bond between them was actually deeper than that. Matt had been born Matt Cavanaugh, but he had taken the name Jensen as a young man to honor Smoke, who had helped out an orphaned boy and molded him into a fine man.

Since Matt had set out on his own, he had been a drifter, scouting for the army, working as a stagecoach guard, pinning on a badge a few times as a lawman. . . . As long as it kept him on the move and held a promise of possible adventure, that was all it took to keep Matt interested in a job, at least for a while. But he never stayed in one place for very long, and at this point in his life he had no interest in putting down roots, as Smoke had done.

Because of that, Matt actually had more in common with Preacher than Smoke did, but all three of them were close. The problem was, whenever they got together trouble seemed to follow, and it usually wasn't long before the air had the smell of gunsmoke in it.

Right now the only smoke in Two Bears's lodge came from the small fire in the center of it and the pipe that Preacher and the Assiniboine chief passed back and forth. The two men were silent, their friendship not needing words all the time.

Two women were in the lodge as well, preparing a meal. They were Two Bears's wives, the former wives of his brothers he had taken in when the women were widowed, as a good brother was expected to do. The smells coming from the pot they had on the fire were mighty appetizing, Preacher thought. The stew was bound to be good.

A swift rataplan of hoofbeats came from outside and made both Preacher and Two Bears raise their heads. Neither man seemed alarmed. As seasoned veterans of the frontier, they had too much experience for that. But they also knew that whenever someone was moving fast, there was a chance it was because of trouble.

The sudden babble of voices that followed the abrupt halt of the hoofbeats seemed to indicate the same thing.

"You want to go see what that's about?" Preacher asked Two Bears, inclining his head toward the lodge's entrance.

Two Bears took another unhurried puff on the pipe in his hands before he set it aside.

"If my people wish to see me, they know where I am to be found," he said.

Preacher couldn't argue with that. But the sounds had gotten his curiosity stirred up, so he was glad when someone thrust aside the buffalo hide flap over the lodge's entrance. A broad-shouldered, powerful-looking warrior strode into the lodge, then stopped short at the sight of a white man sitting there cross-legged beside the fire with the chief.

"Two Bears, I must speak with you," the newcomer said.

"This is Standing Rock," Two Bears said to Preacher. "He is married to my daughter Wildflower."

That would make him the father of the little fella Preacher had seen with Wildflower earlier. He nodded and said, "Howdy, Standing Rock."

The warrior just looked annoyed, like he wasn't interested in introductions right now. He looked at the chief and began, "Two Bears—"

"Is there trouble?"

"Blue Bull has disappeared."

CHAPTER 2

Blue Bull, it turned out, wasn't a bull at all, not that Preacher really thought he was. That was the name of one of the Assiniboine warriors who belonged to this band, and he and Standing Rock were good friends.

They had been out hunting in the hills west of the village and had split up when Blue Bull decided to follow the tracks of a small antelope herd while Standing Rock took another path. They had agreed to meet back at the spot where Blue Bull had taken up the antelope trail.

When Standing Rock returned there later, he saw no sign of Blue Bull. A couple of hours passed, and Blue Bull still didn't show up. Growing worried that something might have happened to his friend, Standing Rock went to look for him.

This part of the country was peaceful for the most part, but a man alone who ran into a mountain lion or a bear might be in for trouble. Also, ravines cut across the landscape in places, and if a pony shied at the wrong time, its rider could be tossed off and fall into one of those deep, rugged gullies.

"You were unable to find him?" Two Bears asked when his son-in-law paused in the story.

"The antelope tracks led into a narrow canyon, and so did Blue Bull's," Standing Rock replied. "The ground was rocky, and I lost the trail."

The young warrior wore a surly expression. Preacher figured that he didn't like admitting failure. Standing Rock was a proud man. You could tell that just by looking at him.

But he was genuinely worried about his friend, too. He proved that by saying, "I came back to get more men, so we can search for him. He may be hurt."

Two Bears nodded and got to his feet.

"Gather a dozen men," he ordered crisply. "We will ride in search of Blue Bull while there is still light."

Preacher stood up, too, and said, "I'll come with you."

"This is a matter for the Assiniboine," Standing Rock said, his voice stiff with dislike. Preacher didn't understand it, but the young fella definitely hadn't taken a shine to him. Just the opposite, in fact.

"Preacher is a friend to the Assiniboine and has been for more years than you have been walking this earth, Standing Rock," Two Bears snapped. "I would not ask him to involve himself in our trouble, but if he wishes to, I will not deny him."

"I just want to lend a hand if I can," Preacher said as he looked at Standing Rock. He didn't really care if the young man liked him or not. His friendship for Two Bears and for Two Bears's people was the only things that really mattered to him here.

Standing Rock didn't say anything else. He just stared back coldly at Preacher for a second, then turned and left the lodge to gather the search party as Two Bears had told him to.

The chief looked at Preacher and said, "The hot blood of young men sometimes overpowers what should be the coolness of their thoughts."

"That's fine with me, old friend. Like I said, I just want to help."

As they left the lodge, Preacher pointed to the big cur that had come with him to the village and went on, "Dog there is about as good a tracker as you're ever gonna find. When we get to the spot where Standin' Rock lost the trail, if you've got something that belonged to Blue Bull we can give Dog the scent and he's liable to lead us right to him."

Two Bears nodded.

"I will speak to Blue Bull's wife and make sure we take something of his with us."

Several of the warriors were getting ready to ride. That didn't take much preparation, considering that all they had to do was throw blankets over their ponies' backs and rig rope halters. Preacher had planned to spend a few days in the Assiniboine village, but he hadn't unsaddled Horse yet so the stallion was ready to go as well.

The news of Blue Bull's disappearance had gotten around the village. A lot of people were standing nearby with worried looks on their faces as the members of the search party mounted up. Two Bears went over to talk to one of the women, who hurried off to a lodge and came back with a buckskin shirt. She was Blue Bull's wife, Preacher figured, and the garment belonged to the missing warrior.

Two Bears swung up onto his pony with the lithe ease of a man considerably younger than he really was. He gave a curt nod, and the search party set out from the village with the chief, Standing Rock, and Preacher in the lead.

Standing Rock pointed out the route for them, and they lost no time in riding into the hills where the two warriors had been hunting. Preacher glanced at the sky and saw that they had about three hours of daylight left. He hoped that would be enough time to find Blue Bull.

Of course, it was possible that nothing bad had happened to Blue Bull at all, Preacher reflected. The warrior could have gotten carried away in pursuit of the antelope and lost track of the time. They might even run into him on his way back to the village. If that happened, Preacher would be glad that everything had turned out well.

Something was stirring in his guts, though, some instinctive warning that told him they might not be so lucky. Over the years Preacher had learned to trust those hunches. At this point, he wasn't going to say anything to Two Bears, Standing Rock, or the other Assiniboine, but he had a bad feeling about this search for Blue Bull.

Standing Rock pointed out the tracks of the antelope herd when the search party reached them.

"You can see they lead higher into the hills," he said. "Blue Bull followed them while I went to the north. He wanted to bring one of the antelope back to the village."

"Why did you not go with him?" Two Bears asked. "Why did you go north?"

Standing Rock looked sullen again as he replied, "I know a valley up there where the antelope like to graze. I thought they might circle back to it."

Two Bears just nodded, but Preacher knew that his old friend was just as aware as he was of what had really happened here. Standing Rock had thought he could beat Blue Bull to the antelope by going a different way. Such rivalry was not uncommon among friends.

"Did you see the antelope?" Two Bears asked.

Standing Rock shook his head.

"No. My thought proved to be wrong."

Two Bears's silence in response was as meaningful and damning as anything he could have said. Standing Rock angrily jerked his pony into motion and trotted away, following the same path as the antelope had earlier.

Preacher, Two Bears, and the rest of the search party went the same way at a slower pace. Quietly, Two Bears said, "If anything happened to Blue Bull, Standing Rock will believe that it was his fault for not going with his friend."

"He wants to impress you, don't he?" Preacher said. "Must not be easy, bein' married to the chief's daughter."

"He is a good warrior, but he does not always know that."

Preacher nodded in understanding. He had always possessed confidence in himself and his abilities, and he had learned not to second-guess the decisions he made. But he had seen doubts consume other men from the inside until there was nothing left of them but empty shells.

Eventually Standing Rock settled down a little and slowed enough for the rest of the search party to catch up to him. The antelope herd had followed a twisting path into the hills, and so had Blue Bull as he trailed them. Preacher had no trouble picking out the unshod hoofprints of the warrior's pony.

The slopes became steeper, the landscape more rugged. In the distance, the snowcapped peaks of the Rocky Mountains loomed, starkly beautiful in the light from the lowering sun. They were dozens of miles away, even though they looked almost close enough to reach out and touch. Preacher knew that Blue Bull's trail wouldn't lead that far.

The tracks brought them to a long, jagged ridge that was split by a canyon cutting through it. Standing Rock reined his pony to a halt and pointed to the opening.

"That is where Blue Bull went," he said. "The tracks vanished on the rocks inside the canyon."

"Did you follow it to the other end?" Two Bears asked.

"I did. But the tracks of Blue Bull's pony did not come out."

"A man cannot go into a place and not come out of it, one way or another."

Standing Rock looked a little offended at Two Bears for pointing that out, thought Preacher, but he wasn't going to say anything. For one thing, Two Bears was the chief, and for another, he was Standing Rock's father-in-law.

"Let's have a look," Preacher suggested. "We can give Dog a whiff of Blue Bull's shirt. He ought to be able to tell us where the fella went."

The big cur had bounded along happily beside Preacher and Horse during the search. He still had the exuberance of youth, dashing off several times to chase after small animals.

They rode on to the canyon entrance, where they stopped to peer at the ground. The surface had already gotten quite rocky, so the tracks weren't as easy to see as they had been. But Preacher noticed something immediately.

"Some of those antelope tracks are headed back out of the canyon," he said to Two Bears. "The critters went in there, then turned around and came out. They were in a hurry, too. Something must've spooked 'em."

Standing Rock said, "There are many antelope in these hills. Perhaps the tracks going the other direction were made at another time."

Preacher swung down from the saddle and knelt to take a closer look at the hoofprints. After a moment of study, he shook his head.

"They look the same to me," he said. "I think they were all made today, comin' and goin'."

He knew that wasn't going to make Standing Rock like him any better, but he was going to tell things the way he saw them to Two Bears. He had always been honest with his old friend and saw no need to change that policy now.

"What about the tracks of Blue Bull's pony?" Two Bears asked.

"He went on into the canyon," Preacher said. "Can't see that he came back out, so I agree with Standin' Rock on that. The way it looks to me, Blue Bull followed those antelope here and rode up in time to see 'em come boltin' back out. He was curious and wanted to see what stampeded 'em like that. So he rode in to find out."

"It must have been a bear," Standing Rock said. "Blue Bull would not have been so foolish."

"Blue Bull has always been curious," Two Bears said. "I can imagine him doing as Preacher has said." He looked at the mountain man. "As you would say, old friend, there is one way to find out."

"Yep," Preacher agreed. "Let Dog have Blue Bull's scent. If there's anybody who can lead us right to him, it's that big, shaggy varmint."

CHAPTER 3

Two Bears took out the shirt Blue Bull's wife had given him from the pouch where he had put it and handed it to Preacher. Preacher called Dog to him, knelt beside the big cur, and let Dog get a good whiff of the shirt.

"Find the fella who wore this," Preacher said. "Find him!"

Dog ran into the canyon, pausing about fifty yards in to look back at Preacher, and then resuming the hunt.

Preacher swung up onto Horse's back and nodded to Two Bears.

"He's got the scent. All we have to do is follow him."

They rode into the canyon, moving fairly rapidly to keep up with Dog. Now that they were relying on Dog's sense of smell rather than trying to follow tracks, they could set a slightly faster pace.

The canyon was about fifty yards wide, with

rocky walls that were too steep for a horse to climb, although a man might be able to. Although there were places, Preacher noted, where the walls had collapsed partially and horses might be able to pick their way up and down as long as they were careful.

Preacher frowned slightly as he spotted a shiny place on a flat rock. The mark was small, barely noticeable. Preacher knew that the most likely explanation for it was that a shod hoof had nicked the rock in the fairly recent past. Blue Bull, like the rest of the Assiniboine, would have been riding an unshod pony when he came through here.

So another rider, most likely a white man, had been in the canyon recently. Preacher couldn't be sure it was today, but the evidence pointed in that direction. The antelope herd had started through the canyon, only to encounter a man on horseback. That had startled the animals into bolting back the way they had come from.

Then, Blue Bull's curiosity aroused by the behavior of the antelope, the Assiniboine warrior had ridden into the canyon as well, and . . .

Preacher couldn't finish that thought. He had no way of knowing what had happened then. Blue Bull could have run into the same hombre. There might have even been more than one man riding through the canyon.

This was Indian land, maybe not by treaty but by tradition, and the ranchers in the area had always respected that because of the long history of peace between the whites and the Assiniboine. They had never stopped white men from crossing their hunting grounds, as long as everyone treated each other with respect. It was possible some cattle had strayed up here from one of the ranches, and cowboys from that spread had come to look for the missing stock.

However, that bad feeling still lurked in Preacher's gut. It grew even stronger when he saw Dog veer toward a cluster of rocks at the base of one of those caved-in places along the canyon's left-hand wall. There was no hesitation about the big cur's movements. He went straight to the rocks and started nosing around and pawing at them.

"Your animal has lost the scent," Standing Rock said. "There is nothing there."

"We better take a closer look," Preacher said. He glanced over at Two Bears, who nodded. The chief's face was set in grim lines, and Preacher knew that his old friend had a bad feeling about this situation, too.

The search party rode over to the side of the canyon. Nothing was visible except a pile of loose, broken rocks, some of them pretty big, but the way Dog continued to paw at the stones told Preacher most of what he needed to know.

"Move those rocks," Two Bears ordered.

"But—" Standing Rock began. He fell silent when Two Bears gave him a hard look. Scowling, Standing Rock dismounted. He went to the rocks and started lifting them and tossing them aside.

Several other warriors got down from their ponies and moved to help him.

They hadn't been working for very long before Standing Rock suddenly let out a startled exclamation and stepped back sharply as if he had just uncovered a rattlesnake.

Preacher leaned forward in the saddle to peer into the jumble of stone. He had a pretty good idea it wasn't a snake that Standing Rock had come across.

It was a foot.

Visible from the ankle down, the foot had a moccasin on it. The rest of the leg to which it was attached was hidden under the rocks.

The other warriors had recoiled from the grim discovery as well. Curtly, Two Bears ordered them to get back to moving the rocks. They did so with obvious reluctance.

Everybody knew what they were going to find. It didn't take long to uncover the rest of the body. It belonged to a young Assiniboine warrior. The rock slide that had covered him up had done quite a bit of damage to his features, but he was still recognizable. Standing Rock said in a voice choked with emotion, "It is Blue Bull."

"He must have been standing here when those rocks fell on him and killed him," one of the other men said.

"Why did he not get out of the way?" another man wanted to know.

"There must not have been time," Standing Rock said. "My . . . my friend . . ."

Deep creases appeared in Preacher's forehead as the mountain man frowned. He said to Two Bears, "Somethin' ain't right here. You mind if I take a closer look?"

"Go ahead," the chief said with a nod.

Preacher dismounted and approached the dead man. Standing Rock turned to face him. The warrior's stubborn expression made it clear he didn't want Preacher disturbing his friend's body. Like all the other tribes, the Assiniboine had their own rituals and customs for dealing with death.

"Standing Rock," Two Bears said. "Step aside."

"I won't do anything to dishonor Blue Bull," Preacher said to Standing Rock. "It's just that I don't think this is what it seems to be. Look at how he's layin' on his back with his head toward the wall and his feet toward the middle of the canyon."

"That means nothing," Standing Rock snapped.

"I think it does," Preacher said. "Let's say he came over here and was standin' facin' the wall for some reason. When those rocks came down on top of him, likely they would've knocked him face-down. If he heard the rocks start to fall and turned to try to run, not only would he be facedown, his head would be pointed toward the middle of the canyon."

"You cannot be sure about these things," Standing Rock insisted.

"Maybe not, but I think there's a pretty good chance I'm right. What it really looks like is that somebody dragged Blue Bull over here, then climbed up the canyon wall to start the rock slide that covered up his body."

Two Bears said, "He would have had to be unconscious or dead for that to happen."

Preacher nodded.

"Yep, more than likely. Maybe we can tell, if you let me take a good look at the body."

"He was my friend," Standing Rock said. "Stand back. I will do it."

"Sure," Preacher said. He moved one step back, but that was as far as he went. He wanted to be able to see whatever Standing Rock found.

Standing Rock knelt beside his dead friend and looked him over from head to toe.

"There are no injuries except the ones the rocks made when they fell on him," Standing Rock announced.

"Turn him over," Preacher suggested.

Standing Rock sent a hostile glance at the mountain man, but he did as Preacher said and gently took hold of Blue Bull's shoulders. Carefully, he rolled the body onto its left side.

A sharp breath hissed between Standing Rock's clenched teeth. Preacher saw what had prompted the young warrior's reaction.

A bloodstain had spread on the back of Blue Bull's shirt, just to the left of the middle of his back.

In the middle of that bloodstain was a small tear in the buckskin.

"A knife did that," Preacher said. "Somebody stabbed him in the back, probably out in the middle of the canyon, and then tried to hide the body."

Two Bears said, "That would mean . . ."

"Yep," Preacher said. "This was no accident. Blue Bull was murdered."

The big man paced back and forth angrily. Despite his size, his movements had a certain dangerous, cat-like quality to them. His hat was thumbed back over his blocky, rough-hewn face.

"Let me get this straight," he said. "You didn't have any choice but to kill the Indian."

"That's right, Randall," replied one of the men facing him. "He seen us. He might've gone back to his village and warned the rest of those redskins that we're up here in the hills."

The eyes of the man called Randall narrowed as he stared coldly at the two men he had sent out as scouts.

"There are several big spreads bordering the Indian land," he said. "And Two Bears doesn't mind if the punchers who ride for those ranches cut across the Assiniboine hunting grounds. You *know* that, damn it! We all do. So what in hell made you think that running into a lone warrior was going to cause a problem?"

The two men, whose names were Page and Dwyer, shuffled their feet uncomfortably. They didn't like being in dutch with the hard-bitten ramrod of this gun-hung bunch that waited in the hills for nightfall.

Thirty men, along with their horses, stood around in whatever shade they could find, watching as Randall confronted the scouts. The others were every bit as rough and menacing looking as their leader.

Page had spoken up earlier. Now Dwyer said, "You weren't there, Randall. You didn't see how spooked that redskin acted. He knew somethin' was up, I tell you. Page and me did the only thing we could."

"And we covered his body up good and proper," Page added. "Nobody'll ever find him."

Randall said, "You seem mighty sure about that. You know that as soon as the rest of his people miss him, they'll come looking for him."

"They won't find him," Page insisted.

Randall wanted to say something else. He wanted to cuss the two fools up one way and down the other. Instead, he just jerked his head in a curt nod and said, "You'd better hope they don't. Finding one of their own warriors stabbed in the back is likely to spook them a lot more than running across a couple of riders would have."

Earlier, when the two men had come back from scouting the approaches to the Assiniboine village, they had brought an Indian pony with them, trailing from a rope lead held by Dwyer. When Randall had demanded to know where the animal came from, they had hemmed and hawed around for a minute and tried to say they found it, but it hadn't taken long for his cold stare to get the truth out of them.

They had run into a warrior in a canyon that cut through a ridge several miles from the Assiniboine village. The Indian kept asking questions, the scouts claimed, so Dwyer had distracted him while Page got behind him and put a knife in his back. Then they had dragged him over to the side of the canyon and caved in part of the wall on him. Chances were they were right about nobody finding the body, at least not in time to have any effect on the mission that had brought Randall and his men to this part of the territory.

With the matter settled for the time being, unsatisfactory though it might be, Randall turned and stalked away to give himself a chance to control his anger. He looked up at the sky.

In a couple of more hours, it would be dark.

And once night had fallen, he and his men could ride down out of these hills and do what they had been sent here to do. That thought put a faint smile on Randall's rugged face.

The prospect of killing always did.